The Spinster and The Earl

Book 1
Gentlemen of Honor Series

by

Beverly Adam

Lachesis Publishing Inc

www.lachesispublishing.com

Published Internationally by Lachesis Publishing Inc.
Rockland, Ontario, Canada

Copyright © 2013 Beverly Adam
Exclusive cover © 2013 Laura Givens
Inside artwork © 2013 Giovanna Lagana

A catalogue record for the print format of this title is available
from the National Library of Canada

ISBN 978-1-927555-29-3

A catalogue record for the Ebook is available
from the National Library of Canada
Ebooks are available for purchase from
www.lachesispublishing.com

ISBN 978-1-927555-28-6

Editor: Joanna D'Angelo

Copyeditor: Giovanna Lagana

This is a work of fiction. Names, characters, places and incidents
are either the product of the author's imagination or are used
fictitiously, and any resemblance to any person or persons, living
or dead, events or locales is entirely coincidental.

Dedication

Dear friends and family, this book is dedicated to you.
May God always fill your hearts with gladness and love.

Acknowledgments

My thanks to the creative team at Lachesis Publishing Inc. You turned a good story into a wonderful one.

Coming Soon

Book 2: Gentlemen of Honor Series

The Lady and the Captain

Book 3: Gentlemen of Honor Series

The Widow and the Rogue

THE SPINSTER AND THE EARL

Chapter 1

It was early morning, but dark clouds had already begun to gather above the rolling, green hills of Urlingford as a young messenger with scruffy, red-thatched hair arrived at Brightwood Manor's front door. He hastily explained his mission to the downstairs maid, who led him into the dining nook. Lady Beatrice, the mistress of the house, sat sipping her tea, having just finished her early morning repast.

The lad, who looked to be all of seven years, took off his cap, and respectfully bowed to the elegant lady seated calmly before him, her thick, midnight hair braided in a coronet around her head and her bright, green eyes expectantly waiting for him to speak. He took a deep breath and let it out quickly. "Mum says it be time for you t'come, my lady. The new bairn's ready to be born."

She smiled reassuringly at him. "Tell your mother I'll be attending her in a trice, Ennis. And you've done well, lad."

She picked up a hot scone and a thick wedge of cheese from the side table and passed the food to the young boy, who stared up at her with wide, blue eyes.

"Yes, ma'am. And thankee, m'lady." He nodded as he hurried out the door to bring back the good news that the Spinster of Brightwood would be attending his mother's bedside.

Lady Beatrice turned and called to her companion, Druscilla Pruit, who had been mending clothes by the hearth fire. "Mistress Ryan is about to deliver her baby. Would you be so kind as to fetch my satchel, Dru'?"

She waved a hand vaguely in the direction of her chambers upstairs where she kept her clothes press.

"Of course, my lady. But don't you think it would be best for me to come with you, ma'am? 'Tis dreadfully improper the way you go gallivanting about the countryside unattended," said the companion with a sniff of disapproval. "And for sure now your father wouldn't approve of your venturing out alone. You never know what dangerous brigand might try to harm your ladyship. A wealthy heiress such as yourself, why she ought to be more careful with her person. There be villains aplenty who might do you a wrong turn out there on those deserted roads."

"Really, Druscilla." Beatrice sighed. "You'd think I was an infant still attached to my nurse's apron strings with the way you blather on. Now do stop all this worrisome prattle and fetch my satchel."

She began pulling on her gloves, her companion's warning not ruffling her in the slightest. The village was a small hamlet of little interest to anyone, except to those who dwelled there. And no real thief worthy of his name would dream of stealing here, she told herself with the self-assurance of the highborn who had always been well protected. "Ye best fetch my shawl, too. It looks as if a tempest is settin' to brew," she called out to the maid's back, her Irish brogue making its accustomed appearance.

Despite the dogged determination of the strict English governess her father had foisted upon her as a child, she continued to speak and act like one native born to the Emerald Isles. A fact her Irish father often remarked upon in sad lamentation.

"Such a pitiful waste o' good blunt . . ." He'd shake his graying head in regret. "I thought to find ye a proper English gent to marry after that woman had finished with ye. But *musha, musha,* what's to become of ye? There be no gentleman of proper rank t' fix your cap upon here. If there'd been one, I'd have ferreted him out by now. And when we go about, none of them English beef-eating squires will have ye with that heavy brogue ye carry so proudly on your tongue. I've been asking m'self over and over again, what's to become of ye, daughter? What's t' become of my lass?"

He would then walk away dispirited by his daughter's apparent stubbornness to not bend to English fashions.

Upon fetching her mistress's shawl, Druscilla won her way into accompanying Beatrice to the birthing. She made the dire promise that if she did not attend, she'd tattle to Lord O'Brien about some of his daughter's unladylike adventures.

Resigned to her companion's presence, Beatrice permitted her to accompany her. The two ladies arrived at the front door of a peat-heated sheepherder's cottage where the Ryans awaited their arrival with unconcealed relief.

They entered the cottage where the Ryan's large brood of children warmly greeted them. Several of the littlest ones pulled on her skirt, reminding her of the first time she'd helped deliver a baby in the family with her friend, the healer, Wise Sarah Duncan, and her mother, Gladys Clogheen of Varrik-on-Suir, who'd mentored her in midwifery and taught her healing ways.

Beatrice was not as exceptional a healer as Sarah, but she was a gifted midwife, and she loved children. Not only was it her duty to be able to help her community, but it gave her joy to help bring a new life into this world. Beatrice examined the laboring mother. The time to push the babe out was fast approaching. She checked the baby's position and came to the worrisome realization that it planned to be born in a breech position. That meant the baby's buttocks were presenting and its feet were low in the mother's pelvis.

"You know my sister, Fiona, my lady," said her companion nervously. "She up and birthed her bairns in less than an hour she did . . ."

The mother groaned and squeezed her husband's hand.

"We always knew that our Fiona," continued Druscilla, "was built like a barn door and as fertile as a potato field. But we never knew how prolific she'd be until her tenth came into the world. Well, that last one for sure almost didn't make it, my lady. It tore m'sister almost in two, birthing out our young Ian. Why, she bled for almost a full day after that . . . and the midwife had a right time of it, getting the bleeding to stop. Almost thought we'd lost her, we did."

The laboring mother moaned again, an overwhelming contraction overtaking her body. Her face damp with sweat, she turned pleading eyes to Beatrice. This baby was to be her tenth, as well.

Beatrice smiled at the woman reassuringly and turned to glare at Dru', warning her with her eyes to keep quiet or else.

The burly, red-haired father of the brood, who had been standing vigil for hours beside his wife and holding her hand, nodded to his pale-faced family.

"Right, you lot, it be time for us to go." He gently kissed his wife on the forehead. "You're doing fine, Maureen darlin'," he said tenderly. "I'll be back as soon as word is sent that the baby's come."

He then looked down earnestly at his eldest daughter who sat next to his wife, a young woman who had already started a family of her own and had a steady head on her shoulders. "You'll stay, Mary, and send word to us when the bairn's born, won't ye, lass?" he asked.

"Aye, I will, Da." The dutiful young woman nodded, reaching for another cloth to cool her mother's head.

"I'll not be leavin' her." She then threw a quelling glance at Druscilla.

Druscilla, oblivious to the somber atmosphere of the room, nor to the warning looks thrown her way, paid no attention.

The children were on the verge of becoming quite sick and the blatherskite's chatter had been frightening them out of their wits as they watched their beloved mother reach the most difficult part of her labor.

"We'll be going, then," the father said and exited the room with the other children following single file out the tiny cottage door.

Beatrice could not fault them for leaving. Normally, the tight-knit clan stayed to welcome each new bairn into the family. But this time with the difficulty of the breech and Druscilla's gory descriptions, she could not imagine how anyone could bear to be in the room unless one had a cast-iron stomach,

She gently reached her hand inside the laboring mother, hoping that the baby had turned. It hadn't. And the good Lord help her, it was still coming into the world the wrong way.

"When Fiona wouldn't stop bleeding, we sent for the priest to give her the last rites. I never was so scared in my entire life. My sister just bled, and bled, and then she bled some more . . ."

"Druscilla," cut in Beatrice, searching for an excuse to send her wearisome companion away. "I've forgotten an important instrument I'm in need of at Brightwood. Would you be so kind as to fetch it for me from my clothes press? It looks like a, uh . . . a funnel."

"Of course, your ladyship. If you're quite certain you won't need me."

"Quite certain, Dru'," she said firmly. "And take the pony cart, won't you? The baby won't be coming for some time yet," she lied.

[17]

She heard the eldest daughter give an audible sigh as the cottage door shut, the tension in the room easing noticeably. "I'm going to need your help," she said turning to the young woman. The contractions had been coming strong and steady and she noticed the mother beginning to feel the urge to push.

"You're going to have to hold your mother up as I try and ease the baby out. I'm afraid it's decided to come out into the world feet first, m'dear." The young woman nodded with understanding, helping her mother sit up.

Maureen gripped Beatrice's arm and whispered, "Please, please get this babe out . . . oh-oh, I need to push . . ."

"Hold back, Mistress Ryan!" Beatrice urged, hurriedly washing her hands once more in the hot, soapy water beside her.

She then put her hand inside to see where the baby was. A foot popped out, and she felt a tiny heel. She heard the mother's panting.

"Now," Beatrice said, "this time when you feel the urge to push, you push with all your might. Do you understand, Mistress Ryan?" The pale-faced mother nodded and began pushing.

Beatrice gently pulled the baby out by its feet. The buttocks appeared soon afterwards and then in cork screw fashion, the rest of the child began to slip out.

"That's wonderful," she said, praising the mother. "Let the contractions do the rest of the work. You're delivering this baby beautifully, Mistress Ryan."

Her hands firmly held the tiny baby's body as the mother continued to labor. She watched as the shoulders began to make their appearance and quickly reached for a towel, holding onto the baby as she turned it 180 degrees, keeping the back upward. An arm appeared and was easily delivered, and then the other arm.

But the tricky part of delivering the large head was

not to be so quick. The baby's chest was free and the wee bairn was making able attempts to take its first breath before being completely delivered outside its mother. Beatrice reached her hand over the baby's face, bringing a finger on either side of its small nose and gently squeezed the nostrils shut to prevent the baby from breathing in clotted blood and choking. She then carefully guided the newborn's head through into the world.

"It's a girl!" she heard the baby's sister exclaim with delight.

Beatrice opened the child's mouth, spread her nostrils, and patted her back to encourage her breathing. A moment of worry flew threw her mind, but then the baby took her first breath. A wail was heard as the baby cried out with a set of healthy lungs, letting her tiny presence be known.

Smiling, Beatrice efficiently cut the umbilical cord and washed the newborn in a clean basin of warm water, taking care with the clean rags provided, finally wrapping the newborn in a warm lambskin bunting. She brought the child to Maureen's open arms, and joined the delighted laughter of mother and sister,

Quickly dealing with the afterbirth, and checking that both the mother and child were doing well, Beatrice took a moment to admire the now sleeping baby. Maureen tenderly kissed her daughter's delicate, wispy locks of bright red hair.

"Aye, one can see she's a Ryan already. Just look at that bonnie red hair," she said and congratulated Maureen, who was beaming despite her exhaustion. It had been one of the most challenging births she'd ever attended and certainly one of the most rewarding.

* * *

Over a tankard of ale, the proud parents asked her to be their new daughter's godmother. Considering the position an honor, she accepted with pleasure and offered to have the baby baptized in what had once been her own christening gown, a long hand-crocheted garment of snowy white satin, lace, and ribbon.

After she toasted her new goddaughter, she took her leave. Refusing the family's kind offer for a ride home on their nag, she began to return by foot to Brightwood Manor. "Oh, bother!" she muttered as tiny drops of rain splattered against her cheeks. She shivered a little for good measure as a chilling wind blew past, whipping up layers of her long skirts.

Dark clouds had been brewing overhead since the beginning of the day. They now rumbled ominously as she walked the barren dirt road leading to the parish of Urlingford. Hastening her pace, she walked towards the local tavern, The Boar's Teeth, in hopes of reaching it before the tempest arrived in full force, bringing with it a certain drenching.

Looking out over the rolling hillsides, she spied the small village of Urlingford snugly situated at the bottom of a green valley. It looked to be a good brisk half hour's journey. A cluster of whitewashed homes and the tall, square church's steeple were the only buildings that recommended the tiny village. Sturdy, thatched farm houses were dotted about the countryside. The thriving sheep trade was the main staple of living for the village. She had just come from one of these small sheepherding farms.

She sighed as she wrapped her shawl more securely around her head, preparing for a very wet walk to the village. Fat droplets of water splattered her face, as she received her own baptism from the darkening sky. She could barely make out the imposing silhouette of Drennan Castle, shrouded as it was in the approaching storm's gray mist.

The once imposing gothic castle had been strategically built on one of the highest hilltops in Urlingford. An ancient relic, the keep had originally been an intimidating fortification with six stone towers. But time and neglect had taken their toll as two wings of the castle were on the verge of collapse, which left just one wing stubbornly refusing to crumble around the dying earl and his two loyal servants.

Strange, but she could vaguely make out what appeared to be a human shape standing by the stone boundary wall. She squinted up at the hill . . .

It appeared to be a tall man wearing a great over-cloak, leaning on a walking stick. The form she saw was a familiar one, although blurred by the rain, she recognized it belonged to none other than old Dermott James MacCallan, the last Irish born Earl of Drennan. These past two months a cancerous growth had been eating slowly away at the venerable old gentleman's spleen.

Beatrice had called upon her friends Gladys and Sarah to help her attend him, along with a very properly certified doctor from Dublin. But it had all been to no avail. The old gentleman was too far gone to be saved by any herbal potion or new scientific methods. The best they'd been able to do was ease some of his suffering.

As for his family, they had been nowhere to be seen throughout his long, painful illness. All and sundry knew he had no living descendants of his own flesh. But his three well-titled sisters, who had sons and daughters to provide for, finally deigned to pay their ailing brother a visit. Aye, she'd seen many of his relations come and go this past fortnight full of feigned solicitude and familial affection for the dying lord.

"Come to pay our last respects to our brother," they told her haughtily when they approached the death bed. Their faces were appropriately solemn and sad.

[21]

But if truth be told, a more meddlesome bunch of vultures she'd never encountered before, and she'd seen plenty of them when attending to the very ill. The siblings came dressed in the black of mourning to sit beside the dying earl, advising the old gentleman to whom he should leave his title and estates. They quarreled amongst themselves in front of him until he could tolerate it no more.

"Cease! You are driving me to bedlam itself with all your cackling prattle!" he shouted, punctuating his words with the loud smack of his cane against the side of his death bed.

He reached out and pulled a bell rope, summoning his head butler, ordering the lot off to the dowager house conveniently situated on the other side of the village to await his impending end.

He told them, "I want to die in peace. I've already made up my mind as to who shall inherit my place on this earth." And with that remark, the vultures abruptly stopped. With offended sniffs and grumbling huffs about their ungrateful brother, they left him alone. None of his sisters knew his choice and he adamantly refused to tell.

"You'll have to wait until my last will and testament is read," he said, and with a dismissing wave of his hand, bid them a final farewell.

"Merciful hour!" Beatrice muttered, her eyes widening in surprise. "For sure now, and what be the old gentleman after in this uncertain weather?"

Then, another figure made its unexpected appearance. This form was much smaller, it appeared to be in the shape of a small diminutive person standing beside the bent form of the much taller old lord. Goose-flesh prickled up and down her arms and an uneasy feeling settled in her chest. She drew the long ends of her heavy, wool shawl more closely about her for comfort.

'Twas said in the village that leprechauns once lived beneath the hill long before the castle had been built, in a network of mystical caverns full of riches beyond anyone's wildest imaginings until the invading Drennan clan, a warring tribe of barons and earls, dared to build their own fortified keep directly on top of the wee people's sacred home. The old story went that in a quest for revenge, the fairies placed a powerful *gessa*, a dooming curse, upon the entire clan. From then onward, a slow and certain decline occurred about the castle, as bit by bit, decade upon decade, the once great keep began to crumble after one disaster or another be it by fire or flood. In one more decade, nothing would remain of the castle but a pile of stone and rubble.

"Aye," said Beatrice half-aloud to herself. "And when the old gentleman dies, the *daoine sidhe's*, the fairies' revenge will be complete. For there were no offspring from the old lord."

She shivered and berated herself for her own grim fancies. "But don't you start believing any of those fanciful tales or you'll find yourself as witless as the rest of them. Why 'tis pure superstitious nonsense, nothing more."

The intriguing question as to the true identity of the second silhouette did cause her to stop and look back at the ancient castle. It was queer that the old earl was out in this dreadful weather, ill as he was.

And to what purpose would a small village lad and an old ailing lord be about on a day like today, she frowned, pondering to herself, with the heavens on the verge of tearing wide open?

But, faith now, mightn't the old lord have called out to a passing lad to aid him in returning to the relative safety of the intact part of the keep? Only, why was he outside in the first place? But even as she posed these worrisome questions to herself, she pushed through brambles and twigs in an effort to find a way up to the castle keep.

She reached the stone wall marking the castle's boundaries after taking one last slippery step. She stood at the same spot where she had last seen the two silhouettes. To her chagrin, she saw neither hide nor hair of the lord of the castle, or for that matter, his mysterious companion. Standing in the damp mist she looked miserably down at the ground hoping no one would spot her.

"'Tis intolerable enough to be uncomfortably soaked and wearing mud-filled shoes," she told herself. "It would be even more dreadful if I were to appear before the earl's household like some bedraggled creature that's been lost in a storm."

She maneuvered carefully around the wall and as she did so a shiny, round object lying on the ground caught her attention. It blinked enticingly up at her. Bending over, she palmed it.

Rubbing the splattered dirt off the smooth surface of what now appeared to be the face of a gold coin, she wondered who might have dropped such a valuable item? In the middle, a square hole had been bored, elegant Gaelic words were etched around the rough edges. The script read, *"Where there be gold, there be the shee."*

Swallowing, she finished the translation with sinking dread, *"And with gold there be the fairies!"*

Whirling around as if a thousand tiny eyes were observing her, Beatrice's heart leapt to her throat. And for the first time in her twenty-four years, she found herself shamelessly afraid of the unknown. An unknown that was so uncertain and frighteningly otherworldly that it made her tremble.

"Musha, musha, 'tis the curse of the Drennans I've clasped in m'hand!" She gasped in horror.

She ran over to the wall of the castle that overlooked

the foaming sea below. She drew her hand back and pitched the coin in. Drawing her shawl protectively about her, she then flew down the castle hill as if the hounds of hell were snapping at her tender heels.

Unbeknownst to her, Beatrice's life had suddenly changed in a magical way she would never in a million years have imagined.

Chapter 2

One week later, Beatrice stood at her market stall selling her spun wool. She had been selling her wares by the village harbor since she was old enough to have her own flock of sheep. The sun shone down on her from a cloudless sky. The warmth suited her mood as she gave a friendly nod to several traders she knew. The market was filled with people ready to make a bargain. It was going to be a profitable day.

A fisherman with missing gaps in his smile approached her.

"I'd like to buy some of your finest wool, my lady," he said smiling at her. "I hear you sell the best there is t' be had in Urlingford. And me wife, well the fine woman wants to knit me a shirt to keep me warm, she does. And as I've just come into a bit o' luck, I thought I'd oblige her and buy the wool from you, ma'am."

"They say I have the finest, do they?" she asked, pleased. "Well then, I hope your wife's fingers are nimble enough to work with these soft beauties, because they may glide right off her needles."

"Aye, have no fear on that account," the man said, nodding. "She's one of the best knitters here about and no wool has been known to slip out of her quick grasp."

Obligingly, she showed the seasoned fisherman her wares.

He chose the very finest wool that she had to offer, a lovely angora fleece carted and dyed a becoming shade of dark red. He then reached into his tin fishing kit and produced a coin, the exact same cursed gold coin she'd tossed away. Quite obviously, the fisherman could not read the script.

Eyes wide with surprise, she stared at the small bit of metal in the rough callused hands of the old man.

"How . . . how did you come by that coin?" she asked, not daring to believe her eyes that it was the very same coin she had discovered that stormy night on the grounds of Drennan Castle, and shortly thereafter tossed into the sea.

"I caught it." The fisherman grinned with relish. "Cut it out from the belly of a fish! For sure 'twas like the miracle of Jonah, the finding of it, my lady."

"Aye, it was," repeated Beatrice in a murmur and numbly took the coin without another word.

All that day she tried to rid herself of the coin. At first she thought to be rid of it quickly by dropping it into the begging cup of a poor man, but it was not to be that simple. The beggar took it and rented himself a room for the night from the local innkeeper, ordering a big meal to be sent to his room. The innkeeper's wife, upon spying the coin in the till, scooped it up and handed it to her wastrel son. His father, the innkeeper, had disowned his son when the young scoundrel almost drove them to ruin with his gaming and wenching ways—and them with three young lasses to wed! Ah, but a mother will always forgive her son.

"Take it before your Da sees me . . ." she whispered. "You're as thin as a twig. Haven't you been eatin', Brian?"

He shook his head and said, "No, I'm starvin', M'ther."

She sighed the sigh of a long-suffering woman, and drying her tears on her apron said, "Take this then . . . go and buy yourself some food. I'll not let you fade away before me eyes."

She handed the magic coin over to him. He kissed his mother on the cheek in gratitude and cheerfully walked towards the market. But before he reached the stalls, he quickly spent it on his knees, gambling on dice.

The coin was snatched up by the gambler, a local sheepherder, who brought it home. Upon hearing coins clanking in her husband's pocket, the sheepherder's wife plucked it out to pay the back taxes due on their small cottage. The king's tax collector then passed it over to the regiment's captain to buy supplies.

The captain in turn handed the coin over to his requisitions officer to buy new wool blankets for their horses. The officer took it and headed straight for Lady Beatrice's booth to buy the best to be found. And since she could not refuse the English officer his request, she took the coin into her hand with a pasted smile on her face. Blasted coin! She would have to try again.

At accounting time, when she came home from market, there it sat on the very top of the stack. It gleamed up at her, the stamped letters shining magically on its face, mocking her efforts

"The devil take it!" she softly swore upon espying the coin. The servant, Ian, who was helping her load the wares onto the cart gave her a queer look.

"Where did this come from, Ian?"

"My mother brought it, my lady," he said. "She wanted to pay you back for the help you gave when my sister's baby was born. It was a miracle, the finding of it. She said she was scraping off mussels below the harbor wharf when it struck her on the head. Someone had tossed it away. Can you believe it, my lady? Why would anyone throw a gold coin away?"

She could not give him a reply, for she had been the one who'd tossed it. She held the coin in front of her face and said, much to the lad's astonishment, a very bad word in Irish.

Angry, she spoke to the coin, "You little bugger you . . . *Imigh leat.* Clear off . . . ye'll not get the better of me! I'll be rid of you yet!" She would have melted the coin and given it away, but she was afraid of the uncertain power that lay within its golden form. Eventually, she grew weary of tossing, throwing, and spending it. The cursed item became a simple meddlesome trick played upon her by the wee folk. One she was unfortunately stuck with for the time being.

And the fey, she doubted not, were watching and having a jolly good laugh over her sudden bursts of colorful language.

* * *

It had been almost six Sundays since that fateful night when she'd found the magic coin at Drennan Castle. The old Earl of Drennan had died the next morning and she'd been stuck with that terrible bit of magic ever since.

She now crouched by the stone wall dividing her property from that of the late earl's, taking steady aim at a plump grouse, the coin clanking noisily against her shot pouch.

"Faith, 'tis almost as irritating as using this useless bit o' metal," she said aloud, grimacing contemptuously down at the ancient flintlock she'd been forced to use for hunting. The ancient relic in her hands had been used in combat long ago, when her father, as a young man, had been a merchant sailor in his majesty's service.

The flintlock had a long, narrow barrel, and a heavy, metal-tipped butt, which had served oftentimes as a club when the pistol was unloaded and required for immediate defense. The firing-arm was difficult to use, its weight heavy and cumbersome in her small feminine hands. Her father, Lord Patrick O'Brien, refused to entrust her with a decent weapon, ignored her pleadings by saying, "Ladies have no business handling weapons in the first place, lass. 'Tis dangerous to entrust one with one."

To which she'd retorted tartly, "Then I won't be one, Da. Treat me like you would any other young gentleman in your household."

He'd heartily laughed, told her she was a scheming hellion, and sent her on her way with this ancient relic of a blunderbuss.

"The unfeeling rascal," she mumbled as she reloaded the pistol. Her father knew she would not be able to take a decent shot with this outdated bit of metal. It'd be a minor miracle if she hit anything.

She crouched now by the edge of a marsh. Mist rose up from the water, obscuring the landscape, which bordered the property of Drennan Castle and Brightwood Manor. Tall weeds hid her from view as she spotted another prey, a large, speckled pheasant, roosting but a few meters to her right in marsh reeds. It would be lovely to have some fresh game on the table tonight and this bird looked to be nice and plump, perfect for basting over a peat fire.

Taking careful aim over the musket, which had no sights, she fired.

To her amazement, the rusty hammer sprang forward the first time she pulled the trigger, igniting the flint in the powder pan and miraculously sparking to burst forth the shot with a smoking *ka-bang!* She felt the gun tremble as the musket ball cannoned out of the barrel. Her hand kicked backwards as the weapon sprang forward. Powder smoked the air around her, creating a cloudy haze.

"Oh, hell and damnation!" a deep male voice bellowed out into the mist as the frightened neighs of a startled thoroughbred peeled in the air.

[30]

She looked up in time to see a wall of shiny black horse flesh and spurred boots flash in front of her surprised eyes. Muttered angry curses could be heard over the horse's panicked whinnies as both rider and steed galloped towards a nearby stone wall. Abruptly, the animal stopped, bolting away from the solid obstruction placed in its path.

The hapless rider, who'd miraculously been able to keep his seat till then, was effectively tossed, his mount kicking up its hooves at the obstruction. He, the unfortunate master, continued to sail over the stone impediment landing with a solid splash into a nearby bog.

"Merciful heavens!" She gasped, and ran to the edge of the pond where sat the thrown victim.

A stranger glared up at her. His dark blues eyes, the same sparkling shade as the marsh lake on a cold day, silently accusing her.

She stood as motionless as a statue, her pale, oval face unflinching at the sight of blood gushing down his leg. Her own green eyes, the color of the hills behind her, blinked back at him. Brushing aside long tendrils of black hair, which had escaped out from under her hunting hat, she observed him.

She made not the least sign of distress by either crying torrents of remorse, or attempting a delicate feminine swipe of the fevered brow. She merely lifted one of her dark, perfectly arched eyebrows and stared.

Although she wore a fetching hunting jacket of dark red wool, the same outfit, in fact, she'd ordered from Dublin with its matching tartan hat, she could tell by the stranger's sour expression he thought her some sort of monstrous creature.

"Sir, are you well?" she dared to ask, trying to remain calm while her insides tumbled nervously about, secretly relieved to see that he was alive.

"No, the devil take it. I am not!" he spat out wincing.

"*Demme*, my leg is throbbing dreadfully. And you, madam, are clearly some sort of half-witted, featherbrained female to think otherwise. Indeed, if I felt any worse, I'd no doubt be lying completely unconscious at your feet!"

"I better help you up, then," she said, biting nervously down on her lower lip, while secretly dreading getting any closer to him. She knew from past experiences that the English were not a good-natured people. And this one apparently was not about to become an exception to the rule. And what would ordinarily have been a perfectly tranquil day of hunting was now ruined.

She sighed to herself as she drew closer. She knew immediately that her first assumptions about him were correct. He was indeed English. There was no question about his nationality. And just to make matters more disagreeable, undoubtedly some sort of well-titled English gentleman. A fact that clearly evinced itself by the well-clipped, cultured accent she'd heard when he spoke, and by his top-lofty manner towards her, his supposed inferior, an Irish gentlewoman.

His impeccable attire, although now thoroughly mud-stained, clung damply to his masculine form like a second skin. The tailoring of the riding outfit was evidently the workmanship of an expensive London tailor, such as Schweitzer and Davidson, or perhaps even that newcomer, Guthrie, she'd been reading about. Indeed, no good Irish tailor worth his name would have considered using such superfine material for a common riding jacket. A good Irish country tailor wisely knew that during a fast-paced canter across the damp, green hills, the suit would become irreparably soiled. "Why waste good material?" a tailor would argue with his clients. When good, sturdy wool and leather are plentiful on the isles, why not simply put them to good use?

Aye, she nodded. And this stranger's clothes were better suited for the more sedate gentlemanly pleasures of a calm dry trot in a fashionable London park. Slim chance of a healthy mud-splattering there. But it was not his stylish clothes, nor the fact that he was probably a powerfully titled Lord Somebody or Other, which troubled her. It was the manner in which his right leg sat at an unhealthy angle. It denoted a serious injury. He could, she knew, become permanently crippled from such a tumble if his leg were not properly tended.

"Do you intend to assist me, or are you planning on standing there awaiting this muck to bury me?" he asked with dry humor. "For if you must know, 'tis dreadfully wet and cold." He indicated the bog, which surrounded him, raising one muddied hand for her inspection. "And as for its fragrant bouquet . . . well, I do believe only a swine would denote it as pleasant to the finer senses."

He had not been gilding the truth, she decided moments later, her own pert nose wrinkling at the putrid smell of various decaying elements, which created the bog. Because he was by all accounts badly wounded, she waded in, not wishing to risk his catching some deadly wasting sickness brought on by a sudden inflammation of the lungs. She had enough laid at her doorstep as it was. She needed no further trouble, such an English nobleman becoming seriously ill, to add to it.

Carefully balancing herself with her *shillelagh*, a long, polished, walking stick made from the branch of an ancient oak tree, she checked the depths. It was not unknown for bogs to turn into unexpected deathtraps. Bogs often acted as sinkholes and many an unwary traveler was known to have been suddenly sucked down by them. Fortunately, the stranger had landed in a rather shallow one. There appeared to be no imminent danger of any unexpected sinking.

The long walking stick she used was one of her father's making and she always took extra care to carry it with her when hunting. Never once had she imagined there'd come a day when she'd use it to wade into a bog to rescue a strange Englishman. Aye, if she'd had an inkling of what would occur to her this morning, she'd have stayed securely at home in her warm bed with Druscilla attending upon her with hot cups of fortifying tea.

She stood beside the fallen stranger and visibly swallowed. She found herself staring down at the lower half of his face. A red, puckered scar ran jaggedly down what would've undoubtedly been one of the handsomest faces she'd ever seen, if it hadn't been so badly marred.

Guessing him to be in his late twenties, the English lord had sharp, broad lines for cheekbones and a fine high brow full of intelligence, which rose above startling, sapphire, blue eyes. But the puckering, white line running down one side of his face ruined the effect. An evident reminder of what, no doubt, had been a violent and most dangerous encounter. Unconsciously, half-afraid, she lowered her eyes protectively away.

"I see you've halted once more," he drawled, his voice tinged with cool amusement. "Undoubtedly upon espying that little souvenir, which I've been branded with, you hesitate." He gave a half-pained laugh, wincing as he did.

"'Tis really nothing to concern yourself, ma'am. A mere memento I picked up hastily on the Peninsula. A gift, one of his majesty's own, a green-horned lieutenant gave me in the heat of battle. The swashbuckling jackanapes didn't know how to wield his sword and struck me instead."

"But . . . you're English," she said, protesting at the idea that he'd been harmed by one of his own countrymen. Only the enemy, she'd been taught, was capable of such wanton recklessness. For everyone knew that the French were a cold-hearted, bloodthirsty bunch of butchers. Not worthy to be called part of the brotherhood of men.

"Just so . . . you'd think he'd have taken greater care around his own kind, wouldn't you? But alas, no. And as you can see being English made me just as vulnerable as any other man around a sharp swinging weapon," he replied, dismissing the subject as of no further consequence.

"Now, if you'll kindly give me your arm, I'd like to get out of this mud bath before it becomes the next Brighton fashion."

Obediently, she stepped forward, leaning down with the support of the walking stick. She managed to pull him up into a half-standing position.

He towered a full hand above her. This astonished Beatrice. She was considered to be quite tall for a woman. Most of the men in the village were the same height or shorter than she. It was an enjoyable asset she took advantage of when bargaining and trading with them. She winced a little and looked up at him as he tightly gripped her shoulders.

He leaned heavily into her for support. She straightened her back, feeling his hard male body brush-up against her. She tried to put a little distance between them, but he clung tenaciously to her like a drowning man to a floating piece of buoyant driftwood. His scarred eye looked down at her with what she thought to be a glint of humor, as if he knew how the intimate contact of their two bodies meeting made her feel. However, when he took his first tentative step forward, he grimaced in genuine pain, hissing air between clenched teeth.

"Agggh. . . ." He breathed, cursing vehemently under his breath.

Raising her eyes heavenward, Beatrice chose to ignore the roasting language. She assisted him to a sitting position upon a clover bank and walked purposefully to her game bag. Removing a leather wine sack, she poured strong spirits over a sharp hunting knife. She moved towards him, a grim look of purpose tightening her mouth.

"Are you preparing to polish me off?" he asked sardonically, eyeing the sharp weapon in her hand. "You're not some sort of Irish druid looking for a blood sacrifice, are you? I think I've already spilled enough today to satisfy even the most demanding of goddesses, don't you agree, ma'am?"

She ignored his jibe. Dreading the next step, she surveyed the area she assumed had been hit by the musket's shot. Her hand shook a little.

"You'd best show me where it entered," she said, licking dry lips. She tried very hard not to envision what she must do, the digging out of odd-shaped metal bits.

If he were in pain now, the thought of her digging embedded bits of metal out of his flesh was even less appealing.

"We, um . . . wouldn't want to risk your becoming sick," she added, positioning her knife over the wound, readying herself.

"If, ma'am, you mean that I might develop gangrene," he cut in, "you may stop your fretting. By some holy miracle you missed." He pointedly nodded towards his horse, which stood a few paces off calmly grazing on a patch of green clover.

"'Twas the damnable fall from my mount, Mercury there, which lamed me most. I must add for vanity's sake, 'tis the first I've ever felt that less than enviable sensation of flying. An experience, I can assure you, that I'd rather have passed."

"Well, then," she breathed, dropping the weapon, "if you'll pardon me, sir, I best be off to fetch our *cailleacha*, the village witch. We'll need her assistance and a pony cart."

He stared at her blankly. A dark, bushy eyebrow lifted in a question mark.

"Did I hear you correctly? You intend on having a witch see to tending my injury?"

"The cailleacha, to be exact. She's our best and most learned wise-woman," she said, straightening up as she heard the challenge in his voice. "Surely you've heard of Wise Sarah? She's quite renowned."

"Apparently not," he replied dryly.

"Wise Sarah is a gifted healer," she explained, wondering what the English gentleman actually knew about the parish he'd stumbled upon. "We put our complete trust in her. 'Tis she who's called upon when we're either ill or seriously injured. She's one of the wisest women I know. You can trust her, sir. She'll do a proper job of tending your wounds."

She hoped for some sign of acknowledgment on his part of the healer's abilities. However, he appeared to be entirely unimpressed, his mouth tightening into an even, firm line of masculine disapproval.

"Let me assure you that Mistress Sarah has studied the art of healing for many years under Gladys Clogheen of Varrik-on-Suir," she continued, trying to reason with him. The older, wise woman, who had trained Wise Sarah, had an even more renowned reputation as a healer than the young witch. Many sick came from far flung parishes all over the Emerald Isles to seek her wise healing advice and help.

"In fact, 'tis well known that 'twas she who brought up the lady," she added, waiting for a light of recognition to warm his frosty, blue stare.

All and sundry knew the tale of how Gladys Clogheen had adopted the foundling left on her doorstep and brought her up to become a great healer. It was a tale storytellers relished repeating, because the old crone and pretty child made the villagers wonder if perhaps the foundling was not a changeling in disguise. Perhaps one who had been brought to the witch's door to learn her magic in order to one day take it back to her own fairy kind?

"No doubt you've heard of her?" she asked hopefully.

His stoic face gave not the least indication he'd ever heard of either women, nor of any of the other famous healers, which were known to populate the more remote parts of the isles.

"Evidently not," she said with finality, dismissing him as an ignorant bore. She had wasted enough time with him. It was time to leave. She stood up, taking her walking stick in hand, preparing to set off for the village and the cottage belonging to the healer. As far as she was concerned, the sooner Wise Sarah took this arrogant English stranger off her hands, the better. She took a purposeful step forward and almost tripped. Something held her back.

She glanced down at the hem of her walking skirt. The stranger audaciously held it and her tightly in place. His grip, surprisingly strong despite the obvious pain he was experiencing.

Long lean fingers kept her in a controlled reign, his hold worthy of any good whip, well accustomed to maneuvering the ribbons of a high-strung thoroughbred. She doubted not that he could tumble her with a mere yank, if he should so choose.

The long jaw line of his mouth jutted out at a stubborn angle as he said, "I'd prefer a physician tended me, ma'am, not some witch." His teeth ground together against the pain that rolled through him as he shifted his body. He tightened his grip, his knuckles turning white.

"Truly, sir, there aren't any. At least not in this parish," she amended, hoping that would at last settle the matter. "And the doctor that is known about here is a worthless drunk of a sawbones. He'd bleed you to death before he healed you."

The skeptical look of disbelief the stranger gave her said loudly he thought she was purposely trying to force some imagined storybook character upon him. The childhood vision of a cackling old hag, who'd use frog gizzards and bat wings in innocuous brews clearly clouding his prejudiced thoughts.

"Upon my word, I am not trying to bam you. We haven't any need for your so-called men of science here. Wise Sarah, our healer, can properly tend you," she said once more, tugging at her skirt to see if he'd release her. "Now, if you'll kindly excuse me, I really ought to hie myself to the village and fetch her."

"I don't want some female witch doctor. I want a man of medicine," he muttered once more. "During the war, I allowed no one to touch me."

"No one?" she asked, skeptically eyeing the jagged scar. Someone had to have at the very least tended that little souvenir of his.

"Except Davis. He's my man at arms. I only permitted him to tend to my needs. Thankfully, his mother was an excellent seamstress and taught him when he was a lad how to make a straight stitch." He glowered at her accusingly. "And now, ma'am, you expect me to submit to some female witch with no real knowledge of medicine. Save perhaps how to cure a few harmless warts. I think not!"

Her fine eyebrows snapped together. It was becoming abundantly clear that more than just his bones had taken flight. What common sense the Englishman may have had had flown, as well.

The open wound on his leg looked worse than it actually was, she told herself, having seen and tended to far worse when her father invited friends for their hunts. The dangerous jumps over the usual obstacles of hedges, harrows, and fences, were always bound to produce at least a couple of casualties each year. It was considered part of the excitement and thrill of the hunt to see if one was skilled enough to finish the course still seated, having successfully preserved one's fragile neck. The fox serving as a convenient excuse for the exhilarating gallop in the open countryside.

The wound, she surmised, would only need a little sewing up. The lamed leg, however, appeared to be either broken or badly twisted. It was an entirely different matter. It would need to be carefully tended, set back into place, and soon. Suddenly, without any sign of warning, she placed her firm, long, white fingers upon him.

"What are you about?" he asked, wincing as she firmly grasped his leg, feeling along for any breaks.

Quickly, she dug deeply into his flesh, felt the torn ligament, and jammed it back into place. He tried to reach her, to make her leave him alone, but it was too late. Stunned, he released the hem of her gown with a loud yelp and promptly keeled over in a dead faint of excruciating pain.

"The devil take it!" she muttered under her breath and gently pushed him off.

Chapter 3

When next the English lord opened his eyes, he thought he had died and gone to heaven. For standing over him was someone who could only be described as an angel. "Soft blue eyes the color of cornflowers and hair the shade of a golden halo. Speak, vision. Tell me, have I passed away? If it be so, then I only desire to lie here and look upon your angelic face."

The vision gave a soft laugh, revealing two darling dimples, one on each side of her near perfect, pink, porcelain cheeks. She placed a cool compress on his forehead. "Nay, sir," she said, a light brogue filling her gentle speech. "You're not yet gone. Merely come to Brightwood Manor, are ye, sir. The mistress of this grand house, Lady Beatrice O'Brien, she be. Why, 'twas she who brought y' here."

"Ah, I see . . ." He nodded, recalling the events leading up to his swoon.

He glanced around the room. He glimpsed a simple clothes press, washbasin, chair, and the smiling angel. No dark-haired vixen in sight.

"I should like to thank the lady of the house myself for bringing you to me." That and it would give me a sporting chance to throttle her, he silently added to himself.

"Pray tell, where is this paragon of virtue with whom I've had the greatest of misfortunes to meet?"

"Lady Beatrice," the vision called to a dark shadow standing by the door. "The English gentleman, he be up now, my lady, and he's asking after you."

He watched intently as the lady stepped into the room. She carried in front of her a fresh batch of bandages and a mixture of poultices filled with pungent herbs.

"Thank you, Sarah, for calling me," she said observing the man warily, not certain what to think of someone who looked completely at ease lying in a strange bed, half-undressed, as if it were his own.

With his leg elevated on a pile of pillows, he reminded her too much of a rajah she'd seen once in a picture book, expecting to be waited on hand and foot by his devoted harem. Sun-bronzed skin peeked shamelessly out of his open starched shirt, the hard-earned muscles he'd developed on the Spanish Peninsula rippling with each gesture, added to the illusion.

Faith, he really was one of the handsomest specimens of manhood she'd clapped eyes upon since the war against Boney started, despite that nasty looking scar he wore. She had to admit, even if he were a bit of a tiresome bore, he was pleasant to look upon.

Distracting herself from the sight of his almost bare chest, she nervously recited by rote her planned introductions. "Sir, I am Lady Beatrice O'Brien, mistress of this house. And this delicate beauty standing beside me is our healer, Mistress Sarah Duncan. I must add she's the same witch who had the kindness to sew your leg up for you."

Wise Sarah gave a deep curtsy and smiled warmly at him. Her light blue eyes, the same shade as bluebonnets, sparkled down at him in warm welcome.

"Indeed," he said looking in astonishment at the lovely vision. She didn't appear to be someone who'd choose to seek out the more unsavory parts of life, let alone be seen boiling a cauldron of eye of newt under a full moon.

"Mistress Sarah, you must amuse our patient here sometime with tales of how you manage to stay aloft at night on your broom," said the lady of the house with a bemused smile. "I must tell you your patient is vastly interested in such witchery and would be delighted to be instructed about your more unusual practices."

"Now, Lady Beatrice." The pretty healer laughed in feigned indignation. For most of her life Wise Sarah had lived under superstitious peasant eyes. She knew the numerous wild tales concerning her adopted mother and herself.

"I've told ye before that we modern day hexes don't use those uncomfortable conveyances anymore. Why they proved to be far too drafty and terribly dangerous to ourselves. What with one good gust of wind there's been many a good hex that's gotten herself lost over the North Sea." She laughed and winked impishly at the lady of the house, relishing the silliness of her own tale. She and her adopted mother had never touched a broom, let alone tried to make it fly, except to clean their plain plank floor.

"Nay, dear lady and lord, we modern sorceresses ride about in smart pony carts these days like the rest o' ye mortals. It being far saner and safer. Though 'tis true, less romantic."

The stranger smiled at her quaint explanation, flashing a row of healthy teeth. "But all the same, ma'am, despite your being a witch. Demme, if I'm not grateful for the service you've rendered me by tending to my leg."

The pretty healer blushed under the handsome English stranger's praise. "It was nothing, sir. Truth be told, it was mostly Lady Beatrice here who did the work, putting your leg back into place and binding it tight like she did. Aye, 'tis she you ought to be looking to when giving your thanks."

His arctic blue eyes turned themselves upon his nemesis, the lady of the house, or the *"vanithee"* as he'd heard the servants refer respectfully of her in whispers. She stood proudly erect wrapping her title as lady of the manor about her like a protective cloak. Her bright green eyes the same shade as new leaves, carefully watching and observing his every word and gesture, her body rigid in anticipation to what he would say. It would be quite easy for him to slight her in front of the wise woman if he wished. But he did not.

"Tell me, is there no master of the house to greet me?" he asked, wondering if the lady was married, intrigued by her apparent aloofness. It was as if she had no one but herself to answer to for bringing home a stranger. Would not someone, her guardian or husband perhaps, wish to speak to him? To assure himself that such an unknown English stranger would not bring harm or scandal to his household? Surely there was someone?

"Aye, there be one," the lady answered. "My father, Lord Patrick O'Brien. He is the master here. He'd like to have greeted you in person, but at present himself is suffering sorely from the gout and begs that you excuse him. In his absence, he requests that you accept his daughter's welcome." She then gave a short bob, in lieu of a proper deep curtsy of welcome, which was normally the due she gave to guests in her father's house.

His eyes narrowed, he'd not missed the slight. "Ah . . . yes." He nodded with understanding, his voice liquid cool, chilling the peat-heated room. "Considering that it was a member of his household who shot me off my mount that would be the least one could expect him to do. Don't you agree, my lady?"

She gasped, stepping towards the ungrateful English dolt. She clenched her hands at her side, ready to give him a proper show of her famous spinster temper. "If ye'd only taken the time to look before ye leaped, we wouldn't have had to put ye in this bed. And I'd not be saddled with the obliging care of ye!"

"Please, Lady Bea—," intervened Wise Sarah, placing herself strategically between the attacking hostess and her wounded patient. "Behave yourself! Now what will your da say when he up and learns you tried to attack this wounded gentleman? And this time in pure aggression, if you please. One would think that you truly wished him harm."

Chastised, Beatrice obediently took a step back. The last thing she desired was to have her father's wrath fall upon her head. He'd warned her that if another one of her notorious escapades brought any disgrace upon the family name, he'd see to her punishment himself. A dire threat she knew he would follow through with if she were not careful.

She sighed audibly, her hands were tied. She could do nothing to dislodge this ingrate. And once more she regretted her part in acting the Good Samaritan to this English pudding-headed lout. She ought to have left him in the muck and mire where she'd found him, instead of seeing to it that he was brought here and properly tended.

The wise woman prudently stepped in, sensing that she was the only one to bring any calm back into the room. She put forth the question that both she and her irate friend had wished to know since the moment they'd set eyes upon him.

"Pray, sir," she said smiling, "now do be after telling us of your name and heritage. Are ye, perchance, of noble birth?"

The stranger bowed to the beauty as much as he was able, a handsome smile curving his lips into a welcoming rogue's grin.

"Fair lady, you have before you a newly named peer of the realm." He paused dramatically before his title, glancing at the other lady to assure himself she was paying equal attention. "I am your new neighbor, the eleventh Earl of Drennan, Captain James Huntington. And your most obedient servant."

Unified gasps of shocked surprise were heard. Stunned, Beatrice touched the gold coin she carried in her pocket. It singed her fingertips, and as if struck, she fell slightly forward.

Noticing her ladyship's distress, Sarah leapt to her aid, leading her to a nearby chair. She felt her friend's erratic pulse and noted the pale color of her normally rosy cheeks, sure signs of shock.

"I think it'd be best if you lay down, Lady Beatrice. All of this has been too much for you, my lady. 'Tis I who'll hie to Lord O'Brien and tell him of His Grace's decision to stay here."

"Thank you, Mistress Sarah, 'tis kind of you." Beatrice nodded, weakly rising on shaking limbs. Giving a lopsided curtsy, she quickly left the room, feeling the earl's blue eyes follow her as she walked out. She dared not look at him lest she betray herself and her secret.

Heart in her throat, she entered her private bedchambers. She vividly recalled the stormy night when she last saw the old earl and the little man, and the trembling fear she felt then came back with full force.

In the beginning, she'd contemplated telling Wise Sarah, but decided that it was too dangerous to involve her curious friend. For although she was a witch, Wise Sarah was an innocent do-gooder whom the whole village fiercely protected as they would any of their own. The beautiful witch was a bit odd to be sure, but a marvel at healing nonetheless. The village people were secretly proud of her renowned lifesaving skills.

As for calling upon her father for help, that was unthinkable. Lord Patrick had enough trouble trying to keep straight the days of the week, let alone be forced to deal with something as strange and queer as a leprechaun's curse.

Aye, ever since her mother's death last winter from cholera, Da's forgetfulness seemed to have grown. And what if the good people, as the fairies were called by the village people, decided to make off with him? None would be the wiser. Her father had become recently very mysterious about his comings and goings, until she knew not where he went.

Nay, she decided, she dare not tell him.

She rolled the coin in her hand, feeling its rough edges and the smooth, flat surface. Her fingers traced the ancient letters forming the words dictated no doubt by the fey themselves. But what to do? Dare she give it back to the new earl? Surely that would be the best way of ridding herself of it? By right of succession, it logically belonged to him. She nodded as she gave it some thought.

But how does one go about giving back a magic coin that's cursed to its rightful owner? And how would one return it so that the owner did not suspect something was amiss? Aye, she had to think of a plan using great finesse and cunning to accomplish the deed, so that he would never suspect that the coin was cursed.

* * *

That evening, having dined alone in her room, she stayed awake and plotted. When at last the candle beside her bed sputtered out, she'd devised an ingenious way to return the coin to the one she decided by hereditary rights was its true owner.

At cock's first crow, she awoke and set her carefully devised plan into motion. Once dressed, she went down to the kitchens to supervise the cooking of the morning's first meal. The turf was loaded into the oven fire and the cook, Mistress Sullivan, awakened by her anxious mistress, sleepily aided her. Everything had to be perfection for her plan to work, even serving the right food mattered.

On silver platters, she laid out fried eggs, toast, and rounds of roasted Brobdingnagian beef, poached, red herring, and a dish of turf-fired, spring potatoes. To this, she added strong drink from her father's cellar. These she carefully set on the large, rolling tea service.

"But, mistress," protested the cook, as her lady moved the tray towards the door. "It isn't proper for ye t' be bringing the tray up yourself, m'lady."

"Proper or not, 'tis I who'll be giving His Grace his morning meal this day, Mistress Sullivan," answered the *vanithee* of the house with a decisive nod. "And I'll not be hearing any more ridiculous arguments against my doing so."

The cook gave her the same look she'd given her when Beatrice was a mere slip of a lass caught stealing sweets from her kitchen. It bespoke of her intimate experience of knowing her mistress was up to something not entirely befitting the lady of the manor.

She frowned back at the disapproving cook. "Nay, don't be getting yourself into a pet, Mistress Sullivan. You're forgetting His Grace is bedridden and his man has not yet arrived. One can hardly expect him to appear at the table in the state that he's in. He must, therefore, be waited upon by someone."

"Aye, your ladyship. But another could easily take the tray up for ye. There be plenty of servants here to do it for ye. It isn't right ye being up there alone with the 'andsome earl. He's an unmarried gentleman, don't be forgettin'. And I've heard the gossipmongers say he's got no lining to his purse." The older woman shook a serving spoon at her mistress in warning.

"I shall be perfectly safe in my own home, Mistress

Sullivan," Beatrice replied pertly.

The old woman shook her head at that. "And I thought after all your boastful protestations that you've had no wish t' be wed, ye'd want to be more careful . . . indeed, take my word for it, m'lady, a gentleman of his class knows more tricks abed than he does standing aground on his own two feet!" She nodded with a conviction of a woman who knew the ways of the world. "Aye, ye best be careful that he donna trick ye out of your virtue whilst supping on those tender morsels ye fixed for 'im, lest he up and mistakes you as part of the meal you fixed!"

"Now you're prattling on just like Druscilla," said the lady of the house, wiping her hands on her apron. She smiled at her cook in a teasing manner, knowing full well the rivalry between the two for her attention.

"That chatterbox ye be comparing me to! What an insult! She was born to be a blatherskite, the flighty pea brain. But meself, I what's known ye since ye were knee high in short skirts, am warning ye. Be careful, Lady Beatrice O'Brien," she said removing a bit of batter from her face. "Or I'll be baking your wedding cake before the day's through."

Unheeding of the warning, Beatrice proceeded to roll the tray away.

* * *

Standing in front of the door, she met the wise woman. The fair-haired healer also had a tray. It was laden with a far simpler meal of toast, boiled egg, and Indian spiced tea. Stubbornly, she stepped directly into the pretty witch's path.

"Out of my way," she commanded, one hand on her hips in an imperious gesture that dared the pretty healer to defy her order.

"But I—"

"Move. The earl will be needing a man's meal. Not something fit for feeding a wee bairn."

Her rival glared and folded her arms defiantly. "His Grace asked me to bring it himself, Lady Beatrice."

"Aye, to be sure he did," answered the lady of the house with a sharp nod of her head. "But 'tis I who'll be relieving you of that tempting duty." She gave the witch a none-too-gentle shove away from the door. "Off with you, now. I'm sure Lord Patrick will only be too pleased to partake of the lovely tray you fixed."

The beauty protested, tapping her tiny foot. "But he be my patient. 'Tis you who are in the way, my lady!"

Ignoring her friend's protests, Beatrice placed her own carefully laden tray up against the door. Facing Wise Sarah with well-practiced determination, she said in a voice that brooked no nonsense, "You may be my friend, Mistress Sarah Duncan, but I'm asking you once and for all to move. Or beware . . ." She lifted her eyebrows ominously and paused for effect. "As a lady, I'll be forced to up and write your betrothed, Master John Maxwell, about your flirting ways."

Wise Sarah's light blue eyes darkened with terror. "You wouldna dare," she whispered, her face paling at the mere idea of her betrothed, who was on a ship somewhere loyally fighting the French, hearing of a harmless flirtation with her handsome patient.

"Aye." Beatrice nodded knowingly. For if Master John Maxwell suspected the new Earl of Drennan had paid his beloved any attention beyond that of a patient for his physician, he'd likely jump ship and return to Urlingford to tear the poor English lord's legs off, limb from limb, with his own powerful blacksmith hands.

Not that she'd ever write the fiancé of the witch's harmless flirtation. Although there were many jealous, green-eyed lasses in the village who might've delighted in so doing, attempting to steal the witch's betrothed away from her at the same time. But she wasn't one of them. And Beatrice had to play the scene to her advantage or be under the vexing power of the magical coin, quite possibly forever.

"You win." The wise woman sighed, giving in to the mistress of the house's demands. She took her tray and backed away from the door.

Head held high, she proudly departed down the hall towards Lord Patrick's quarters where she passed her tray to the master of the house's valet.

The victor boldly stepped up to the door and knocked. A deep male voice within gave leave for her to enter.

The Earl of Drennan sat in bed, his back supported by a pile of pillows. He held a pipe between his teeth, seemingly unaware of the confrontation that had just taken place outside his bedchamber door. Despite the jagged scar that ran down his face, his features were not entirely displeasing in the early morning light.

His voice sounded deep and welcoming in the peat-heated room. "Are congratulations in order? I believe you just won the tussle with Mistress Duncan."

He eyed her and the feast she had prepared with open appreciation. At first he'd been suspicious of her unusual warm greeting, but upon seeing her and the food, he decided the lady was here on a mission of goodwill. They both looked delicious.

"And upon seeing what you've prepared for me, I must confess that I'm delighted that you did so."

She gave a graceful curtsy at his approval. She'd taken extra care that morning with her toilette, carefully choosing a pretty, linen dress that matched the color of her light, mint-green eyes, while daringly letting her usually tightly bound black hair curl down the sides of her face. It was, she'd reasoned, important that he find her in her best looks for her plan to work. The small gold coin in her pocket made her ever mindful of the important task ahead.

The fact that her heart beat a quick staccato when she was near him or that a light of excited interest sparkled in her eyes, she told herself, had nothing to do with it. This adventure must be carried out with the same finesse she used in bartering wool in the market place. She had to get rid of the dreadful object and the dangerous curse it carried as quickly as possible.

She lifted the domed silver lid off the warming dish. "I am at your command, sir," she said, hovering over the tray with an empty plate in one hand, serving fork in the other. She stood at mock attention, awaiting his orders.

"Let's see, sergeant," he said, eyeing the platters. "Everything seems to be in Bristol fashion. Load up all your ammunition, and don't be too thrifty with the, uh . . . ," he pointed to the whiskey and winked, "the special ammo. We don't want to disappoint the troops."

"No, sir." She snapped a stiff-armed salute with the tray's lid. She filled a silver goblet bearing her family's coat of arms for him then poured a dish of tea for herself.

He raised his goblet in the air. "To the chef and all those who fought bravely to serve it." She smiled in return, raising her fine porcelain cup hand-painted with pale, pink rosebuds and gold trim.

"To our guest, the Earl of Drennan, may he enjoy a healthy life," she said, toasting in return, watching him devour his meal.

He chewed the food, savoring the delicious flavors of the prepared fare. He did not bother with the salt and pepper. But he did pause long enough to compliment her on the food.

"Mistress Beatrice, demme if this isn't the best meal I've had the pleasure of enjoying these past six months or more. Far better than the bland gruel I've been feeding myself at the castle, which apparently my late uncle had lived on before his death. Not to mention the weevils I obediently consumed as an officer in the service of his majesty's infantry. But now I must set an example, for the men you know."

He smiled, taking a bite of the perfectly poached herring as his stomach gurgled with satisfaction, proving his point. Quite clearly it was to his benefit to stay at Brightwood Manor.

"Excellent, superb, prime," he muttered between bites. "All of it tastes as if the gods themselves prepared it, ma'am." He barely glanced at her, so intent was he upon his present pleasure.

Lady Beatrice daintily ate her toast and sipped her tea. It was not becoming for a lady to be seen drinking and gorging herself with food. These two rules of decorum were the few feminine virtues her mother had managed to instill in her before she passed on. That she did not dance particularly well, nor sew, draw flowers, or sing like a nightingale mattered not at all. To her thinking, what was important for the Mistress of Brightwood Manor to know was how to run a vast estate whilst sick abed with a raging fever, being able to entertain a manor full of demanding guests for an entire rain-filled week, and to play a quick-paced game of whist while bandying interesting stories in French with her nearest neighbor.

These peculiar talents were the finer ones she counted upon daily to profit her family. They were qualities her mother had encouraged, believing that a young lady must be both a brilliant conversationalist and an accomplished estate manager. While some gentry lived off their inheritance with little idea as to how to make it more profitable, Beatrice's family was already seeing to her future and that of the next generation to follow. She bordered on being a paragon of perfection any young lady in Ireland might have chosen to follow. That is, if the young person didn't mind being branded a bluestocking by more envious, lesser-talented ladies of society.

A single-mindedness of thought, which any man might've envied, led Beatrice to make wise investments and helped her achieve well-defined goals. And at that precise moment all her energies were centered on one task only, ridding herself of that accursed coin. With that single goal in mind, she picked up a small, silver pitcher containing her father's favorite brew and presented it to him.

"Some whiskey, Your Grace? It be one of m'father's own making. Some say 'tis the best in all of the Emerald Isles."

The earl took a sip. *Nectar of the gods.* He smacked his lips in satisfaction. "Not just Ireland, dear lady. But all the rest of the Union, as well."

His dark blue eyes twinkled with delight. It had also been one of the strongest brews he'd ever chanced to taste.

"I'll take that as a compliment. And seeing how it came from an English lord, a grand one at that." She poured him some more of the potent brew.

He looked at her with a trusting smile of approval. She was almost sorry for what she was about to do. He really hadn't been such a make-bait since his arrival. Of course, he'd been a bit arrogant and full of himself, but then weren't most men? He drank down another dram.

"Sir, you must be terribly thirsty," she said pouring him another.

He waved a hand over the goblet to stop her, his eyes blurring. "I think I've had my ration, sergeant. Don't want to deprive the rest of the men."

"I'll have you know that this is 'elixir,' my dear Captain. And do you know your English word for whiskey comes from our Gaelic one for '*the water of life.*' So, one can therefore assume that one can never have enough. And as for the rest of the other brave gentlemen being deprived, no need to worry, Your Grace. There be plenty for all. We O'Briens see to it that our men are well watered and fed."

She had heard men were more apt to do one's will when filled with strong spirits. She hoped as well that he wouldn't notice her odd behavior. She needed him to be malleable and uncaring about what occurred about him for her plan to work.

He grinned, and firmly placed the drinking cup back on the table. His head felt light and he said in slightly slurred words, "I'm certain 'twas found to have extraordinary powers. But, I think I ought to pass-s-s . . ."

Undeterred, she took the drinking goblet and placed it beneath his numbing lips. Batting her long lashes at him, she did her best to be as coquettish as any young lady flirting behind a fan at her first assembly ball. She'd been waiting for this opportunity, now was the moment to seize it.

"Lord O'Brien will be dreadfully disappointed if you didn't drink another dram." She pouted prettily. "Why 'twas he who sent it up with his best wishes for your improved health, Your Grace."

James gave a lopsided, half-drunken smile at her. She looked so pretty sitting beside him, coaxing him. Demme if the chit didn't have pretty green eyes, too. Such a tiny waist she had. He hadn't noticed before. Why the vixen was almost winsome in both her attire and manner. Aye, she was most becoming this morn.

"That s-settles it!" he said in a half-drunken slur. "It would be intolerably ill-mannered of me if I were to insult my host's offering of goodwill." He took the goblet and drank smoothly down the rest.

The moment had arrived for action. She stealthily removed the cursed coin from her apron. She leaned closer to him, holding her breath as she daringly hid the magic coin amongst his bedclothes.

"There," she said breathlessly, her heart pounding in her ears from the near danger and deception. "I best take my leave and go tell Father how much—"

She chanced a glance at him and forgot the rest of her words of farewell.

He was looking into her eyes through a drunken fog, silently caressing her, without touching. He ran his eyes over her long dark hair, the soft curves of her oval face, down the line of her smooth, pink cheeks to her softly parted lips. An intoxication only a woman could give him pricking at his baser appetites. His head spun.

She held her breath and stared up into his handsome eyes. In one spectacularly impulsive moment, she wanted him to cover her mouth with his, to discover that heady feeling of being passionately kissed.

As if reading her thoughts, he lifted his hand up and removed the hairpins, which held back her hair. With one gentle tug, the long strands fell down about her shoulders. Her head felt suddenly lighter.

Encouraged by her silence, he combed his fingers through the glossy tresses. He placed his other hand firmly around her waist, pulling her up against his body. She took in a breath, surprised by the bold gesture.

"You are invitingly delectable," he whispered in her ear, his breath smelling strongly of whiskey.

He began to gently nibble on her earlobe, lowering his head, placing a series of small kisses along the column of her exposed neck. He murmured between kisses, "Delicious, soft and warm . . . absolutely enticing."

She whispered back, "Thank-you," briefly remembering the first time he'd placed his hands around her, how her body had quickened at the feel of his body brushing up against hers when she helped him out of the bog.

Gathering her hair, he gently moved it to one side as

he continued his exploration along the nape of her neck. When he reached her shoulders, he gently tugged down the muslin covering, causing her to shiver at his touch. He bent his head and began kissing her again . . .

She delighted at the feel of his lips against her skin, each kiss causing her pulse to quicken and her heart to pound in anticipation. Finally, wanting his lips on her own, she took his head into her hands and forced his bleary eyes to look into her own.

She commanded him, "Kiss me."

Obediently, he complied, his mouth descending on hers, his tongue gently coaxing open her mouth. He tasted of a mixture of tobacco and whiskey. His mouth savored her lower and upper lips as he sucked on them, awakening long forgotten feelings she'd tried to forget when she vowed to become an independent spinster.

She felt his hand reach inside her bodice and fondle her breast. In a gentle circular motion, the soft pad of his thumb applied pressure, rubbing her nipple. Involuntarily, she let out a soft moan of pleasure.

The sound of the outer chamber door clicking open, however, pushed away all thoughts of any further kisses or heated embraces. Startled, she backed out of his arms.

Not bothering to knock, Wise Sarah strolled in dressed in her best Sunday frock, a blue homespun gown lined with fine Irish lace. She wore a winsome smile and turned to speak to her patient, but the words she'd prepared died on her lips.

Head sunk to one side, the Earl of Drennan lay openmouthed like a dead fish in deep slumber. A drunken snore buzzed the air about him.

"Oh!" she muttered, surprised, spun on her heels, and walked out, slamming the door shut behind.

And that was a grand shame. If she'd but lingered a moment longer, she'd have seen a sight worthy of remembrance. Her friend, the renowned Spinster of

Brightwood Manor, that waspish maid of virtue, slid off the bed and onto the floor in a breathless heap.

Eyes closed, the lady of the house sent up a prayer of thanksgiving. "Praise be the good Lord above for small favors," she whispered leaning her head weakly against the wall for support. "He fell asleep."

So once again she'd miraculously managed to slip through the manacles of holy wedded bliss. For if she had been found lying in the handsome earl's bed kissing him, letting him fondle her body, she surely would have been trapped in a marvelous scandal.

Aye, even the becoming witch would have reported her to her father. For such scandalous behavior as being found in a bachelor's bed was not tolerated by the upright religious folk of Urlingford. But as the earl had fallen fast asleep when the witch entered the chamber, there was no reason to question her slightly ruffled state or the flaming color in her cheeks. She nodded in sober solemnity. A blessed angel from above was watching out for her this day.

And with a triumphant smile, she reminded herself that not only had she not been found in the earl's arms by the witch, she had skillfully rid herself of that blasted coin.

"Aye, and I wish him good fortune with it," she murmured, and left the room with nary another thought about what she had just said and done.

Chapter 4

It was not, however, the noise of his own snoring that awoke Captain James Dermott Huntington, the new Earl of Drennan. Much like the princess who could not lie asleep on a pea, he could not slumber with a magic coin in his bed. It poked. It prodded. It intruded upon his person until he could bear it no more. He'd slept on the rocky ground of the Guadarrama Mountains more comfortably than in this bed.

"What in blazes!" he muttered, searching for the intruding object. What was it? A protruding nail? A lost cuff link? Any number of small items came to mind as he searched madly under the coverlet till at last—

"Voilà!" He clasped the rough-edged object in his hand. He examined it closely. It glowed a shiny yellow in the afternoon sunlight, its magic qualities hidden cleverly beneath its smooth, golden surface. Pleased, he pocketed the yellow-boy telling himself it might bring him some much needed luck. He then pulled on his morning dressing jacket and as he did, glanced out the bedchamber's dorm window.

Outside, the lady of the house, Lady Beatrice, stood by a bed of roses, pruning the dead blooms. Her hair was primly tied back, completely hidden by a straw longhorn hat. A pity that, he thought, observing her movements. It would've pleased him to see it in the sun flowing like long black waves of smoke down her back. He grimaced. He was waxing poetic over none other than the person who'd been the cause of his present cumbersome injury.

"She's nothing but a shrew," he told himself firmly. "Your reasoning must've been badly addled by Lord Patrick's elixir, old boy. 'Tis a sorry day when you have difficulty telling the difference between a beautiful Irish colleen and a cold-hearted wench, such as she."

A problem, no doubt, brought about by months of all-male companionship endured on that rock in Spain. Not to mention the strong potent drams consumed earlier that morn. Apparently, he had not learned how to resist the temptation of too many tumblers of spirits.

He put a hand to his temple and felt a dull throbbing there. It matched his confused state of mind. For which was the dark-haired lady below? Was she the enticing lass with the soft lips who'd been ready for a passionate embrace this morning? Or was she the aloof, frostbitten spinster who'd so rudely shot him out from under his mount? The perplexing questions were worthy of the boggy marshes of Ireland where he'd been unceremoniously thrown.

Befuddled, he reached for the cold compress that'd been thoughtfully left by his washbasin. He placed it on his forehead and laid his head back. His recline was short-lived, however, for the sound of the garden-gate swinging open alerted him to the presence of another entering the garden below.

A tall dandy strolled into the ladyship's flower garden with the air of one who expected to be always the praised tulip in it. What's this? A suitor for the lady's cold hand? The earl rubbed his eyes clear of sleep. And without any thought for the lady's privacy, the seasoned soldier drew out his field glass from his kit beside the bed and fixed them upon the colorful popinjay.

Immediately noted was the rather large beauty spot the jackanapes sported. It stood out, a small dark mound on the dandy's pasty white chin.

"My word! 'Tis as big as my little finger!" James exclaimed out loud, focusing his field glass more firmly upon the byword for bad taste.

The object of his interest, one Squire Herbert Lynch by name, bowed over Lady Beatrice's gloved hand. The dandy wore a superfine morning jacket of striped pink and yellow, with large shoulder pads. His long, spindly legs, the envy of any stork, were gartered in yellow silk clockwork stockings and beribboned in bright pink at his knees. Yellow shoes buckled with shiny brass, the kind one usually wore to a ball, completed the gentleman's elegant attire. His yellow teeth smiled down at her from his pasty face.

Lady Beatrice still wore a pair of soiled garden gloves. Belatedly realizing his intention to make a gallant gesture over her hand, she removed one. The tall, thin pole of a gentleman buzzed around her like a bee to the lucrative honey pot with his lisping compliments.

"M'—m'dear, you are a breath of fresh spring air this fair morn," he said, affectedly forming his body into the perfectly required serpentine S. He drew her hand into his own. The wax padding he wore braced underneath his coat cracked audibly from the sudden strain.

"*Là,* you must show me the newest addition to your garden, Lady O'Brien. 'Tis been bandied about that you've added those dear little flowers from the Netherlands. Even my ward has asked if she mightn't pay a call in order to see them. But knowing that you did not wish to be troubled, I told her firmly no."

"But you shouldn't have, Squire Lynch. I'd have been delighted to show them to young Mistress Kathleen. You must tell her when you see her next that she is always the *bienvenue* at Brightwood. Faith, I do find her youthful company to be most pleasant and refreshing."

She smiled brightly, all the while grimly remembering his young ward's sad face. Although an heiress, young Mistress Kathleen Dargheen, seemed beggarly as far as familial affections were concerned. The village gossipmongers had long ago noted the sad fact that Squire Lynch had appointed himself the orphaned child's guardian only so that he might try and squander away his ward's fortune before she reached her majority. The dreadful unfeeling man was sure to ruin the lass's future.

She herself had met the child at a soiree held at the squire's home. She recalled a pretty child with silky, honey-colored hair and a pair of china blue eyes looking sadly out at the world, silently proclaiming to all and sundry her dismal state of neglect. Even the faded silk bonnet tied around her tiny chin bespoke of her greedy uncle's evident uncaring negligence of her. Immediately, she'd felt a certain kinship with the heiress. She knew herself what it felt like to be only wanted for one's money and not for one's self. She tried, therefore, to show kindness to the child as often as possible.

Lynch interrupted her thoughts, audaciously squeezing her captured hand. She took a shallow breath, resisting the more natural urge to slap him. Indeed, men like the squire were becoming increasingly more and more tiresome. Taking up her valuable time with their romantic nonsense, forcing her to listen endlessly to their ridiculous odes to her dark eyebrows and long raven hair.

The most dreaded of all these admirers, however, had to be the overzealous singers who frequently caused her to lose a good night's sleep. They, unfortunately, appeared regularly beneath her window, rain or shine, to sing in quivering trebled voices, dreadful ballads of undying love. Such untalented amorous screeching, assured to put her in a foul mood the next day, was probably the worst part about being a wealthy spinster. The last troubadour who'd had the audacity to wake her up in the middle of the night, had inspired her father, Lord Patrick, to deal with him himself. So disgusted was he with the grating noise of the singer, he'd thrown the entire contents of his chamber pot down on the hapless head of the screeching gentleman below.

She shook her head with resignation and carefully removed her hand from the Squire's clammy grasp.

Faith, if only her great aunt had left her very small fortune to her father, instead of her. But nay, the shrewd old bat had bequeathed all her earthly riches to her strong-headed, but nonetheless beloved, niece.

"Undoubtedly foreseeing what a bumble-broth it would create," she muttered under her breath in an exasperated sigh.

"What did you say, m'dear?"

"The um—flowers are over here." And she led him to a bed of tulips.

She had sent for the bulbs directly from Amsterdam herself. They were one of the few delights her wealth had brought. The bright petals of red, yellow, and white bobbed in the wind creating a colorful display for all to enjoy.

"These are my favorites. Such cheerful colors, don't you think, Squire?" she asked, trying to divert his attention away from herself, pointing to the flowers on their right-hand side.

"Yes, lovely, m'dear, lovely . . ." He nodded, barely giving them a glance, his weasel-like eyes focusing upon her right ring finger. For blinking in the sun was a large emerald ring of considerable worth.

In rapture, he breathed in deeply the scent of wet spring roses and tulips around him, wrinkling his long white nose as he abruptly let loose a thunderous, *"A-choo-"*

"God protect you, Squire," said Beatrice politely, wiping the spray away with a gloved hand. He simpered and gave her what he thought to be one of his most winning smiles, a yellow-toothed grin of favor.

The earl watched in fascination as the thin, choleric dandy led Lady Beatrice around a tall hedge into a more secluded part of the garden. The tall hedge blocked his view from the manor. He could no longer watch the proceedings.

Reaching into his pocket, he thoughtfully rubbed his fingers against the gold surface of the coin, feeling the rounded edges against his fingertips.

He wished the lady would send the spindle-legged macaroni on his way. The sight of the man gave him a headache. Even as these wishes passed through his thoughts, he heard a terrified scream, followed by what sounded like a loud, but very distinctive *ka-splash* of water. He grinned happily. The sound was very reminiscent of his own recent dip in a certain marsh bog.

Seconds later, a thin figure came scurrying out from behind the tall, obstructing hedge. The white blur in a pink-striped coat ran helter-skelter, yelling at the top of his voice. "Shrew! Witch! Hoyden! Bi—" and other various colorful epithets about the lady.

Looking down at his dripping, dirt-sodden coat and stained satin shoes, the shaking squire moaned aloud in deep despair, "They're completely and utterly ruined! You've destroyed m'beauties!"

He fell to his knees and keened at the expensive loss.

Lady Beatrice appeared next. She walked slowly, dragging the wet hem of her walking gown. Her hair dripped water droplets down her face. Upon espying the kneeling Lynch, she mumbled some angry words and charged towards him ready to tear the jackanapes to pieces.

He caught sight of her and let out a squeak of fear, making a frog's leap safely away from her. With an agility that astonished those who watched, the squire safely landed on the other side of the stone gate surrounding the garden.

Face flushed with rage, the insulted lady shouted over at him from the other side. "Be assured, sir, if I had my firearm, I'd use it and give the crows a pudding! Serving your skinny, white carcass up as an entree!"

She spat at him and wiped her tainted mouth across the sleeve of her dripping gown, vividly recalling the repugnant shock she'd most rudely received.

She had been innocently standing in front of a small, bronze statue of a shooting cupid, looking down at the flowering water lilies she'd most recently had planted in the reflecting pond, when the damned jack-straw had taken advantage of her immobility and pressed himself upon her. He had grabbed her slender shoulders, so that she was forced to face him, and in so doing placed a slobbery wet-dog kiss upon her mouth.

Outraged, and without any thought to the consequences, she gave the scurvy knave a most satisfactory push into the reflecting pond. Unfortunately, she'd received a good drenching at the same time.

Seeing the evil intent on her face, the squire swung up onto his nag. He failed to make it completely over the saddle. Half of him now sat astride Flossy, a plump chestnut brown mare of advanced age, known to be the most sedentary, gentle mount in the parish. The other half dangled in midair, his skinny, striped-clad backside swaying temptingly back and forth.

Noticing the half-mounted gentleman's predicament, Beatrice calmly and deliberately opened the garden gate.

"Nice, Flossy. Get-EE-up, girl," urged the frightened Lynch, his Adam's apple bobbing up and down in quivering fear.

[65]

She walked near. Spying a riding crop hanging from a nearby post, she snatched it down. Her emerald eyes reflected her inner thoughts as she approached. They snapped with sweet, dark thoughts of revenge.

From his precarious perch, the coward squeezed his eyes shut. She approached the horse and raised her crop.

"Ohhh—no-o!" squealed the squire.

Smack! The whip fell squarely upon Flossy's ample back flank.

The docile mount reared. The squire screamed. And together horse and rider galloped off down the main road towards the village.

It was later reported the lads at The Boar's Teeth rescued him for a quid each. No real harm done, except to the lining of the gentleman's purse.

Watching the horse canter down the road, the offended lady was satisfied that the audacious jackanapes would never bother her again. She emitted one last angry huff, and whipping her damp skirts around walked back to the manor house. Her revenge would have been complete, had not she heard a deep, masculine laugh coming from above. The manly laughter forewarned her that the entire debacle had been witnessed by another.

She stopped in mid-twirl and looked up at the second-story window. A pair of twinkling blue eyes met her light-mint green ones. He smiled with piratical amusement down at her.

The deuce! The English earl had obviously been witness to the whole dreadful fiasco. Embarrassed, and feeling strangely discomfited that he should be witness to her loss of temper, she continued towards the house, unable to muster any verbal display of anger. Instead, she hurriedly entered Brightwood Manor, giving the back garden door an indignant slam.

* * *

Captain James, the Earl of Drennan, set down his field glasses, a calculating gleam still shining in his shrewd, sapphire eyes. Some of those niggling questions about her shrewish character had been clarified by my lady's display of unrestrained temper towards the squire. It was evident she needed a firm hand to bring her to heel. Despite the minor character flaw of her evident dislike of gentlemen, her wealth had not gone unnoticed. And he sorely needed a wealthy wife. And as for Lady Beatrice O'Brien, well, one day she would need a husband. So, why not him?

He had a title to offer that was above her own. His nationality as an English subject guaranteed her children would be treated better than had they been born of an Irish father. Aye, it could be a very good match for both of them. He stroked his scar thoughtfully.

Besides, the winning of her cold hand in marriage would prove to be a most interesting campaign, worthy of a seasoned strategist such as himself. That is, if he decided to set himself to the task of wooing her. But to do so would require finesse, planning, and help. The kind of help that he'd had when planning a siege against the crown's enemies in Spain. He would have to send for his valet, ex-corporal in arms, Edmond Davis, immediately.

Through Davis, the earl cunningly set about vicariously spying upon Brightwood's household, his manservant bringing back daily reports concerning the running of the manor. Their main focus of interest was Lady Beatrice, herself.

Acting as his intelligence officer, Davis gleaned from the servants that they took their orders not from the master of the household, but from the *vanithee*, the young mistress. It was reported that Lady Beatrice did the accounts, oversaw the welfare of the tenants, and made the estate profitable. The people at the manor both respected and pitied her, having concluded long ago that her ladyship would never find her way to a secure marriage bed.

"The lady was once betrothed to a Viscount Linley," Davis said handing his master the morning gazette. "'Tis said to have been a suitable match, what with the lady's dowry and his adequate title."

He bent over and whispered in confidence to his master. "As it happened, sir, she called the wedding off. It was the night of the ball, when they were to have announced their impending nuptials. They say she suddenly received a letter telling her he'd run off to join the Royal Hussars."

The valet shook his thinning blond head in disapproval. "Such scandalous behavior, sir. What bad form to break the engagement the night of the ball held in its honor. Dreadful."

"And very cruel," added the earl. "Hmm . . . but that might work somehow to my advantage." He puffed thoughtfully on his pipe, a burning itch beneath his bandages causing him to point to a carved, silver-handled stick nearby shaped to resemble a hand. "Would you be so kind, old chap?" Davis handed him the scratching cane, the irritation serving to remind him of who had brought about his present discomfort.

"Continue, Davis. You were saying?"

"Oh, uh, right, Capt'n. The lady cried off and has ever since been safely on the shelf, so to speak. The nub of it being that she's taken a certain dislike to any of the gentlemen her father has presented her. Especially detests, they say, the English ones. Her almost-betrothed having been one himself."

"But what of her family? Are they not distressed by her still unwed state? If she's as wealthy as you imply, Davis, surely they would wish to see her well settled.

And try to create some sort of suitable match for her?"

"Aye, you'd think, sir. But 'tis only the lady's father, Lord O'Brien, and a widowed aunt, I hear, who wish to see her tie the knot. The rest of the family are praying she remains permanently dressed in virginal white. They'd like to have a share of her vast fortune. Not that she shows any signs of popping off to the nether world, sir."

"But the lady is still young and fit and surely could be convinced to marry if a suitable husband was found."

A knock on the chamber door interrupted him. Druscilla, Lady Beatrice's paid companion, brought in the morning tray. The earl looked the silver platters over. The menu was an exact replica of what he'd eaten the day before, which meant the same hands had prepared it.

The companion glanced unabashedly at ex-corporal Davis. Ever since the solidly built English valet had arrived at Brightwood Manor, she'd found ways to be as much in his company as humanly possible. She'd set her cap on this stiff gentleman's gentleman since the day she clapped eyes upon him. She always wanted to marry a nice solid man such as he, and there weren't too many of her own station here for the taking.

She giggled as she accidentally brushed up against him, setting the silver tray on the table next to His Grace. Her smile was genuine and slightly bucktoothed, as she bobbed a curtsy to the two gentlemen and left.

When she'd gone, the earl casually asked, "Is it considered part of a lady's companion's duties to bring a gentleman his morning mess, Davis?"

Puzzled, his man inspected the platters. If a two-headed snake had been served instead of the usual rumps of roast mutton, he could not have felt more discomfited. It had been bad enough that the woman had practically wiggled her bottom at him, but then to bring his master's morning mess in, as well. Gads! It was intolerably impudent!

"Nay, Capt'n—I mean, Your Grace. It isn't considered part of a lady's maid's duties, or responsibilities to serve a gentleman. Unless he be her mistress's husband, sir," he said stiffening. He silently rebuked himself for permitting the lady's companion entry to the usually exclusive all-male domain.

"Just so, Corporal Davis." The earl nodded. "Just so." And without another word, he tucked into the delicious food with unfeigned relish.

* * *

Lord Patrick O'Brien's gout had been easing quite nicely, and he felt fair pleased with himself as he ambled towards Drennan Castle's ruins. It was nearing the hour of nine and a cool night wind blew dead leaves around his horse's feet. Lord Patrick, an old, stout gentleman, carefully walked the animal through the maze of fallen square stones while holding onto a walking stick. The ruins had once been part of the castle's stone walls.

He heard a twig break and froze. Had he been followed? Perhaps a cutthroat purse-snatcher hoping to catch him out here alone was even now about to pounce upon him? Tensing, he let go of the horse's leash and put a hand on his sturdy blunderbuss.

A familiar young trebling voice called out, "Who goes there?"

"'Tis I, lad, your master, Lord Patrick," he replied roughly, easing the weapon down again.

A slight lad of thirteen stepped out from the shadows. Tommy Flander's freckled face greeted him with a broad grin of welcome. His own rude weapon, a large pitchfork, he carried defensively in one hand.

"Aye, so it be. 'Tis grand seeing your lordship up and about again. Bessy's not been making her best. It was as if she knew you weren't here to test her out, my lord."

"Is that so, Tommy, me boy? Well, now that be a grand shame, especially when I'm certain you kept her going at a fine trot."

The lord picked up a tumbler full of freshly brewed whiskey from a rough hewn table. He drank, swishing the liquid around in his mouth as he did so, tasting the flavors. "You fed her plenty of the secret ingredient like I told you to, lad?"

He touched the distillery's copper belly as if he were milking a cow of the most temperamental variety.

"Aye, my lord. Though 'twas difficult warming her with the wind blowing about tonight. And I'll be telling you, true, the moon was full-hitched in the sky. Afraid I was. They say the wee folk dance here when it be like this."

The lad glanced superstitiously at the half-ruined parts of the castle. In the moonlight, the ruins loomed forbiddingly in the quiet. Rumors had been spread aplenty and as fertile as the meadows in spring, as to the certain downfall of the Drennan clan. The talk now was that the new lord's recent fall from his mount had not been an accident.

For all the village knew that Lady Beatrice was one of the best shots in the parish. If she shot his lordship down, it was certain he would have been greeting the heavenly saints themselves that morn, instead of lying in a comfortable featherbed at Brightwood Manor as a convalescing guest. "Nay," cackled, Mother O'Donnell, a wizened lady of some advanced years. "'Twas them rascally wee folk who'd whispered a word into the horse's ear, which brought about his lordship's present condition." Young Tommy, one of the avid listeners, believed the old woman.

He turned to his master. "'Tis been ever so quiet since the new earl settled at Brightwood to heal, m'lord. Faith, been right silent enough to wonder if the banshee wouldn't howl at us at night in mourning for them noble dead knights buried over there."

He nodded in the direction of the castle's silent cemetery, fearfully eyeing the tilted tall grave stones of long gone lords and ladies. He took a step back into the warm firelight. Their ghosts were rumored to walk about on nights such as this, capering with the fairies under the moonlight.

"Nay, lad. There's naught to concern yourself in that quarter. Dinna you know that the ghosts like it when it be quiet. 'Tis said to give them a bit o' rest. Though if one had seen me lass come running from here, you'd think she'd seen one of the fey herself."

He winked at the servant and said in a voice full of confidence, "As long as we leave them in peace to do their fairy craft, there be no harm in putting ourselves under their protection. Why, tonight we'll even leave a jug offering out to keep them from making mischief. I hear they take to a fine brew. And I'd like even to go so far as to say ours has begun to taste, quite magical."

Lord Patrick took another sip from the jug, not a wit concerned for the fey sprites that might dwell in the ruins, or the ill effects drinking would have on his gout. For, was it not his own levelheaded daughter who gave him the idea of moving his poteen-making operations here? What with the whole village full of superstitious heathens, he'd chosen the best spot in Urlingford to secret Bessy. All the credit was due to his brave girl coming home pale-faced one rainy night from the direction of the supposedly bewitched castle's haunted ruins.

At first he'd thought some foul play had been used against his strong-headed lass and had started to order his outriders to chase out the villainous rogues that had dared to frighten her. But she'd stopped him in mid-stride, her face rosy with shame, as she confessed she'd merely been frightened by the storm's loud flashing show of thunder and earthshaking lightning.

Now that was an astonishing bit of news. His strong-willed lass had never been inclined to be afraid of anything in her entire life. Brought up as an only child, she had learned to stand on her own two feet, without the protection or interference of bothersome siblings. She was quite fearless. Not even as a wee chit when she got stuck in a ram's pen by accident, was she afraid. She'd merely blinked those bright green eyes of hers twice at the beast, daring it to charge and calmly walked out the gate as if taking a sunny Sabbath stroll to church. The doting father was certain that a braver lass than his Beatrice could not be found in the entire parish.

He knew then that her fright had to have something to do with the castle. What, he was not certain. The castle was mostly in ruins, unoccupied with the exception of two remaining towers inhabited at the time by the old earl and his elderly servants. But knowing his lass to have a level head about her, he'd reluctantly accepted her moonshine of an excuse and developed his own brilliant plans for the ghostly ruins.

"Aye," he mused drowsily as he snuggled up against Bessy's warm copper belly. I'll have to get m'lass a husband. I canna have her continually running around the countryside like some wild hoyden. For sure, I am that tired of the lads at the Boars Teeth making fun of my Bea' and those foppish suitors of hers. I have to find her a proper gentleman, one that can stand on his own two feet. Best I shut my eyes and do some thinking about it in the morn." And with that resolve in mind, he drifted off into a drunken slumber.

Chapter 5

The following evening, Lord Patrick found himself seated comfortably by the turf fire of his own manor home deciding the fate of his only daughter. Lord O'Brien, the Earl of Drennan and Beatrice drank to the younger lord's good health with contraband Spanish port, the bottle having been graciously provided by his recovering guest. Since it might be a crime either to keep it or to throw it away, the two lords decided it was best if they drank it then and there.

"*Slainte*," she heard her father say in Irish, toasting the earl's health.

"To your own good health, sir," answered the younger lord, raising his glass in turn. Primly Beatrice sat frowning at her father for disobeying Wise Sarah's orders of no strong spirits.

She'd tried to ignore them, but made a poor attempt of reading a tome containing recently translated Irish folklore. Irish legends were currently à la mode with scholars. Until now they had not been translated from the original Irish. The particular legend before her was a recent publication sent directly from a press in Dublin connected with the Institute of Ancient Irish Lore. But her thoughts refused to remain focused on the giant warriors of old for long. They kept straying towards a far more contemporary personage. Principally, this ruggedly handsome lord sitting calmly, talking with her father.

She listened as her father said, "I suppose once when your lordship is fit again, you'll be wanting to kick up your heels a bit. The gossipmongers have it that you came directly here upon learning of your uncle's passing. By now, a young buck like yourself must be after wishing to be back in London with the ton."

The earl shook his head in negation. "Far from it, sir. 'Tis doubtful I shall ever return to my former home or life. No doubt the moneylenders have long ago confiscated what few possessions I owned," he openly admitted.

"When I bought my stripes, I'd been running neck-high for some time in dun territory from gambling debts and living beyond my meager means. I behaved like a complete make-bait." As way of explanation he added, "I am the youngest of three sons. 'Twas very decent of his majesty's service to see to it I did not scorch myself any further into Newgate Prison. When I joined up, those money lending sharks no longer could pursue me. I was under his majesty's protection. While in the army, I reformed, learning how to handle responsibility, becoming the wiser man you see today."

"But what of your family? Surely they'd welcome you with open arms now that you're an earl?"

"Miracles have been known to occur," said James with an unemotional shrug.

"Mayhap you're thinking of returning to that fine regiment of yours? I hear from your man Davis that ye were a Jim-dandy fighter." The old lord winked, taking a puff from his clay pipe.

The younger lord smiled at the compliment, his eyes falling upon Beatrice's dark, shiny head. She pretended to be absorbed in her book, feeling his eyes observing her, carefully hiding her own interest. She knew so little about him. She listened intently to their conversation.

"My decision depends on a sundry of variables, Lord O'Brien. None of which exclude my choosing to make my permanent residence the family's ancestral castle here in Urlingford. Living there does, I must admit, have certain advantages. One, of course, having such charming neighbors such as yourselves nearby."

She looked up, startled. Charming? No one had ever used that term in connection with them before. She'd heard gentlemen say several flowery and exaggerated compliments to her. This, however, was the first she'd heard anyone consider using more personal terms than one would use with, say, a well-trained pet.

Her eyes met his. Unbidden, her cheeks flamed. It'd been two days since she'd felt his arms around her waist when she'd asked him to kiss her. The embrace was not one she could forget. It burned in her thoughts, reminding her how she had completely forgotten herself in that moment. If she was not careful, she'd soon find herself doing more than just looking at this appealing gentleman . . . she would find herself back in his bed. No, that would not do at all, not unless she wished to give up her independence and wealth to a man.

Observing his daughter's flushed expression, Lord Patrick helped himself to the port decanter. He turned to Beatrice and said, "Daughter, would ye be so kind, darlin', as to fetch m'wrap? I feel a chill creeping up my back."

"Aye, Da," she answered, forcing herself to move towards the door, reluctant to miss the conversation between the two. She sensed her sly fox of a father was up to something. He usually never played the part of a feeble old man afraid of catching a sudden chill. There'd been many a day when she'd seen him wander about on horseback with nothing on but a thin, frilled shirt. Now what the devil was he about?

Lord Patrick called out after her as she prepared to reluctantly leave the room. "And be a good lass and close the doors behind you. There's a fierce draft coming from the main hall."

She nodded, but sensing something was afoot left it open a crack. She fully intended to listen at the door.

The old lord set aside his drink. "Now, you were saying that you might stay on. May I ask what it would take to entice ye to stay, Your Grace?"

James, the Earl of Drennan, ex-captain of his majesty's service, swirled the ruby liquor in his crystal tumbler. He was enjoying the moment. It'd been a long time since he'd gambled, having decided upon buying out of his majesty's service that debtor's prison was not the sort of quarters he wished to find himself in. He'd given up the heady addiction. Leaning back comfortably into his chair, he decided it was the moment to pass the first ace of information to his partner, Lord Patrick O'Brien.

"'Tis simple, sir. I've need of a wife," he stated plainly without any further to do.

"Oh, so that be the way of it. And might I be so bold as to ask what qualities ye'd be after in seeking one, sir?"

The young earl took a light sip from the tumbler and looked the lord directly in the eye and said without bluffing, "She must be rich."

"To be sure," nodded the old lord sagely, "you've only the castle estates and another smaller one, I hear, in the next parish to live on. And although they'll bring you a tidy sum, I imagine your lordship will be needing plenty of gilt to make your life more comfortable." And thinking of the decaying castle, which the younger lord was considering turning into his permanent residence, he added, "Not t' mention more habitable."

Lord Patrick scratched underneath his graying beard in thought.

"Hmm . . . there be rich brides aplenty to be had around London and Dublin. Aye, ye could do very well indeed by tying the knot with some rich cit's offspring. What with your title, the ladies would line up for the privilege."

The young earl shook his head and gave a feigned doleful sigh. "And she must be of Irish lineage. 'Tis not been bandied about, but my title requires that I marry an Irish lady of blue-blood. My uncle, you must understand, detested the thought of the title passing completely into English hands. In order for me to inherit, he put in his will that I must marry—"

"An Irish lass of good lineage." The old lord nodded, finishing the thought. "Aye, I ken to your problem, lad. There are no Irish blue-blooded lasses left for the having around these parts, except my lass. . . ."

All of a sudden, he beamed. He looked the young earl over with a speculative gleam in his merry, green eyes, the very same color as that of his unwed spinster daughter's, only more full of good humor.

"But, say no more. I believe I've the perfect bride for ye. Aye *begorra*, I'll even see the lass leg-shackled to you m'self!" he said, clapping his thighs in evident delight as he thought of one particular dark-haired lass with a quick-spirited temper and gilt aplenty to spare on a crumbling ancestral castle. And this lass was of a very good Irish lineage, even if he did say so himself.

"I thought you might," answered the earl, waiting for the old lord to mention the lady's name. He kept a poker face of indifference. Lady Beatrice was the winning royal flush in Lord Patrick's hand. If he'd managed to win the old lord over in accepting him as a suitor for his only child, then he'd overcome one of the biggest hurdles in his campaign.

Lord Patrick did not have a chance to utter his daughter's name when the doors swung open and a vexed Lady Beatrice strode into the room.

She pushed her father forward and brought forth the errant wrap, which he'd let slip down his back. With a huff under her breath and a word about "addlepated old men," she marched out of the room again.

Lord Patrick turned with a half-apologetic smile towards his guest. "Mind, you'll have to be persistent to catch her. This lass, well, she's got a wee bit o' bad temper. And to my dying shame she's known as—"

"The Spinster of Brightwood Manor," supplied the earl with a hint of boredom in his voice. "And before you ask whether or not I'm interested in courting her, the answer is . . . aye, sir . . . aye. For I'm very much set in getting my own way." He ran a finger slowly and meaningfully along the jagged white line on his face.

Bushy white eyebrows lifted with concern. "Sir, we're speaking of wooing and winning me only daughter and heir. Not of fighting them rascally Latins."

"Oh, are we? Ever since I got nearly shot out from under my mount, I've had difficulty telling the difference." The earl sighed as though the evening had been entirely too tiresome for words and he now meant to seek the assured comforts of bed. "My humblest apologies, Lord O'Brien. I see now you only meant to speak of your eligible daughter in passing." He raised a hand to summon his man to aid him.

"Nay, sir. Sit down, if you please," the defeated father protested, waving his hands for him to sit.

"You've the right of the matter. Me lass is a bit unruly and, as ye can tell, hard won the shameful name she's now called. I donna suppose you've heard, but she was almost betrothed once to another worthy English gentleman of title. But he called it off at the last moment and ran off to join the army instead. Aye, and ever since she's been wearing that horrid mantle of spinsterhood."

"My word, sir, that is a bit harsh. The lady has undoubtedly been unjustly maligned," said the young earl yawning effectively behind his hand. "What I've seen tonight was pure daughterly affection and modesty of spirit. Indeed, the more I see of the lady, the more resolved am I to woo her. Is it not you Irish who say, 'Never take a wife who has no faults?' Demme, if I'm not willing to take her as I find her, sir."

He'd thrown down his last trump. He wanted the wealthy and charmingly sharp-minded Lady Beatrice O'Brien. And if the sparks of attraction between them yesterday in his bedchamber were any indication to go by, she'd make the perfect spouse for him. He waited, his fingers clasped comfortably around the tumbler, confident that soon the game would end and his suit would be accepted.

It did not take long for Lord Patrick to come to a decision. He had a cantankerous daughter, which no man, as yet, had managed to get close to. And yet within three days' time, this English lord had managed to get the saucy, sharp-tongued lass of his to prepare his morning meal not once, but twice. Aye, he nodded thoughtfully with wonder. Who knows what might happen if the English earl decided to become better acquainted?

As for Beatrice, by the holy rood, the lass needed a husband! Brushing aside the fact that both his daughter and the earl were of hot, unruly dispositions, the old lord spat into his hand and held it out to seal the match.

"My lord, 'tis a match made in heaven," James said. A faint sardonic smile lit his rugged face as he heartily spat into his own palm and slapped his future father-in-law's hand. They shook forcefully. The couple was now as good as promised to each other.

* * *

The next morning the earl's sweet success with Lord Patrick was singed with the aroma coming from his morning tray. The smells rising from the silver serving platters served were not what one would call appetizing.

Lifting the lids off, he quickly discovered why. The

toast was burnt to a crispy black and the herring smelled, although poached, as if it had come from a slop pail. Next to that was watery gruel that someone had decided to pass for half-cooked porridge and a muddy-colored cup of East Indian tea, tepid, no doubt.

"Davis," he said, holding his nose. "Return this pig's slop from whence it came and bring me back a proper mess."

"Aye, aye, sir," agreed the valet, wrinkling his own nose in distaste. It was worse fare than what they had eaten in Spain.

"So, my lady, you've declared war upon me," mused the earl as he read the epistle included. It informed him that the sooner he was able to remove himself from Brightwood Manor, the better. "Well, we shall see about that." Rolling the parchment into a tube, he set it on fire and calmly lit his pipe.

Down in the kitchens, the culprit watched with barely-restrained satisfaction as the somber faced Davis returned the tray. "Without His Grace's compliments."

Her companion, the love-struck Druscilla, tried to aid the valet. But the stalwart corporal brushed past her, turning his ramrod back on her in silent dismissal. Evidently, he believed she had played a party in the plot to sabotage his master's morning mess.

When he disappeared through the pantry door carrying a freshly laid tray of his own making, the wretched companion burst into a torrent of tears.

"Oh, come now, come now," reproved Beatrice, patting her on the back. "Making a watering pot of yourself will do no good. 'Tis ridiculous, all this remorse. Truly, Dru', he doesn't merit your eyes turning that most unpleasant shade of red. For sure now, in a sennight's time you'll realize that you're far better off without him."

The companion shook off her mistress's consoling

hands. *Bedad,* her lady had no heart! It was made of pure Canamara stone!

The young companion drew herself up and looked her mistress directly in the eye. "I know you think me a right fool, my lady," she sniffed, "but you needn't have played such a mean, spiteful trick. Just because you're planning on leaping apes in hell doesn't mean the rest of us have to, as well!"

Shocked, Beatrice stood stone still. Her companion had said what no one had tactfully dared since her broken betrothal a year ago. If she had slapped her on the face, Druscilla Pruit could not have wrought her revenge any better.

Druscilla, frightened by the calm look on her mistress's pale face, began to plead for forgiveness, saying she hadn't meant to say such cruel words. Beatrice paid her no heed and walked away.

In the privacy of her chambers, she gave herself a long study. Gone along with pretty bouquets and romantic girlish dreams was the dimpling round face that had been hers when she'd made her first debut in Dublin. In its place a thinner, more pronounced oval. High cheekbones had replaced the dimples of long ago and her green eyes stared back at her knowingly.

She undid the knot that held her hair in place. Long, black, silky strands fell in lustrous waves down her back.

"Viscount Linley used to say that it reminded him of crow feathers, fine black, shiny and glossy." She ran her fingers through the tresses, remembering her ex-fiancé, an arrogantly brutal English youth whose passion for spending money and gambling held his heart's sway more than she ever could.

"Aye, me darling, and 'twas you who helped send him away," she thought, staring at her reflection, the dimple from her youth faintly making its appearance at the corners of her generous mouth. "To think that no one knew that it was I who secretly arranged for his commission in the army. None found out, not even Da. For the money I bribed the army with had come hard won from the wool of my own sheep."

She grabbed her pillow and threw it joyfully into the air.

"The Spinster of Brightwood Manor. Ha!" Adroitly, she landed a blow against the bedpost. Bursting, the pillow's feathers flew every which way in a white flurry.

Laughing giddily, she twirled around dizzily under the rain of white plumage until landing with a muffled, "Oomph," she fell backwards onto the soft, downy mattress of her chamber bed.

* * *

The earl watched from his usual post by his bedchamber window. His field glass against his eye. Lord Patrick sat astride a horse loaded with a sennight's worth of provisions and a bedroll. His Grace's eyes gleamed with anticipation. It appeared the devil's own luck was with him. The old lord was about to make one of his famous disappearances. Already having devised the next step in his carefully laid plans, he gave the awaited command to charge.

"Davis, quick man, fetch my evening clothes. And then send for two servants to carry me down. Tonight I dine alone with Lady O'Brien!"

"Aye, aye, sir," saluted his servant and left to look for help.

* * *

The lady of the house sat in her father's chair at the head of the table. She leaned back, perfectly content to be alone. All those who could order her about had left, including her friend the wise woman.

While her father was preparing for one of his mysterious walkabouts, Sarah had informed her she'd received an urgent message from her mother, the renowned healer, Gladys Clogheen of Varrik-on-Suir. Fearing that the old wise woman was ill and dying, she'd left posthaste on the next carriage heading north.

Beatrice had watched with barely contained satisfaction as her father and friend disappeared down the road. Turning with one final wave, she'd fair danced up the manor steps to her long awaited liberation.

"Freedom," she hummed contentedly to herself. "Aye, 'tis truly grand to be doing for once as one pleases."

Soon the leading strings of proper conventional manners would be snipped off completely. She was on the verge of becoming that most dreaded of all females, *an original*. No man, be it squire, earl, or duke, would dare to court her then. It would be just too risky. Rich or not, a gentleman wouldn't want to marry such an uncertain oddity. Aye, they'd wonder what dangerously outrageous ideas might enter into her head.

Once she turned five and twenty, she'd finally have a free hand with her dowry. She could cast off the shackles of propriety and start to build cottage schools, create a dispensary, and hire skilled Quakers to work their art of silk weaving using her newly planted mulberry trees to feed the worms.

Oh, there were at least a half dozen other modern enterprises she wanted to put her hands and blunt into. So many things she'd been denied a chance to investigate and finance because she was of the gentler sex, and her father's ward. She just needed to be patient. A mere six more months and she'd be completely free to do as she pleased with her wealth.

And as for that tiresome English earl—bah! That fop could do her no harm! Just because her father had given him leave to court her didn't mean that he'd have the slightest chance of getting her.

She had tripped gaily up the steps to take her midday meal, blithely without another thought to anyone reporting her actions. She'd sat down in her father's now unoccupied chair dreaming of her freedom.

Her happy reverie, however, dissolved as a commanding voice boomed out orders in a most regimental manner. "Straight ahead . . . maarch!"

The sound of uniformed feet, scuffling towards the dining room, could be heard. Suddenly, the French doors sprung open and in entered none other than the devil himself, the Earl of Drennan.

Turning, she stared in openmouthed astonishment as two servants carried her guest, like a princely maharaja upon a red-velvet throne chair, into the room.

Waving his walking cane about, he boomed out instructions. "To the left now. Steady on, men. Ahh . . . splendid." He nodded pleasantly to her in acknowledgment. A bright, red, smoking jacket enfolded his broad shoulders as he waved his polished cane about in greeting.

"It would appear that I'm just in time to join you for supper, my lady."

She bristled at the idea of being *"his"* anything. He paid no heed at her disapproving scowl. He pointed to the chair next to her own. The empty chair was decorously removed by a servant and his chaise carefully settled into place.

"Là, I do hope the chef hasn't burnt anything tonight," he said in an even, conversational tone. "You must know, ma'am, I was served the most appalling meal this morning. 'Twas most criminal what it did to my delicate digestion. And I fear, my dear," he added in cool, even tones, "that if I'm served the same pig swill again, I shall be ever so vexed."

He gently patted his walking-stick with measured significance, the scar below his eyes giving him the look of a man ready to fight his way to a decent meal.

Beatrice winced uncomfortably. As an honored guest, he had the right to demand punishment for the insult served. Indeed, if he so desired, the earl could complain to her father about her lack of cordiality. And Lord Patrick, being a lovingly stern parent, would then be forced to see she was given the thrashing she deserved.

"But, ahh . . . such delectable smells." The earl sniffed, the mouthwatering roast mutton garnished with carrots and turnips filled the room with its delicious aromas. He looked under the hot serving trays. "It appears that all is well once again in your ladyship's kitchen." He nodded to one of the servants to serve him. "Aye, 'tis wondrously edible, m'dear."

"I'm delighted you find it thus," she said gritting her teeth, trying not to be disconcerted by his arrogant appearance.

"But from what you've just disclosed, my lord, I wonder if you mightn't reconsider taking your leave to return posthaste to the more certain comforts of your own home."

James raised one dark sardonic eyebrow at her impertinence.

"I shall return to the castle soon, but as I've said before, there are so many attractions to my staying here. Including, if I might be so bold, the daughter of the household."

"Là, sir," she said, rolling her eyes at the pretty comment. "Next you'll be telling me I remind you of the fabled Queen of Sheba."

"Nay, Lady O'Brien, I do not seek any riddles where you're concerned. Though to be truthful, I'd hoped you might divert me out of my present doldrums."

Disconcerted, she looked down into her lap. She'd tried unsuccessfully to forget that but two days ago she'd been alone with him in his bedchamber. And if he meant diversion to mean . . . her cheeks heated warmly at the remembrance of the passionate embrace they'd shared.

His voice took on the pompous tones of an elder speaking to a child. At the same time, he summoned the valet to pour him some more wine. "I'd hoped you'd play a few hands of cards with me. However, knowing so few ladies of my acquaintance who are as logically minded as myself, I thought that perhaps you would not wish to—"

The phrase "as logically minded as myself" lodged itself in her thoughts in the same manner a cannonball might in the first volley of war. The badly worded insult caused Beatrice's long, slender fingers to tighten around the arms of her father's chair. She listened to him continue to rattle on in a bored lecturing tone about the mental superiority of the male species.

Midway between his tiresome discourse on the size of a lady's head, which was obviously much smaller than a man's, and therefore meant only for thoughts concerning child-rearing, sweets, gowns, and music, she felt something inside her snap. Her notorious temper, which she'd managed by some small act of willpower to keep in check until then, bubbled up into almost volcanic proportions, forcing her into a hasty decision.

"Your Grace." She breathed deeply, squelching the desire to say, *Your extreme pompousness.* "I gladly accept your invitation to play a few hands with you, sir." She released her tightly held breath. "Shall we say this evening when the clock chimes eight?"

"With pleasure, ma'am. I look forward to it," he replied, bowing to her as his fingers stroked the rough edges of his lucky gold coin.

* * *

[87]

Rain beat against the manor walls as the tenth Earl of Drennan and Lady Beatrice O'Brien, the Spinster of Brightwood, played in the yellow drawing room. The walls of the room were hung in yellow silk and with its ceiling of octagon compartments, it was considered to be one of the most agreeable rooms in the manor house.

A peat fire had been lit and a playing table set cozily beside it. A screen had been setup so that the couple might play in some privacy while those attending them stood beyond to be summoned at the slightest whim of the couple.

Dressed in full evening attire of black velvet breeches and a cut away black-swallowtail coat that stretched at his broad shoulders, the English lord looked, even in Beatrice's critical eyes, quite dashing. She blinked at him for a moment as he held open a cedar box containing the pasteboard playing cards. She picked out a deck and began to shuffle.

He studied her, as with intense concentration she shuffled the cards. Her hands lifted and dropped the boards into place with the adroit expertise of a seasoned card player. The lady apparently was no stranger to the game.

"I see, ma'am, that you've had some experience."

"Yes," she nodded, intent on starting, "we're not so unlike the ladies in England, my lord, who think nothing of putting their families into great debt with the turn of a hand. The only difference is that we Irish win or lose, do it with a bit more panache and a lot less money. Shall we begin?"

"Whenever you wish." He flicked a hand eloquently as if the evening held little import to him. He adjusted his splintered leg more comfortably on the chair beside him. She asked him to cut the deck, and turning over the last card, she established the trump. They began.

Picking up her hand, she smiled at him, her pearly

white teeth glistening as she smugly waited for him to discard his hand.

She waited and revealed her own. "*Ecarté!*"

"So it is," he replied dryly, a hint of boredom lacing his words. "But do let us play another hand or two. I'm just beginning to warm to the cards."

They played again, and yet again she won without half trying. It was as if she could never lose. It made no difference how bad her cards were, his were always worse, and the game would once again miraculously play in her favor.

"It appears lady luck favors you tonight," he commented, gathering the deck for the fourth time.

"Aye, that it would seem, Your Grace," she agreed, sorely tempted to add that any simpleton could memorize the table of correct plays. Faith, he ought to have won at least one hand by now. That is, if he didn't discard his most important cards so foolishly in the first toss.

"Shall we play a different game?" she suggested, wondering if her good fortune, if indeed that was what it was, would hold out.

To lose so many times was almost unpardonable. Unless the gentleman was a complete dolt and had no head for keeping track of his cards. Perhaps the strong whiskey he drank as religiously as medicine now had begun to addle his brain?

He put his hand in his pocket and felt the rough edge of his lucky coin. It warmed the tips of his fingers. "Do you gamble, Lady Beatrice?"

"On occasion, I've been known to place a shilling or two on the table," she answered cautiously. A dim spark of delight dancing in her eyes, she might just have found a way of ridding herself once and for all of this English nuisance her father thought to foist on her. Coyly, she added, "Mind, m'lord, I gamble only when doing so will be to my advantage."

"But, of course, my dear. Why then I propose we wager for what our hearts truly desire." He smiled, a soft edge of amusement in his voice. "I suspect in your case, my lady, you'd like to be well rid of my esteemed presence."

She glowered at him. Of all the tactless, bumble-headed things for this impertinent make-bait to say. To think she'd helped drag him out of that muddy bog and brought him to the shelter of her own home. The ungrateful lout!

He frowned. "Perhaps I am wrong about your wanting to be rid of me?"

She tightened her mouth into an angry disapproving line. She glared back at him.

"By Saint George," he continued, "I could've sworn your note this morning said you wanted me as good as gone. Did I misread it? In which case, I owe you an—"

"Aye, so I did," she snapped, wishing she wasn't so readable, or that he wasn't looking so innocently perplexed.

"But do be after telling me what reward you'll be seeking in this gamble, sir?"

"Why, I thought you'd have guessed by now." For a moment he dropped his foppish facade and looked directly into her startled green eyes. "I want nothing more or less than your dear self, Lady O'Brien."

"The devil you say!" she spat, giving a warning nod in the direction of the servants around them, including her own companion.

Druscilla, unaware of the danger her mistress was encountering with the earl, stood in a nearby corner shamelessly flirting with Davis.

The earl shrugged, as though he were talking of merely inviting her to tea.

"Of course, it would be at a suitable place of my choosing. As for the rest . . ." His gaze strayed from her startled emerald eyes down to the low décolletage of her gown. Creamy, white breasts rose with an indignant intake of breath from beneath the lace lining.

"The rest, I believe, will depend on how well we manage together, won't it?" he finished with a suggestive wink.

"For certain, Your Grace," she mocked, her tongue at last finding its habitual sharpness, carefully slicing the words out evenly. "And I'll even clean out your castle, if you like."

Aye, she told herself. The silver-tongued rake didn't fool her not one wit by his so-called desire for her. Too many empty-pocketed, money hungry fops had paid her court. No doubt he was like the rest, sniffing out the silver, which clinked so thunderously around her purse strings.

This English dandy was no different. All she needed was for him to confess his true reason for courting her. Then she'd go directly to her loving father with the truth. And the revelation would put an end to all this foolishness.

She leaned across the table and whispered, "What be ye really after? You needn't be afraid of telling me. I promise I'll confide in no one the truth. Not even my father will know the real reason for your courting me."

He threw back his head and laughed. His laughter rumbled merrily in her ears. "My lovely colleen, do distrust me. For in the end, I'll have you!"

"You'll what?" she asked, raising her voice. She dared him to repeat his audacious words.

"'Tis best I show your ladyship." Swiftly, he breached the remaining space between them. Grasping her shoulders, he pulled her forward, half-lifting her out of her stiff-backed chair. Before she could utter a protest, his mouth descended on hers, sealing her surprised lips with his own ardently warm ones.

Stunned, she at first tried to draw away, but the heat of the kiss sparked the hidden embers she'd thought to have successfully doused. A hot, tingling sensation invaded her entire being, rekindling the burning desire she had felt in his bedchamber.

She unwittingly uttered a soft sigh. And upon hearing the sound, pulled back out of his arms as if she'd been slapped, her breath coming out in short pants.

"Do you need any further proof of how much I desire your company?" he asked, taking out a monogrammed handkerchief to give her.

"Nay," she said, wiping angrily at her now swollen mouth, pretending that the kiss had been horridly bitter instead of alluringly sweet. Her hands were shaking and she could feel her cheeks were red hot.

"I see," he said. "Then you believe in the old adage that the mouth that remains closed is a melodious one."

"Aye, Your Grace. But there be another even better." She nodded, her voice dripping with biting sarcasm. "That a man ties a knot with his tongue that his teeth can never unloosen."

"Yes, the Celts do have a way with adages, don't they? But perhaps, my sweet, my tongue would do better elsewhere?" He gave her a roguish smile and a flash of white gleaming teeth.

She would've retorted something equally pointed, but it suddenly struck her how silent the room had become. The normally soft murmurs of conversation between the servants standing discretely behind the screen had ceased. All in the room were straining to hear the words that passed between the Earl of Drennan and the mistress of the house.

Belatedly realizing that something was amiss, Druscilla hurried over to her. She stood at the ready, at the slightest nod from her mistress to administer to His Grace, the Earl of Drennan, a proper kick to the selfsame nobleman's shins.

The couple might have received permission from

Lord Patrick to court, but there were, until the day the banns were published, certain proprieties to be followed, even by an eccentric spinster and a handsome earl. And he had just now stepped over the boundaries defining discreet gentlemanly behavior.

"Do you wish me to ask His Grace to take his leave, my lady?" Druscilla whispered nervously into her ear.

"Nay, the uh—earl was only making a feeble point, Druscilla. A lesson, I assure you, he'll not be repeating," answered her mistress, a slight tremble in her voice betraying her normally calm facade.

She nodded in the direction of the earl's man servant. "You may return to your conversation with Master Davis. There is no need for anyone to question what has passed here."

"But, ma'am," whispered the maid, reluctant to leave her mistress's side. "He made an improper advance upon your person."

Beatrice nervously swallowed, forcing the rest of her statement out in a faked lighthearted manner. "Really, Dru', my father, as everyone well knows, gave the earl permission to court me. Therefore, nothing unseemly passed between us just now."

"Well, then, my lady, I best fetch your shawl. I expect you and His Grace will be wanting to take a little walk in the garden." The companion sniffed, properly shocked.

"That won't be necessary. It's rather cool outside. And we intend to play one more hand of cards."

Beatrice sighed to herself. Oh, if only she could be rid of the knave. Then her life could continue on the calm steady course that she'd set for it. Waving her fan back and forth, she tried to calm her nerves as her acknowledged suitor picked up the strewn deck.

The cool manner in which he dealt the deck reminded her that she needed only to play out the next hand in order to gain back the slippery control of her once well-ordered, tranquil life. Squaring her shoulders, she claimed her own set of cards. A soft gasp escaped her lips. There lay in her hand a series of unmatched low numbers of no particular suit. They gleamed mockingly up at her.

She glanced back hopefully at the earl. His rugged face revealed nothing about his own hand. If he had any feelings about the game, he kept them well-hidden, letting nothing about his silent demeanor betray his thoughts about his own cards.

He discarded one last time.

The moment had come to reveal their hands. Slowly turning his over, he showed his points and uttered simply the single word of triumph in French, "*Gagné.*"

Hands shaking with frustration, she ungraciously slapped her own worthless cards down on the playing table. "Good-evening, sir," she whispered and silently walked out, the soft rustle of her skirts the only noise in the room as servants retreated to their own quarters.

They left him with Davis to enjoy his victory alone. In the flickering light of the smoking peat fire, the earl spread his cards out, tapping the four winning points. He'd shrewdly gambled on her assumption that he was a foppish dolt who didn't know an ace from a queen. He, of course, had won.

"If my luck holds," he said aloud to the empty room as he flipped his lucky gold coin in the air, "I may win myself a bride, as well."

Chapter 6

Lord Patrick moved uneasily from foot to foot as he stood among the bulbs his daughter dug around. His dog, a high-strung black and white border collie, sat at his feet anxiously wondering why his master had stopped in their usual walk about the manor.

"Have a spark of sense, Bea'. The earl's not one gentleman we wish t'insult," he pleaded. "We can't afford to offend him. Your reputation has come down as it is."

She gave her father a scathing green-eyed stare. "Pray tell, what exactly do you mean by that?"

"Bedad lass, the whole village has heard of your kissing him. They'll be wondering why we're not visiting there. Whether once again you've been jilted, or something or other." He mopped his head in frustration. His daughter's peccadilloes were working on seeing him buried.

"Faith, I can't even pop m'head in The Boor's Teeth for a tranquil pint without some jackanapes making some sort of witty jibe about m'daughter's game-of-the-hen ways . . . demme, if they all don't think you'll burn in hell for not marrying."

"You can attend, Father," she said, lifting her chin in challenge. "But as for myself, I refuse to do His Grace's bidding."

"But, darlin', the gentleman asked me if you'd be willing to be the hostess of his fine fête. And I told him that you'd make a grand one."

"Then you shouldn't have spoken for me. 'Twas

[95]

unfair. I loathe him."

"Aye, anyone can see that." He sighed. "But he—"

"Tell his lordship that I'm not coming," she said with a final toss of her head.

Lord Patrick frowned down at her, his bushy, white eyebrows meeting in the middle of his forehead. "He's out yonder, awaiting your answer." He nodded in the direction of the garden, his voice rough with impatience. "You can hie yourself over there and tell him yourself that you're not coming. I'll not play messenger for ye, lass."

"He's outside waiting?" she whispered, almost dropping her trowel.

It had been almost three sets of Sundays since she last saw him. He'd packed his belongings the day after the card game and departed without so much as a by your leave. Now, as if he'd just paid a call but yesterday, he'd returned as coolly as water from a mountain spring to visit her.

"Well, are you going to see him?" asked her father, softening at the thought that his high-strung daughter had finally met her match.

"Aye," she said, deciding to settle the matter with the English lord once and for all. She'd tell that arrogant son of Cromwell how to go about hanging himself! She snatched off her gardening gloves and tossed them in her basket.

Her father watched with parental affection as she marched off with a quick swish of her skirts to find the earl. Softly chuckling to himself, he remembered how for the past fortnight his usually indifferent lass had fair jumped out of her chair whenever a visitor came to call.

"Just like a cat, all spit and fire, she was. Hissing at everything and nothing, an' a saying she didn't care for the man."

"Ha!" He laughed. "And I'm a blind old fool. Musha, 'tis a pleasure to see her come alive again."

He nodded his graying head and pulled out his long dhudeen pipe. A rewarding cloud of fragrant smoke soon circled his head. Mayhap for the first time in five years he could finish carving that cradle he'd begun. He smiled dreamily, thinking of the grand babies he hoped to bounce on his knee one day. With a soft whistle to his dog, he went in search of his carving tools.

The earl stood by a white rose bush admiring its perfectly unfolded leaves. He turned at the sound of her approach and leaned casually on his walking stick. He was wearing a morning coat of superfine gray that stretched at his broad shoulders, his immaculately starched neck-cloth done in the complicated occidental, contrasted with the dark tan of his sun-kissed skin.

He raised his tall, beaver hat as she approached, looking directly into her wide green eyes. His blue ones sparkled down at her as if they'd just heard a splendid joke. "Ah, Lady O'Brien." He bowed.

"Your Grace," she replied stiffly, lowering her lashes as she made a proper curtsy of welcome. "My father tells me that you wished to speak with me, sir."

"That I do," he answered, his eyes taking in the green morning poplin she wore. The simple puffed sleeves encased her narrow shoulders and the tight square bodice tapered sharply into a v-line around her waist, billowing over the heavy folds of her stiff, white petticoats and clean apron. Stiff, just like her pale, tight face. Except her cold airs could not hide the contrary lushness of her youth, her rose-colored lips, and the bright color of her emerald eyes. Neither could she control the wanton long black tendrils that had escaped once again from her tight coiffeur, which now pleasingly framed her face.

He itched to put his hands around her tiny waist. But her cool, green eyes forewarned him that such a gesture would not be welcome.

"I've been considering our wager," he said nonchalantly tugging at one of the pearl buttons of his leather riding gloves.

She looked up at him, his words at last having caught her attention.

"I thought perhaps it best for me to invite you to my home to act as my hostess," he continued, clarifying the matter. "During the upcoming festivities to celebrate my new peerage, I shall have need of one. I'd hoped you'd accept to play the part."

"Aye, to be sure. That's what you thought would be best," she murmured parroting him, a tinge of anger framing her words.

What she really yearned to know was where had he been all this time? Why had he not paid a call? She would rather have her favorite ewe roasted than confess that she'd thought of him.

He stood so close to her, much too close—she could feel the barely contained energy beneath the perfectly-attired gentleman.

She strolled over to her tulips to distract herself from him. His closeness clouded her thoughts. She needed to give herself time to think. He may have won the card game, but he hadn't won her. And to top it off he'd gone away and completely ignored her!

Having some guile of her own at her disposal, she said, "But I wonder, Your Grace, what would happen to your fine plans, if for example, I were to tell Father of our little agreement? Don't you think his honor would be a wee bit offended? Perhaps he'd even consider dismissing you as a suitor for my hand?"

A spark of admiration lit his eyes. Smiling down at her, as though they were talking pleasantly of the unseasonably fine weather Ireland was enjoying that spring, he said, "Faith, I thought Lord O'Brien had told you. But then, perhaps not. What a pity, I thought by now he'd confided in you."

"Told me what?" she asked suspiciously. Her eyebrows raised questioningly, a niggling of doubt making her insist. She sensed he was about to tell her something that he would then hold over her head.

"Why, my dear lady, did he not tell you about the little tête-à-tête he had with me?" he said once more, as if he could not believe she did not already know.

"Let me see . . . oh, yes, I do believe, ma'am, he promised to forfeit to me ten of your best sheep if you decided to bow out of your obligation of fulfilling the role I chose for you," he finished, with a low warning tone of a moral lesson.

"Apparently, my lady, your father is a laudably honest gentleman and believes that one should pay off one's gambling debts. I, of course, heartily agreed with him," he said explaining. "It would set a bad precedent if one did not fulfill one's debt. Don't you think, my lady?"

Beatrice shook her head in stark disbelief. Her own dear father had betrayed her. It was almost too much to bear.

Ten sheep! *Mavrone*, she'd been planning to use all of the flock's wool for the new looms she'd ordered. She couldn't afford the loss of any of the quality fleece. She gulped down her rising panic and squelched her pride, turning pleading, green eyes the color of new spring grass on him.

"Would you be willing to wait till autumn to collect on them?"

She bit down on her lower lip, mentally counting the lambs to be born in the following weeks. The season had only just begun. Oh, so many would be lost! And all because of her arrogant foolishness.

He shook his head, his eyes resting upon her tightly bound hair. "Nay, m'dear, one debt will not settle another. You do understand that, don't you? That your sheep, though they'd be welcome additions to my own flocks, aren't nearly as important as—"

"M'self," she murmured, a lump in her throat, making it impossible for her to utter more. She nodded miserably. Musha, musha, why had she let herself make the expensive gamble? The payment was far too dear. Her well thought-out plans couldn't afford such a setback.

He saw the look of dismay on her face and knew that once again he had won. The matter was settled. She had to capitulate to his demands or lose some of her precious angora sheep.

Nonchalantly, he re-buttoned his riding gloves and prepared to finish the matter with one last parting word of instruction.

"I'll send a carriage for you on the morrow. I want you at the castle before my guests arrive. There's a great many preparations to be made and I'll be depending on your valuable help in this. I suggest, therefore, you bring a small retinue of some of your own servants to lend a hand."

She bowed to his authority, holding her sharp tongue in check. She knew that if she did protest, it would make matters worse. She'd lose the sheep. And as for her father, he had chosen the man's side in the matter. She knew there would be no leniency coming from that quarter if she did not do as the earl bid.

"Good day then, Lady O'Brien. 'Tis been a pleasure to see you again." He tenderly lifted her hand to his. His mouth brushed a butterfly kiss over her wrist. It caused her to shiver and she stared at him wide-eyed, blinking, forgetting for a moment what they had previously been discussing.

Silently, unable to stop the course of events, she watched him mount his gelding and disappear down the road. She could not resist, however, thinking of perhaps faking some highly contagious malady that would send the rogue running for cover. But immediately, she dismissed the idea as worthless. Knowing him, the fox would see through her guile and send for one of his so-called physicians to check on her false condition. The doctor would probably bleed her to death in the process.

No, she couldn't risk it. Valiantly, she consoled herself with the thought that perhaps being hostess would not be so entrapping. That is, if they both managed to keep their hands to themselves.

* * *

Days later, Beatrice looked down at her hands. Small calluses had begun to make their unwanted appearances on her tender white palms. "The devil take all Englishmen," she grumbled, giving a silver coffee pot a hearty rub.

Her shoulders and arms ached from the exertion and there was still a pile of silver yet to be done. She'd started working at first light dressed in her oldest frock, one that should've gone to the scullery maid ages ago. She wore a faded, gray turban wrapped protectively around her hair.

He, that English slave-driver, had set her about making the huge stone pile of Drennan Castle hospitable and somewhat habitable. The roué's definition for the word "hostess" evidently equated with that of "unpaid drudge." Since the moment of her arrival at the castle's front steps three days earlier, she and the half-dozen servants she'd brought with her had been put to the awesome task of trying to remove the thick layers of dirt and cob-webbed grime that covered the ancient keep.

That repairs had been made before she'd arrived were evident, from the solid beams above her head, to the newly laid floors below. The sounds of continuing work echoed throughout as the noise of various hammering and sawing bounced off the stone walls and filtered down to the kitchen where she and three of her maids were hard put to work cleaning, polishing, and endlessly rubbing away the tarnish, layer by layer.

Beatrice muttered between her teeth, "The pleasure of m'company. Ha!"

She'd seen little of his lordly self since her arrival. With the exception of telling her what needed to be done next, the earl barely spoke a civil word to her, as if she were one of his foot-soldiered minions waiting to take obedient commands from their aloof superior officer.

She almost felt like saluting him every time he did show his face. For sure, as the sun rose every new day, he'd find something else that urgently needed to be done. And would she hop to it and see that it was taken care of like a good lass?

She huffed an errant tendril of hair out of her way.

The leading rascal of them all was her own father, Lord Patrick. That sly, old fox had immediately disappeared for parts unknown, after depositing her and the servants he'd been willing to loan on the front portal of the castle. They were unceremoniously left like some parcels he was well eager to be rid of. And to think she'd been concerned for his well-being the day she'd returned the blasted coin to that—that—overbearing, English fiend!

"Aye, I hope they both burn in Hades," she muttered, remembering the fairies, wishing once more she'd never clapped eyes upon the lord and master of this large stone barn. Mucking it out made-up for a lifetime of unsaid penance for the way she'd mistreated the male sex.

Perhaps, she had to admit, she had been a wee bit of a forked-tailed creature herself to those she successfully dissuaded from courting her. But faith, for all her various machinations, she didn't merit this lowly treatment! She sighed, and went back to her rubbing, picturing the earl and her father's smug faces in the reflection of the silver bowl. She simply wiped their existence away.

*   *   *

At luncheon the earl made his appearance. He stood, a tall figure at the kitchen door, his dark-blue linen shirt hanging loosely open at the throat, a few manly hairs peeking through. He surveyed the domestic scene of her and the servants polishing his tarnished silver.

She glanced up at him, her sooty lashes fluttering against her pale skin. It was evident he'd been hard at work from the glistening sheen on his face and the wet dampness on his shirt. His muscled arms, like strong broad beams, were revealed as the long sleeves were rolled up.

"Lady O'Brien," he greeted her. "Just the person I wished to see."

Her heart did a funny little leap. Despite her anger, he looked dangerously attractive. Noticing how dirty her hands had become reminded her to be careful. He was the enemy, the same despicable rogue who'd tricked her into coming here in the first place.

She wiped her hands on a clean rag. Hands on her hips, she confronted him. "So, my lord, what humble task would you be setting me onto next? Digging a duck pond for your carriages to wash in, I suppose?"

"You've done splendid wonders to my silver. A shallow pond to clean carriage wheels would be rather nice. 'Twas not work that I was thinking upon," he said, eyeing the dirty turban covering her hair and the small brown smudge on the tip of her pert nose. "But rather, my lady, food of the nectar—"

"Now you want me to feed you, as well." She gasped, ready to throw her dirty rag at that haughty roughhewn face. The bleeding spalpeen!

His grin broadened at her show of shrewish temper. "Nay, nay, you mistake, sweet lady," he protested, laughing as he put his hands in front of him as if her angry accusations were sharp-edged daggers. "I merely wished for you to join me in the partaking of this hamper."

He brought forth from behind his back a large wicker basket.

"A lady from the village showed up here about five minutes ago. A Mistress Ryan she said her name was. She's a tenant of yours, is she not? She asked me if I'd like to share this with you."

Beatrice's tightly clenched hands returned to her side. The wonderful smell emitting from the hamper was admittedly heavenly. Her mouth watered and any insane thoughts of refusing were immediately put aside by her stomach's loud, rumbling acceptance of the invitation.

"Mistress Ryan is my tenant, Your Grace. But I shall do as she suggested and invite you to partake with me this hamper," she said in her grandest lady of the manor voice, her dirty turban slipping as another errant strand of thick black hair tumbled out, falling over her right eye.

"The pleasure, dear lady, is all mine."

He bowed, a merry twinkle in his dancing blue eyes. "I'll meet you by the south portico in, shall we say, half an hour's time? Thus giving us both ample time to make ourselves um . . . more agreeable."

She nodded, thinking it would take her at least that long to remove the first layer of heavy soot that covered her face, let alone the rest of her. Hurrying to her chamber, she had a basin of hot water sent up with a bristled pig's brush.

'Twas delicious to feel the sticky grime wash away with the rough scrub of her serviette. She felt as though quite a bit of the dust covering the castle had found its way onto her. She dreamed of what a luxury it would be to have hot water whenever one pleased. But as it was still day and the servants were all busy with the reparations being made, it would be wrong to request a hip bath.

The chamber that she'd been given was a pleasant one. Whereas most of the castle seemed on the point of moldering away, this part of the keep had miraculously withstood the test of time. It was through Druscilla that she learned the reason why.

Her companion had managed to wheedle her way back into her mistress's good graces once more by being one of the first servants from Brightwood to volunteer to accompany her ladyship to the castle. She chattered merrily away as she helped her ladyship undo the back of her gown.

"'Tis said to have been the only part of the castle not built on the fairy ford," the maid gossiped. "And your chamber, my lady, was said to have been once occupied by— oh no, I shouldn't be telling you this."

"In the name of all the blessed saints, what are you blithering on about? What is it you shouldn't be telling me?" she demanded.

"Why, what I wanted to say, ma'am, was that . . . well, the rooms used to be one of the late earl's fancy pieces," the blatherskite blurted out without any further constraint. Her mistress might be a bit of a hoyden, but she was still the vanithee of Brightwood Manor, a high born lady of one of the few remaining Irish nobility in the Urlingford parish.

"You didna say," Beatrice whispered with wide, shocked eyes. Her reputation would be in shreds if word leaked out about where she slept. Original or no, she'd not have all and sundry wondering if she was the new earl's light-skirt.

"Aye, my lady. 'Tis said one of them wicked earls kept his French mistress here," confided the companion grimly with a sharp nod. Her own innocent, brown eyes gazing warily about as if a sinful orgy were about to unfold on the middle of the bed.

"Musha, if that be so. . . ." blanched Beatrice. "'tis impossible for me to remain here. But where, oh where, shall I move myself to?"

She'd already inspected the other rooms in the castle and greatly despaired of finding a replacement. The only other habitable chamber was near the servants' quarters and it was even less acceptable for her, being dreadfully dank and a prime spot for catching deadly inflammation of the lung. She shook her head with resignation. She'd have to make do with this room. And to be sure, that didn't prove to be such a tiresome task.

The chamber had a lovely view of the valley, decorated in graceful Louis XV furniture, one of the few rooms that had any furniture or decorations to speak of. The drapes were in faded shades of light pink with silver and white flowers. It proved to be quite pleasing to the eye, even in its tea-stained appearance. If one of the late earls had kept a mistress here, Beatrice had to admit, the soiled dove had had the good taste of a discerning Beau Brummell.

She gestured to Druscilla to help her into a gown, a resounding gong in the hall warning her that time was slipping by. With the help of her maid, she changed into a green walking gown edged in fine lace.

Short country sleeves and a square bodice made the top half of the simple empire gown, the straight skirt falling down from the waist. Her hair was brushed up and a cascade of black curls framed her face. She draped her favorite long black shawl bordered with military tassels around her shoulders, letting the long fringe dangle becomingly down her back.

Pinching her cheeks for color, she picked up her dark green parasol and hurried out to the south portico terrace.

The earl stood with his feet wide apart, hands on hips, waiting impatiently for her appearance. He had changed into a fresh, white linen shirt and tight leather breeches, clothes that most of the working men laboring on the castle wore. At first glance one could easily have mistaken him to be one of the common laborers from the village. But the arrogant tilt of his head told all that here was the proud lord and master of the castle, the Earl of Drennan.

Unwittingly, she returned the charming smile he gave her in greeting.

He gestured towards where the picnic had been spread on a patch of verdant lawn near the portico wall. Ever the soldier, ex-corporal in arms, Joshua Davis stood to one side vigilantly awaiting his captain's orders.

The earl handed her down onto a cushion, a large wool blanket spread out beneath her. With a nod to his man, he ordered the food to be served.

The delicacies that the admirable Mistress Ryan created for the hamper melted in Beatrice's mouth. Ever aware of the lord of the castle's presence, she glanced at him between bites of succulent shepherd's pie.

For an Englishman, she had to admit, he was not unpleasant to look upon. The leather breeches molding to his muscular thighs, which required no extra wax padding, bespoke of a man used to physical activity. They may make him into an earl of the realm, but that could not change the fact that here was a man with the soul of a soldier, a leader of men. She had to admit to herself that enticed her.

They talked about the repairs that had been made that day, and to her surprise, she relaxed under his smile.

It sent warm flutters through her, as the wall she had carefully built around her heart crumbled a little.

"The south wing where we are now shall be completely redone. 'Tis the part which needs the least attention," he said, pointing to the area where most of the reparations had already been made. "As for the west wing to our right—"

"The ruins," she said with a familiar shudder. It was over there that she had seen the old earl on the fateful night that she'd picked up the magic coin.

He nodded, picking up a twig with which to draw a crude map of the castle's keep. "I shall have to let that part of the castle go."

He drew an X through it.

"Why?" she whispered, half afraid, wondering if he knew of the leprechaun's curse upon the castle.

"It's unstable. We've tried rebuilding the walls there, but each time one's completed, it collapses. The foundation shifts beneath like quicksand. My ancestors should never have built on that part of the hill."

"Oh." She breathed, relief flooding her with warmth and confidence. Fleetingly, she looked up at him. Staring at his mouth, she remembered the kisses that they had shared. They had not been such disagreeable experiences. Mayhap, she admitted, they'd been passionately exciting.

"There's something middling strange about that wing," he said, bringing forth his lucky piece from his pocket. He began tossing it up and down.

"Strange," she echoed, staring at the coin as it flipped up, a gleam in the sunlight.

"Aye. Most of the men I've hired from the village refuse to go near there. Some superstitious folderol. They say the castle is cursed." He laughed, thinking of the quaint tale. "By none other than the fairies themselves!"

"But—but 'tis true," she said, and the minute she heard her own words, she clapped a hand over her mouth.

The gold coin stopped its flight and landed neatly into the palm of his hand. He turned and looked at her as if she'd been senselessly struck by a stray moonbeam.

A tinge of color pinkened her cheeks. Merciful hour, how was she to set about explaining that? She lowered her lashes over her eyes, not able to meet his penetrating blue stare.

He placed a hand beneath her chin and forced her to look into his eyes.

She trembled, her heart thumping loudly in panicked fear. The moment to confess about the cursed night she'd picked up the magic coin was now upon her. What was she to say? How could she tell him of the curse?

A little figure dressed all in black appeared ominously at the top of the stairs leading down to the portico lawn. Startled, they both turned to see the tiny black apparition approach them.

A woman's voice boomed out, "What the devil do y'think you're about? Take your hands off m'niece, or by the Holy Mother of God, I'll have ye up before a priest!"

Beatrice paled and softly groaned. She closed her eyes, trying to will the black apparition to disappear.

"What is it?" whispered the earl.

"Mavrone, 'tis she . . . Herself, my aunt and godmother, Lady Agnes Fitzpatrick," she said with an unfamiliar hiccup of dismay. She watched the tiny vision charge down the stairs, long dark wisps of black silk and lace flying upwards like the wings of a small invading bat.

The little woman dressed in widow's weeds was none other than her father's eldest sister, the widow of one of Ireland's most famed sea captains, Lady Agnes Fitzpatrick. She was the only person in all of Ireland who could force Beatrice to behave like a proper young lady and settle down.

"She's—she's your aunt?" the earl asked hollowly with relief. For half a moment, he'd thought she was one of the wee folk come to prove him wrong, and to rain vile curses down upon his head for doubting in their existence.

Unnerved, he stood to meet the much feared lady in black.

"Aunt Agnes," she said, taking a deep breath, "May I present to you the Earl of Drennan . . ."

"I know who he is, Bea'," said the formidable lady, cutting short the introductions. "You are the English lord my brother has given permission to court my niece." She sternly eyed James as he bowed over her hand.

"My brother informs me that you served in the Infantry in Spain, instead of the Royal Navy, Your Grace?"

He nodded. "Yes, ma'am."

"Indeed . . . I shall overlook the mistake for my niece's sake."

"That's very kind of you," said James smiling, equitably regaining his composure.

"Aye, it is," replied Agnes, touching a locket that contained a miniature portrait of her missing husband. "For no finer men exist than those who serve his majesty on the open seas. Now, Beatrice, I'm dreadfully tired from my journey and would like to rest. Please take me in."

"Of course, Aunt Agnes," demurred the niece, while mentally wishing her interfering relative anywhere but there.

Chapter 7

"'Tis a fine tick mattress this be," said the tiny black figure sitting on the end of a four-poster bed. Aunt Agnes moved her widow's weeds out of her face and smiled at her niece as she tested the tick beneath her with one firm push of a small plump hand.

"I'll take this room, Bea' darling. It suits me fine," she said. "That is, of course, if it be agreeable with you, dear."

"As you wish, Auntie. Though, 'tis really none of my concern. For sure now, I'm only a guest here m'self," demurred Beatrice, not wishing to argue with the tiny whirlwind, knowing full well that if she had said she wanted the room for herself, her aunt would summon her at unseemly hours of the night. And when she did, the tiny lady would sound a wee bit like Goldilocks trying to find the right bed.

She could hear her say in that sweet voice of hers, "Beatrice darlin', would ye mind getting a heavier coverlet for your aged aunt? M'bones are chilled." Or, "Bea', sorry to be making such a sorrowful nuisance of m'self. But would ye kindly fetch some planks? Me back's achin' again." And so forth all night, until she finally handed over the desired bed to the headstrong, diminutive lady.

Nay, she best try and save herself late evening trips down the hall by giving her aunt her own bedchamber, a good night's rest being more precious to her than a comfortable bed.

"Auntie dear, would you care to sleep in my room? I'm certain it'll be more comfortable for you than this small chamber."

"Nay," spat the tiny lady. "Tested it already. That bed of yours be made for a pair of soft-bodied lovers. Not a tall fit for a wizened old dwarf such as m'self, darlin'."

Beatrice had the good grace not to say a word.

Did her aunt know her chambers had once been occupied by one of the late earl's paramours? Holy saints above, she sincerely hoped not, or she really would have her and the earl up before a priest!

Lady Agnes's eyes twinkled merrily and with a well-aimed dart added, "Not that anyone would think that you're seeking His Grace's bed. 'Tis been bandied about that you're planning to wither on the tree like an unplucked rowanberry, leaving all your wealth t'them miserable curs we call relations."

"That be no concern of yours, Aunt. And pray tell, as you know that I've no intention of marrying, why you came charging down at his lordship as if His Grace were trying to—to—"

"As if he'd like t'buss you? That'd be fine to be sure. And let the entire village think he was having his way with you before you're even properly married? Never! Ye may be a hoyden, and a bit of a shrew, but we all know you've kept your virtue intact."

"Really, Aunt Agnes—" The shocked Beatrice gasped. "Your tongue has not dulled one wit."

"Forget about m'forked tongue for the moment. Tell me, lass, has he asked for your hand yet? Paddy said that he gave him permission t'court. Well, has he asked you to marry him yet?" questioned the older woman keenly.

Beatrice barely blinked an eye at the question. It was just like her aunt Agnes to be posing questions that were no concern of hers.

"No, he hasn't," she answered primly. "And I very much doubt he shall."

Stubbornly lifting her chin, she moved to open the blue curtains, which covered the windows, hoping to distract her aunt with the view. The drapes had been made up the day before. They fit perfectly with the Chinese screened walls of deep blue, which somehow had miraculously found their way into the castle's stone interior.

"How very droll," said her aunt, looking again at the room. "Did you know, my dear, the Asian style is à la mode with the ton now? I've heard that English dandy, Brummell, is having his townhouse in London redone in lacquered cabinets and sculpted bamboo. But to be sure, your being here, m' dear, with the handsome devil of an earl 'tis nothing more than pure neighborliness. And I suppose the way you've set yourself out to muck this stone dungeon 'tis pure coincidence."

"And how do you know that I've set myself to that task? Mayhap I'm simply here doing the pretty for my neighbor?" challenged Beatrice, lying through her teeth, the calluses on her hands hidden deep beneath her apron pocket.

Her aunt patted her niece's slender shoulders with a small, pudgy hand.

"I know you only too well, darlin'," she said with a loving smile. "Only you'd think t' use bees' wax and lemon on these rough-hewn planks instead of plain pond water. Although your sensible head hasn't seen fit to put a vase of flowers by m'bed." She gave a small sniff of reproach. "Not that I'm complaining, mind."

"I beg your pardon. I haven't had a chance to pick you some posies. I've been too busy scrubbing the floors."

She turned and gazed down at the waters of Kilkarney that wound their way through the emerald green valley of Urlingford. She wearily wished she were already five and twenty and safely on the shelf, so that she wouldn't be

[113]

having this indelicate conversation with her well-meaning, but nosy aunt.

"So, how long are you planning to stay?" she asked, sidestepping the subject of the earl much the way she would a boggy ditch.

"'Tis all business, we are," Lady Agnes muttered, a slight frown of disapproval pursing her thin lips. "How kind of ye to be thinking o'me aging bones. To be sure now, it be almost a pity that m'brother didna have any sons. Mayhap then I'd not have had to leave my own comfortable home for this lacking reception. But he wrote that ye needed me. So whether or non you're wishing me gone, I'm here to stay."

"Da sent for you?" Beatrice repeated, stunned by the announcement. She turned around to stare at her domineering aunt.

It was well known that her father and his older sister barely tolerated each other, being completely on opposite sides of the river on one most important issue—whiskey. The grieving widow of a stern, tea-drinking sea captain, her aunt eyed the spirited brew as the works of the Devil's hands. She could recite by rote the report made by doctors from the West County, which stated that "an increase of insanity was plaguing Ireland due to Methodism and the deadly sin of drinking."

"Aye, I told him that I'd come and help you, darlin'. But mind," she added smugly, "I made that heathen brother o' mine agree to m'conditions first."

"And they were?"

"I made him take an oath that he wouldn't make another drop of that wicked, mind-sapping brew of his until the day he walked you down the church aisle."

She looked at her niece's stunned expression.

"Why, darlin', you're as pale as a sheet. Didna your father tell you of his promise to me?"

"No-o," Beatrice replied weakly with a half-felt

laugh. And if she had known, she'd never have stepped outside of Brightwood Manor's doors.

"It would appear Da's been making quite a cartload of bargains behind m'back lately, including this one."

Only now she realized to what extent her father was willing to go to see her well settled. That troubled her. She didn't like the idea that anyone sacrificed themselves on her behalf. Not Da—not . . . A pair of dark blue eyes appeared in her thoughts, giving her stomach a sharp twist. Not anyone.

Agnes nodded, satisfied with the affect her revelation was having on the stubborn chit. "I've been thinking, Bea', that lovely gown you wore at the assembly ball last harvest. The one I told ye was not suitable for an unmarried lass."

"Yes, Aunt?"

"T'would be most appropriate for tonight, don't ye think? And as you and I will be dining alone with the earl for the last time. Well, to be sure, I was hoping that you might consider wearing it," she said, recalling the pretty picture her niece made in the russet colored evening gown of liberty silk.

Although, to her thinking white would have been the more appropriate color for the unwed heiress. But undeniably, her niece was an original and wore what she pleased. Being so wealthy, no one dared say otherwise when she wore the gown. Aye, her niece's wealth was most helpful at times.

"Very well, Auntie," she agreed, deciding it was best to call a truce or she'd end up dodging her tiny aunt's sharp tongue all night. "I'll wear the gay rag if it'll please you. Not that I see what's so special about the gown."

"Oh, and I want you to wear your rubies," added the matchmaker, shrewdly interrupting. Having her niece look like the rich heiress she was wouldn't do any harm, either. From the amount of repairs currently being done on the castle, it was evident that the new Earl of Drennan needed some gilt. A pretty rich bride would be a decided asset.

*   *   *

The glass window panes glowed behind Beatrice as she paused in her descent down to the main hall. The rout was to be in two days' time. The work in the castle had reached its final frenzied peak of last minute preparations. Tonight would be the last bit of calm before the whirlwind of activities began and the house filled with the expected guests from Dublin and London.

From below she heard her aunt's voice twitter up to her. "Sure now, Your Grace, it must've been grand t' have been a part of such a splendid regiment. But here on the Emerald Isles, ye must be thinking of more peaceful pursuits. And seeing how much m'niece has been so helpful to Your Grace . . ."

She hedged shamelessly on, despite the scowl of disapproval directed at her by the helpful lady herself, who appeared at the bottom of the marble stairs. "Mayhap you should consider putting my niece's hostess talents to the full test. Though mind, I taught her the most practical talents. Aye, I can almost guarantee ye that no English bred debutante will match her in this."

"And what useful talent would that be?" asked the earl, politely interrupting the lady's discourse.

He looked in the direction where the subject of their conversation now stood, shimmering under the light from the candlelit chandelier above them. His warm gaze fell upon the beautiful vision in russet silk coming towards them.

She appeared to almost glow before him in a

sparkling red gown. She wore large, red robin-egged rubies, which sparkled around the column of her creamy neck. Carefully wrought gold-threaded droplets of ruby red gems dripped from her pierced lobes, brushing against her dark black curls. She looked, to put it mildly, spectacular.

Heavens, the earl thought, his eyes fixed upon the vision before him. The lovely, young queen walking towards him was both classically elegant and lushly beautiful. He wanted this Irish goddess before him. His blood throbbed, rising under his skin when she smiled at him in greeting. The devil take it, she was, as never before, the woman he most desired to bed and wed.

Aunt Agnes brought him back to the present, continuing the conversation they had begun before she appeared.

"Faith, sir, didna she tell ye? It was m'self who taught her how to cook."

Aunt Agnes proudly beamed a nodding smile in her niece's direction. She continued blithely on, unaware of the sudden chilling discomfort she brought into the room's otherwise warmed occupants.

"She has the touch of the fairies, my Bea' does . . . her pastries, oh, Your Grace, why they be as light as feathers when she puts her hand to it." She lightly tapped the earl's hand with her fan in a playful gesture of delight. "Aye, 'tis true, in all of Kilkarney there be none who can beat m'niece's cooking."

Beatrice cringed at the compliment, remembering only too clearly the dreadful meal she'd served on the fateful morning the day after her father had given the earl leave to court her. If memory served, she'd managed to create the most spectacular scorched mess one could possibly provide.

She turned large, pleading green eyes towards him. Her tiny aunt's wrath was a terrible thing to behold when properly stirred. It was known to blow into a miniature hurricane, which could cause an entire household to tremble in fear. Facing a firing-squad was more welcoming than a full month of guilt-ridden recriminations and harping from the tiny domineering lady.

"Ah, yes," smiled Captain James, his voice dripping with warm interest, "then perhaps, dear lady, you can persuade Lady Beatrice to lend a hand in teaching my cook some new ways in preparing some tasty treats for my guests?"

Her aunt gave her a beaming smile. Beatrice swallowed her relief, and readily nodded in agreement. She'd been momentarily spared an indoor tempest.

"I would be pleased to help Your Grace," she capitulated and taking his offered arm, they strolled into the dining room. Both castle and master had gone through noticeable transformations. The fop she'd played cards with had miraculously disappeared and suddenly transformed himself into this nonpareil, a gentleman worthy of the renowned English ton, who frequented the court of the Prince Regent.

She glanced up at him, completely bewildered. He looked like a nobleman of the realm. He'd changed from the bragging fool she'd played cards with, into this debonair and attentively charming gentleman. Unlike his more effeminate male counterparts with their beauty spots, powdered wigs, and ridiculous manners of speech, he appeared to be the somber epitome of manliness. A fact her heart did not let her forget, as it quickened at his touch upon her arm when he slowly and decorously led her into the dining room.

Aunt Agnes trailed contentedly behind them, waving a gloved hand for them to continue on without her. She lingered over a small oil painting depicting the goddess of love, a half-naked Venus lying in a pale blue sky discretely covered by carefully placed white clouds. It hung in a small gilt-edged frame near a large flower arrangement. The tiny lady flicked open her pince-nez and gave the small painting a thorough inspection, tsking aloud as she did so.

Beatrice and the earl continued to walk on alone through the French doors into the newly restored dining room.

She leaned towards him once her aunt was out of earshot and whispered, "Thank you for defending me. My aunt Agnes's displeasure can be quite uncomfortable at times."

"No need to thank me. I merely spoke the truth. If I'm not mistaken, it was you who prepared one of the most satisfying meals I've enjoyed since returning to England. It was very, very much to my liking."

He lightly stroked her hand. "By the by, do you think you could persuade Lord Patrick to give me a bottle or two of that most excellent elixir he brews? I find my health has greatly improved upon taking that wondrous potion."

Ever conscious that her aunt was within hearing range, she nodded.

"I'm certain that my father would be more than willing to part with a few bottles, Your Grace. We wouldn't wish you to fall into decline after having made such a remarkable recovery."

She dared a glance at his injured leg and couldn't help but notice how much he had been standing on it while overseeing the repairs of the keep. Certainly, the well-formed muscles belied the fact that it had up until a fortnight before been wrapped tightly in bandages. The only discernible trait that it had been dealt a wounding blow was his slight limp.

"Does it pain you much?" she asked, feeling a twinge of guilt that she had been partially responsible for his misfortune.

"Nay." He shook his head, and upon noting her contrite expression, smiled. "It's almost completely healed. I no longer use a cane and limp but a little. A fact which I credit alone to the skill of the one who set it." He smiled at her warmly.

She had the good grace to lower her eyes, recalling their angry exchange afterwards. "Sir, you are more than prodigiously generous with your praises towards others this eve, even when perhaps they do not merit them."

"Please, do not consider me generous. Seldom do I feel called to be so," he said and lifted her hand to brush a butterfly of a kiss across it.

Her eyes widened. The kiss had been but a mere flutter over her skin, much as it had when he had kissed her wrist in the garden, but each time it sent resounding chills through her.

*   *   *

The rest of the evening was spent comfortably at the table with her aunt regaling them with some of the escapades she'd shared at sea with her legendary husband, Captain Ian Fitzgerald. The couple had sailed the seven seas and lived through many remarkable adventures during their more than two-score-and-five years together. It was only when his ship had sunk during a storm off the coast of darkest Africa did the couple finally part.

"I've traveled to all the seaports of the known world in hopes of hearing of some news of him," her aunt sniffed in mourning, "but it was to no avail. Not a word of him or his crew to be found. They fear all hands were lost in one of them dark unchartered spots off the African coast."

Looking at her aunt in proud widow's weeds, Beatrice for a moment could not help but feel a sharp twinge of sadness and envy. Her aunt, despite her woes, had had companionship, love, and friendship in her life.

But what about me? Beatrice asked herself. *With whom have I ever been able to share all my hopes and trust in? Let alone share all my mundane victories? Thus far, there has been no one.*

She glanced at the tall gentleman at the head of the table and her heart whispered, *But here's a man with whom one could easily share an entire lifetime of adventures, if you let him.*

She shook the thought off, reminding herself of the avarice of men, especially of those who'd previously pursued her. She had but to conjure up the uncomfortable memory of the pinch-faced Squire Lynch's white mouth to turn her rosy dreams of a happily shared hearth into a frightening nightmare.

Bedad, she trembled at the thought of marrying such a worm. No man could be trusted to let a lady live her life the way she wished. For gentlemen wished only two things from a wife—her coin and her offspring.

Aye, she nodded. 'Twas best to remain a spinster maid than to let any man rule over her, or her heart. But even as she reminded herself of these sobering facts, her gaze kept returning back to the earl's face, her eyes straying downwards to his firm lips. For the tiniest of moments she wondered if his kisses would always make her feel heatedly mindless of everyone and everything about her. Undeniably, it would have been interesting to find out.

Her aunt, as though sensing this would be an opportune moment for the couple to be alone, yawned into her hand.

"Oh, my—the journey has quite worn me out," she said. "I believe I shall retire for the night, my dears."

Standing, the earl helped the tiny lady from her chair. He offered her his arm, but she refused it with a gentle shake of the head.

"'Tis kind of Your Grace, but there's no need. I can find my way." She leaned into him and whispered into his ear, "Take your chance with her . . ."Agnes kissed her niece affectionately and said, "I'll be praying to the Virgin Mary tonight on your behalf, Bea'."

"Why, Aunt?"

"Because miracles have been known to happen." And with that dry reply, the lady gave them both a benevolent smile, the same one she would have given if this were their wedding night, and went in search of her bed.

After Agnes left, they sat and companionably drank tea, discussing the festivities planned for the upcoming days and the remaining repairs to be made before the guests arrived. The castle was quiet, except for the gentle tick-tock of the salon clock. It was a comforting sound, the servants having retired for the night.

Druscilla had taken to her bed hours ago with a good book and a hot cup of chamomile tea. No one was going to disturb them. Beatrice's reputation was protected by her aunt's presence in the house and her father having secretly betrothed her to the earl. A secret the entire village was now well aware of after he proudly shared the news at the pub, buying a round for the entire house.

Upon hearing the clock chime the half hour before midnight, Beatrice said, "I believe I shall retire for the night."

With hooded eyes, James nodded an agreement. "I will follow you up. I would not wish for you to trip on the stairs."

Despite his limp, he insisted on carrying the heavy silver candelabra. He shadowed her, his eyes observing the gentle movement of her swaying hips beneath the layers of red silk as she ascended.

His bedchamber was at the end of the hall. She stopped in front of hers. She turned towards him, but before she could speak, he opened the door and stepped into the room.

"I'll make a quick check for rats, shall I?" he said, eyeing the large Louis XV bed.

Not waiting for an answer, he made a token inspection, peering into the dark corners and under the bed with the candlelight, knowing full well the small vermin had long ago fled when the renovations began.

"Is it safe?" she asked, peeking around his back.

"I believe so . . ."

She cautiously entered. She was not afraid of many things, but small furry creatures with long tails and sharp teeth, was one of them. The mere idea of stepping on one or worse, being bit, made her hesitate.

His dark eyes focused on her anxious face in the candlelight. She was standing between the bed and him.

"No harm will come to you," he whispered huskily.

Putting down the candelabra on the side table, he gently touched her face. It was as if he'd been thinking about nothing else for the last couple of hours, but of this moment alone with her. He was taking his chance.

Although she would never admit it, she wanted him to take her into his arms. Deep inside herself she knew it was the reason why she'd come to the castle. Her aunt had been right. She was not there merely to help her new neighbor. She was there because she wanted to be with him. She wanted him to touch her, to connect with him in the most intimate manner a man and woman could by making love.

She looked into his eyes. She could see the desire he held for her in their dark blue depths. He wanted her. The knowledge sent a tingling awareness coursing through her body, heating her blood. His eyes mirrored her own secret wanting.

He placed his hands around her waist and began to kiss her. He stroked her mouth with his tongue, stirring something deep inside of her, a feeling she knew had been missing from her life. It was a wild, heated emotion that she thought to have tamed into submission long ago, but had been reawakened the fateful morning when she gave him the magic coin.

Yes, she silently decided, ignoring the inner voices that warned her against trusting men. *I want him . . . I want to become one with him.*

He began to undress her, loosening the back of the red gown. Gently, he pulled it down over her shoulders until it went over the curve of her hips and finally lay in a pool of silky fabric at her feet. She stood only in her undergarments and rubies.

She heard him suck in his breath as he looked at her and said, "I have desired you for a long time now . . ."

"You have?" she could not resist asking, almost in disbelief. Men were always after her money, not her. This was the first time a man confessed he desired her alone.

"Yes, and believe me, my dear, I have dreamt of you, a great deal, over the past few weeks . . . I have wondered what it would be like to touch you again, to feel your body against mine, and how well our bodies would fit together when I made love to you."

She said honestly, "So have I . . ."

He gave a heartfelt laugh at her words, and rewarded her with a passionate kiss on the lips. Her arms reached up and wrapped themselves around his neck, encouraging him to continue.

"A minute," he said. He removed his hands from her waist, taking off his evening jacket. Lifting his arms up to reveal the hard muscles he'd earned in the military, he shrugged off his white shirt.

He hesitated. "Shall I continue?"

She nodded, comfortably lying down on the bed. She propped herself up with one hand, her eyes taking in the beautiful proportions of the half-naked man standing before her.

There was no doubt she wanted him. Skin bronzed from working outside on the castle glowed in the candlelight. She wanted to touch him, to feel the smoothness of his sun-kissed skin beneath her fingertips, to have his body pressed up against hers, and to feel his response to her touch.

He sat down on the bed next to her and removed the last of his clothing. He was completely naked. Her green eyes shone with approval, taking in the manly contours of his body.

Between the two pillars of his strong thighs and below his flat stomach was his manhood. She stared at it, curious, unafraid. She was a midwife, familiar with the manner in which men and women made love and created children. His had come to life from the passionate kiss they had shared and stood erect under her fascinated gaze.

"You are a stud," she said honestly.

"A stud? You mean like a stallion?" he asked, amused by the word choice. "A rather crude, but pleasant comparison."

"Aye," she reaffirmed. "Despite the nasty scar you wear, nature has definitely favored you."

"And you, my dear vixen, are a living Aphrodite," he said, his voice thick with desire. She looked like the pagan goddess of love, lounging on the bed's rich blue coverlet, wearing only her corset and gems. Her hair was still piled high on her head in the Grecian style, a small ruby coronet crowning it.

He began to untie her corset, freeing her breasts from the confines of the restricting garment, gently cupping them with his hands, weighing them. He bent down and sucked on each nipple, teasing them with his tongue, until she let out soft sighs of pleasure.

He placed his arms on either side of her and

carefully held himself above her. She lay comfortably back against the soft mattress as his hands and mouth continued stroking her body, awakening a swirling desire between her legs. He rubbed himself against her, his hardness causing her to want to press all of herself up against him, until invitingly she lifted her hips. She wanted him to enter her, to answer the growing need between her legs.

"Soon," he whispered into her ear, not wanting to harm her.

He gently opened the lips of her sex to be certain she was wet and ready to take his manhood. His fingers probed, stroking gently at first and then more quickly until she was moving restlessly beneath him, raising her hips so that his fingers would go deeper.

"Please . . ." she moaned, wanting him inside of her.

He smiled knowingly, and kissed her lips, then placed the tip of his manhood inside of her, his breath turning into a heavy pant, not certain if this was her first time, trying not to harm her. A bead of sweat broke out on his forehead.

"There's no barrier," she said, breathlessly, not wanting him to stop. "Lost it ages ago while fox hunting . . . it broke when I landed hard after taking a jump."

Relieved, trying to maintain control, he hissed air out between his teeth, entering her completely, his hands cupping her backside. He rhythmically began to move inside her, his body cradled by her thighs.

She felt his manhood pulse inside her, and while awkward at first, met his thrusts with a passion of her own, the hot waves of desire in her lower region overwhelming her until she heard herself cry out. They continued their coupling until he suddenly removed himself with a shout of his own and spilled out his seed next to her.

Knowing it was her first time, he turned towards her

and began praising her. He reassured her, gently stroking her hair and planting kisses of gratitude. "You're a lovely, desirable woman . . ."

He then stood up and sought out the washbasin. She watched him, admiring the manly grace of his naked body. He returned and gently washed her, rubbing her body dry with a towel. He quickly kissed her and placed the coverlet snugly over her naked body.

Trying to locate her night dress, which hung in a dark corner, he stumbled into her clothes press, "Ouch—" he muttered and rubbed his shin.

He returned to her side with the prized gown.

"Lift your arms up," he said. He helped her put on the gown, awkwardly placing it over her head. A small rip was heard as he pulled too hard. A ribbon lay in his hand.

"Sorry," he said sheepishly, staring down at it. "I guess I don't know my own strength."

"Don't give it another thought. Druscilla can sew it back on tomorrow," she whispered, her green eyes smiling at him, amused by his clumsy efforts to help her.

He became somber, not returning the smile. He looked down at her thoughtfully, wondering how he could protect her if it was discovered that he had been in her bed. What could he do?

"If it is discovered that you and I, um—" He looked at her, unsure how to finish the sentence, for she had not told him how she felt about having become sexually intimate with him.

"Had made love together, yes?" she finished for him, wondering what he was trying to say to her.

"Your reputation would be in shreds. I think, therefore, I should do the right thing by you," he finished quickly. He got down on one knee and did what he thought was the noble thing to do, sacrifice his bachelorhood.

"Will you marry me?" he asked.

She frowned, her face darkening.

"You think I should *marry you*?" she queried, her voice lifting in disbelief. "Because we were sexually intimate?"

"Yes, in a nutshell, that is what I think," he answered a little sharply, his right knee beginning to throb, the same one he had badly twisted when he was shot out from under his horse. "I want to save your reputation."

"Indeed . . ." she said, coolly surveying him.

Her eyebrows lifted, never in the world imaging that a man would so bluntly ask her to marry him right after making love. Not because he loved and admired her. Oh, no—but because the jackanapes wanted to prevent a scandal!

"That won't be necessary," she answered primly.

She pulled the coverlet up to her chin, eyeing him as if suddenly he had turned into one of the despicable rats she had been afraid of earlier. Imperiously she added, "You may leave now, Your Grace."

"What do you mean that won't be necessary?" he asked, feeling as if she'd just slapped him. She was supposed to be breaking down in tears of gratitude and saying yes to his proposal. What the devil! What was she, an unfeeling shrew?

"You needn't sacrifice your bachelorhood, sir, because of me," she explained, discarding the cover in exasperation. "I am a lady. And you are, for the most part, a gentleman . . . I . . . that is *we* . . . do not have to follow the rigid conventions society expects of us and marry. We had an affair. Therefore, what happened in this room concerns no one but ourselves. No one need know what occurred here tonight."

"An affair," he repeated, looking down at her as if she stated for a fact that the Irish gentry had children out of wedlock on a regular basis.

"Aye," she said defiantly, although she felt a lump develop in the middle of her throat after saying it.

"My proposal meant nothing to you?" He almost growled, his face rigid with contempt. "And losing your virginity to me was merely a—a *lark*?"

"No—I mean—Yes." She didn't know how to respond.

She felt a sharp pang somewhere in the region of her heart. She looked down at him, still kneeling on the floor.

Why did he have to look so wonderful? It was so much easier when he was acting like a pompous, good for nothing jackanapes. Why did he have to be so noble about taking her virginity? And why, oh why, did he have to go and propose marriage to her and ruin everything?

They stared at each other, both exasperated with the other . . . both breathing heavily in anger. The very air about them felt thick and heavy with the potent mixture of anger and sexual attraction. Suddenly, he stood up and taking her into his arms, he began kissing her in a way that made her heart sing.

She did not push him away. Instead, she forcefully pulled him on top of her. She wanted him to make her forget herself. She wanted to be simply a woman making love to a man.

His hands moved over her body, lifting her nightgown over her legs. He rubbed himself up against her, skimming her body with his own, until she felt a familiar warmth between her legs . . . but he had not forgotten.

Abruptly, he stood-up.

"Where are you going?" she asked in a fog of desire. "Stay."

"Go to the devil!" he said, biting the words out angrily, snatching up his clothes. He stomped over to the closet armoire and pushed on the back.

"I'm *not* your stud, Madame! I am a man!"

Much to her surprise, a secret door swung open. Naked, he strode into a narrow hall, which led to his own bedchamber. Before she could say another word, it closed behind him with a sharp click.

He left her open-mouthed, staring at the now empty place where he had once stood. Turning on her side, she punched her pillow in frustration and muttered one word, "Men!"

She tried to speak to him the next day about what had occurred between them, but he quietly dismissed the topic as not important.

"Don't trouble yourself with my feelings," he said when she persisted. "Do what you promised and I will consider your debt fully repaid." And she did.

Over the next two days a quiet truce was established between them. She continued to help him prepare for the festivities, secretly regretting the manner in which she had turned down his marriage proposal, wishing she had worded it differently, but wisely she did not reopen the topic.

* * *

Guests arrived at the castle first in a trickle, then in droves, as the week celebrating the twelfth Earl of Drennan's peerage approached. Carriage after carriage arrived at the castle's grand, front entrance. Each arrival represented another cartload of guests for Beatrice to sort out, another limp hand to press, and another deep curtsy to perform. Her childhood governess, a thin, tightlipped spinster her father had imported from England with the express instructions to give her some polish would have been as proud as punch if she'd lived to see how well Beatrice handled all the various titled gentry who made their appearance at the earl's doorstep that day.

She checked the list in her hand carefully, grateful that the number of guests was not quite as high as those invited. Many of the invited, members of the haute-ton, had chosen to remain in London.

The fall season had been in full swing for some time in London. It was approaching the moment of supreme *ennui*, brought on by viewing the same gaggle of lisping debutantes and obnoxiously sneering lords at the same ballrooms and salons day after day. It became tediously boring. A new Irish earl, particularly one who had not only served valiantly in the war but was still alluringly eligible for marriage, was a most intriguing and welcome diversion. However, no one dared to miss a moment of the latest ton events. The impending appointment of the Prince of Wales as the Regent of England had just been announced in the House of Lords.

The old king, whom everyone had affectionately named, *"Our farmer,"* was now said to be madder than a rabid dog. There was talk of having him locked away on a secluded estate and having his son, the Prince of Wales, appointed as regent to reign in his place.

Under the guise of honoring the recently dethroned French court, most of whom had taken refuge in England to escape the terror of Madame Guillotine, the prince planned to celebrate his future regency. The daily gazettes made it known that the future king planned to hold a party at his residency, Carlton House. Outdoor tents, it was being reported, had been set up on the vast grounds. A mere thousand or more guests were expected to attend the lavish banquet and ostentatious fireworks display at the estate. A tremendous crush was naturally to be expected. Anyone whose name could be connected with a peer of the realm intended to be there for the festive event.

Many courtiers murmured to the press that soon their corpulent Prinney would be their new sovereign. Life for the ton would be almost perfect, especially for those who depended on the royal patronage of the prince. Thus, with the announcement of the impending celebrations, not one member of the crème de là crème intended to miss the fête. It might very well be, the London papers said, "The highlight of what was turning out to be a decidedly flat season in town."

It's a blessing in disguise, thought Beatrice when she read the news from her *Dublin Gazetteer.* What with there being only two wings in which to house all the titled gentry who'd deemed it important to make their appearance at Drennan Castle, not to mention the hordes of servants they brought with them to dance attendance upon them, the castle was fast being filled to the brim with guests, despite the absence of many of the invited.

"His Grace would've been better served by a juggler," she told her aunt, glancing down at her guest list.

She checked off another name as she passively watched a carriage deposit its travelers at the front portal. It moved to the right to wash its wheels of the heavy mud collected from the unpaved roads. The newly dug duck pond created for the washing of carriage wheels, she was pleased to note, was being put to use. Her suggestion of having the bottom paved with cobblestones, which allowed the conveyances to easily pass through without getting stuck in the muddy bottom, had been taken into consideration when it had been dug.

"It has struck me as rather odd, Auntie, that not one member of His Grace's family has made the slightest effort to put in an appearance," she said, as the footman came and gave her their august guests' titles. "Not even the usual assortment of poor relations have made an effort to appear. For sure now, 'tis really most peculiar, if you were to ask me."

"Not a bit, darlin'. Perhaps they're all very elderly and infirm, and therefore cannot make the long vigorous journey from London to here," suggested her aunt, explaining the matter away as nothing but a problem of mundane logistics. "Not many my age have the superb constitution I enjoy. Or the wherewithal to stand such long, tedious journeys," she added.

She waved cheerfully in greeting to some elderly dowagers on the steps as she continued talking. "You needn't be worrying that pretty head of yours, Bea'. I've heard the Earl of Drennan's family is all that is supposed to be respectable. His mother is, after all, the Duchess of Huntington. A lady of such rank and prestige that I've heard even royal princesses are afraid to let their shadows cross her path. And as the earl is one of that lady's offspring, his family will not delay laying accolades at his feet."

She patted Beatrice reassuringly on the shoulder. "And for sure, darlin', such an exalted family would know better than we their duty towards their own kinsman, now wouldn't they?"

"Aye," nodded Lady Beatrice in thoughtful agreement, "they're probably just preparing to send some collectively extravagant gift by livery with words of regret." She hesitated, doubt filling her voice, "But still, 'tis odd, Auntie."

Her aunt's assumptions were correct in one aspect. A liveried letter arrived that afternoon from England bearing the dowager Duchess of Huntington's name upon the engraved parchment. Lady Beatrice looked towards the earl who stood by the great hall door reading over the parchment. The messenger stood respectfully to one side to see if there was any reply forthcoming to give to his mistress.

"Will any of your family be attending the celebrations, sir?" she asked, wondering where she would put them if they did decide to make an unannounced appearance. It would mean shuffling everyone about again. Someone's feelings were bound to be ruffled in the process. "Oh, this is going to require the devil's own luck," she muttered to herself, bracing herself for the worst.

The earl heard her and turned in her direction, a half-smile on his rugged face. "You need not concern yourself, Lady O'Brien," he said, putting aside the letter from his mother. "They're not coming. To be truthful, I did not expect them to."

She breathed a sigh of relief at the news, cringing at the thought of one of their guests being forced to vacate their chambers. Some had already looked down their noses at what had been offered. Not knowing that they had been fortunate to be given a bed at all.

"I suppose these meager quarters are what one must expect in a foreign land," she overheard one English dowager say the day before to her maid as she lifted a scented handkerchief to her long white nose upon inspecting her assigned chambers. "These Irish lords are, after all, merely glorified peasants, aping their manners and tastes after us who are in every way their betters."

Beatrice decided then and there that if anyone had to be moved, it would be she of the long nose. "I wonder if the barn's been occupied yet," she mused to herself as she walked away from the English cow. "A little mucking out of the stalls and it would be perfect for her exalted ladyship."

There was no more room in the castle. Even the barrack-styled dormitories, where the male servants slept in bunks and on the floor in bedrolls, were layered with people. Thankfully, many of the artisans and servants who came to the castle to work were from nearby villages and made the daily trips to and from their cottages without any need to pass the night. But if another carriage full of guests should suddenly appear, it would ruin the delicate balance she'd somehow miraculously been able to create in the cramped keep's quarters.

James folded the letter and slipped it into this pocket. He shrugged, as if the matter of none of his relations attending was of no consequence to him. He then turned to the livery and told him, "There is no reply."

The weary servant turned heel and headed towards the kitchens where he would receive welcome rest and food before returning to England.

"Why did you say that you weren't expecting them, Your Grace?" she asked, not knowing how matters stood between him and his august family. He never spoke about them either with warmth or cold derision. It was almost as if they didn't exist.

"The one family member whom I'd have liked to have witnessed this moment has gone on to his glory. And if it were not for that gentleman, I wouldn't be here at all," he said bluntly. His cold glance told more than words of his walled-off emotions concerning his family.

"My uncle Dermott was the late earl, as you may have heard. It was he who also inherited the title unexpectedly when his two elder brothers died. He was, before becoming the Earl of Drennan, the family's priest. It's tradition in my family for younger sons to take the vows of the Church. And as it were, those vows would have been my vocation, as well. That is if my uncle had not intervened and paid for my commission to become an officer in his majesty's service."

Her eyes widened. She was beginning to understand. If it had not been for his uncle's intervention, he would have been expected to join the priesthood!

"And being the lowly third son, my widowed mother

considered me to be the least worthy to merit the great title my uncle kindly bestowed upon me."

She wisely said no more. She stood beside him and understood at last his cool aloofness concerning his relations. Simply said, the illustrious Huntingtons cared not a farthing about one of their own sons, or his exalted new title. They rejoiced not a bit, because he had gone against what his mother had decreed.

One would have thought that a word of congratulations was in order. Or at the very least a small memento of his father's to mark the occasion. Nothing arrived, except this curt message sent to bluntly inform him of the family's refusal to attend the celebrations. They collectively turned their backs on him and his household.

How did he feel about being the proverbial black sheep of that renowned family? To be considered such an outcast even the lowest ranks of the family refused to pay their respects? She could only wonder how he'd managed to remain aloof and untouched by their collective snub.

This stiff, unsmiling gentleman beside her and the one she'd dined with last night, seemed to come from different sides of the same shining mirror. The face and body were the same, 'twas true, but all the spirit and fire of the man was completely different. It was disconcerting to see this sullen gentleman standing rigidly next to her, coolly collected, in complete control of his emotions.

Strangely enough, she wanted the devilish, smiling rogue. The man who'd so audaciously forced her hand over a game of cards, to appear once more. The same man, who with a mere smile and a few teasing words could spark flaming roses in her cheeks and spin her into a dither over whether or not she looked a pretty picture that day.

"Lady O'Brien, you needn't look so concerned. I am

quite resigned to their contempt of me," he explained ruefully. "By not entering the profession that they chose, they believed I became a traitor to my family name. I became better than what I was born to be and made myself the proverbial upstart of the family. I suppose my mother thought my eldest brother, Rodger, the Duke of Huntington, ought to have inherited the title. My second brother, Edward, having properly joined the navy and become a sea captain, wouldn't have qualified."

"That's utterly ridiculous." She gave a half-laugh of disbelief. Surely he was jesting? If anyone merited the title of the Earl of Drennan, to her thinking, he most certainly did.

She recalled all the many improvements he'd made on both the castle and the local estates. They were quite astounding.

She doubted any other gentleman would have had the muster, mettle, and strength to do so splendid a job. By taking firm command of what looked to be a broken-down castle and poorly run estates, he'd begun to make Drennan Castle sturdy and strong once more. The tenant holdings were turning into something more than just promising properties. The wool trade in town was thriving. Plenty of fine, healthy sheep were available to be raised. Hectares of unused plots were being planted with potatoes, insuring a good food source in hard times.

Many thought, upon seeing the improvements, a good firm future was now to be had in Urlingford for anyone willing to work. And all that was due to the new Earl of Drennan's involvement.

"Your not being worthy to be the earl is complete and utter rubbish," she said, a note of derision towards his family in her voice.

She put her hands defiantly on her hips, speaking in a voice she would have used to convince a wool dyer that he was looking at the finest wool in the parish.

"Your Grace, were you not legitimately named your priestly uncle's predecessor before his death? Surely your family is blind not to realize how fortunate it is that the late earl decided to pass the title on to you, instead of deeding it all to the Church, or worse, forfeiting the title back to the crown?"

"Aye, so thought I. But my mother believed it ought to have gone to someone else," he answered in a weary voice. "Never once did she contemplate that I might choose to disobey the family by leaving the seminary. I found a career that suited me better than what they'd planned."

"By becoming a soldier," she supplied.

"Aye. And not of the holy cross, as she had expected. But that of loyally serving king and country."

"She expected you to become a . . . uh, celibate priest?" She almost choked on the words, so improbable was the idea.

Faith, the Duchess of Huntington must have been utterly mad. Try as she might, she could not picture this handsome figure of a man as a scholarly priest living a tranquil life in a tiny country cottage, his life dictated by the whims of the rich patrons of the surrounding parish.

This was not a man who took orders from anyone, unless he chose to. Nay, he would only take commands from someone as grand as himself, someone like Wellington perhaps, or the great Lord above. But as that higher power had not commanded him to take holy orders, she could not imagine anyone else dictating to him that he must take those most sacred vows.

She glanced back up at his saber scar, an outward reminder of his adventurous life. It added ruggedness to his handsome face. No indeed, no one could command this gentleman to do as they wished, unless he chose to let them.

She shook her head. Nay, this was a man of courage and the good Lord above had surely meant by his very nature for him to be out and about in the world seeking adventure and love. It was utterly, preposterously unthinkable that he should have become other than what he had chosen: a soldier, a gentleman, a rogue adventurer.

She smiled, remembering the intimate moments they'd shared together. The way he made her tingle with excitement and expectation like no other man, not even her ex-fiancé, had ever done before. Faith, this third son made a levelheaded spinster think the most wicked of thoughts just by being close to him!

A glimmer of a grin lined his stern face. It broadened into a smile and before she knew it, a low rumble of manly mirth was heard warming the air. His blue eyes sparkled with the joys of life.

"It's a good joke that, isn't it?" he chortled, slapping his breeches that encased his broad thighs. "Me, a priest?"

"Aye, Your Grace, that would've been a merry jest." She nodded, her own light laughter joining his as she smiled warmly up at him. She was pleased to hear him laugh again, even if it was painfully over his family's rejection of him.

"Come," he said, brushing away his gloom with a broad gesture of his arm, taking hers companionably. "Let's go over this confounded list one more time. Demme if we shan't have a glorious celebration. Why even Prinney himself will wish he had attended!"

* * *

The sun broke through the habitual dark clouds of Kilkarney on the first day of the fête. The guests assembled were, for the most part, members of Ireland's gold clover circle, the best the Emerald Isles had to offer. That is, when they were not busy carousing about

London, or any of the other fashionable spots visited by the English court.

Notable among these dandies was the young Irish aristocrat, Beau Champ of Dankeckney House, who was known to keep a brace of pistols loaded and waiting on his supper table in case anyone said something he construed as an insult.

"I heard he even broached a cask of claret one time with a single shot," whispered the footman to the cook, Mistress Reagan, upon the arrival of the gentleman's well-sprung carriage and matching team of grays at the castle's front portal. "The gossipmongers say a bet was made over the shot. He won one hundred guineas." He nodded in admiration.

"Well, lad, he best be behaving himself and not make such foolish bets here, or the master will saber 'im with that walking stick of his," answered the stalwart cook with a disapproving shake of her white-frilled cap. Beau Champ had a tidy brown beard and corpulent round figure. A couple of equally well-fed spaniel dogs trotted closely at their master's red-heeled shoes.

"Who are they?" the lad asked, giving a low whistle of admiration as another white phaeton with a matching team of blacks arrived. It carried one of the most interesting families in Ireland.

"That's Laeticia and Edmund Powers, brother and sister, they be. I've seen them before when I worked in Dublin last season." The cook nodded knowingly.

"He's a magistrate with an estate in County Tipperary. They call the brother, 'Beau Powers.' He's here, no doubt, for the grand hunt the master has planned. Loves his horses and wine, that gentleman does." Mistress Reagan sighed, thinking of the many casks she'd stored in the cellar in anticipation of such gentlemen as Beau Powers. She eyed the country gentleman with approval. He was wearing dark leather breeches, shiny Hessian top boots, and a snowy white cravat.

Beau Powers was one of those rare English eccentrics of the Golden Clover Circle, as the haute ton of Dublin were known as. She'd not mind serving him. Unlike most of these English, feast-swilling absentee landowners who were now in London dancing attendance upon the prince, Beau Powers was not one of those Cromwellian-spawned dandies squeezing all they could from their penniless Irish tenants. The English Beau Powers was an exception. A true gentleman of integrity, who loved his adopted country, Ireland.

"A dandy kind-hearted master you'll find him to be, lad, if you be so fortunate as t' find yourself serving him," she said beaming. She remembered the way he'd heavily tipped her and the other servants the last time she'd worked a party he'd attended. The gentleman had given her a whole guinea for bringing him an extra bottle of claret to his private chambers. Didn't even try and pinch her bottom, neither. Although she wouldn't have minded much if he had, the handsome devil.

"But . . ." She frowned in hesitation, her chubby, round face pinching a little in disapproval at the smiling buxom maid who stood at the ready to take the gentleman's traveling cloak. The young housemaid's cheeks flamed under the dandy's notice.

"I think it be best we lock them young country lasses we hired in their chambers tonight. Who knows which one of these pea-brained colleens will take it into her silly cap to try and slip into that gent's well-made bed? For I'm telling you true, lad, there won't be any bairns born on the wrong side of the blanket coming from *this* castle. Not while I'm in charge here."

The Beau's sister, Mistress Laeticia Powers, followed him from behind, daintily stepping down from the open carriage. Her young, curvaceous figure made her the portrait of a fully clothed Venus come to life. The striking dasher wore a blue traveling gown and sported a wide-brimmed hat bedecked with matching striped bows. She appeared to have just stepped out of the latest fashion gazette in her fine traveling coat. She gave a long, white-gloved hand to the gaping footman who helped her down.

The pocket Venus, upon meeting the new earl, enthusiastically threw her full white arms around him. Beneath her beribboned hat, blonde curls bounced on each side of her round, heart-shaped face as she kissed him on the cheeks in greeting.

"I'm so delighted for you, Captain James," she gushed openly, holding onto him as if she had no intention of ever relinquishing him. Her dimples deepened into a cherubic smile as she gazed up at him adoringly. "So . . . so . . . terribly thrilled t' hear of your good fortune."

She batted her thick eyelashes up at him, her tightly corseted body in the empire style, which had been à la mode since the war's beginning. It exposed to the elements her splendid bosom which brazenly bounced up and down against his starched white shirt with each excited breath. She left no doubts as to her intention of trying to snare his manly attention.

Laeticia knew a good catch when she met one. At the moment, the young earl was considered to be one of the best-titled ones on the marriage mart. And as her family held no peerage, as yet, she was determined to marry into a good family.

"Does she know the master well?" asked the lower footman, visibly swallowing at the sight of Mistress Powers's exposed charms. "I, uh . . . was wondering if she mightn't already have an understanding with His Grace. What I mean is—is she the one he's chosen to be the new mistress 'ere?"

"Nay, lad. She's just making His Grace's acquaintance for the first time. Her brother there is the one who knows him best. They attended school together. The lass is trying to get her claws into him before them shy kittens over there give 'im a try," said the cook. She nodded in the direction of a giggling group of prim debutantes.

The young ladies stood awkwardly by their relations and pale-faced female companions on the bottom steps of the front castle portal, looking like a group of white gardenias clustered around their more colorfully dressed guardians.

"Aye, Laeticia Powers is not the only young lady here eager to get herself attached to the earl. My bets, though, are not on that bold miss," she whispered as Mistress Powers passed them, ascending the stairs, her backside swaying alluringly to and fro like a wide seagoing ship.

Lady Beatrice stood stiffly off to one side, watching the other lady smile in supreme confidence, as if she'd just laid siege to the castle and been proclaimed its rightful queen. Beatrice smiled coolly at the dasher and Laeticia made her obligatory curtsy before entering the castle walls.

"Dark shot though she be, 'tis to my thinking that Lady Beatrice would make the finest mistress of this castle," said the cook with haughty finality. "She has backbone instead of wishbone, that lady does. Not like some of these simpering, pale moths standing over there."

Tom stared at the tall lady in incredulous amazement. He'd heard strange talk concerning the aloof heiress's game-of-the-hen ways at the local inn, the Boar's Teeth. The tales of her escapades with her various greedy suitors were renowned throughout the tiny parish. They were frequently retold with wicked ribald humor to newcomers with unrestrained glee.

Eyeing the unsmiling lady, he could not find

anything desirable in his master shackling himself with such an odd bluestocking. Even if, as they say, she be richer than Croesus himself.

"If I were the earl, I'd be after asking Mistress Powers," he said dreamily watching the back of the stylish Dublin lady disappear indoors.

"Aye, to be sure ye would, untried youth that you be. But the master will be needing a lady with brains and grout. And as Lady O'Brien has plenty of both, 'tis she I be thinking who'd be the best choice . . . but mind, lad, the master best be quick about his business of doing the asking. There be others who are chasing after 'er." She nodded knowingly in the direction of the young, colorful gentlemen assembled around the chattering debutantes.

"Plain spoken and all that dear lady be. Those giddy city chicks and their ne'er-do-well brothers are also in force among the guests. And those spendthrifts are terribly eager to tie themselves to her golden purse strings. Aye, twill be a most fortunate man who nabs her ladyship for his own."

The gentlemen stood about uncomfortably, their mothers having dragged them away from the unprofitable gaming dens they habitually frequented. This in exchange for more profitable introductions and dancing partners for their marriageable daughters.

"Not that I don't think your sister doesn't stand a chance with the earl," one dowager was overheard saying to her heir. She eyed with pleasure her pretty, but slightly bucktoothed daughter, as they waited their turn to greet their host and hostess. "But the word being bandied about, Reginald, is that His Grace is looking for a wealthy bride. As you know, our finances are rather badly scorched. I'm afraid your dear sister cannot compete for that gentleman's august attention," she murmured regretfully.

"However," and at this the mother's eyes lit up with Machiavellian expectations laced with old-fashioned guilt. "If we were to stop paying off your gambling debts, we just might be able to scrape together a splendid enough dowry for one of those other lords over there to take an interest in Felicity."

She leaned into her son with a, 'Listen, this is for your own good,' look upon her full face. She whispered, "Now, if you were to marry a bride with unlimited wealth at her disposal, such as Lady O'Brien, why then it'd be your rich wife's duty to pay off your debts. Wouldn't it, my dear boy? And then we could arrange a proper marriage for our dear Felicity." She gave him an encouraging nod in the wealthy spinster's direction, hoping her son had at last understood the family's position concerning his duty to marry well above his present impoverished means.

"Yes, ma'am," the young gentleman murmured uncomfortably, reaching up to his stiff cravat where a stranglehold on his carefree bachelor days was making it most difficult to breathe. "If you and Felicity will kindly excuse me, Mother. I do believe my man is signaling to me."

"Of course. Do go your merry way. Enjoy yourself, Reginald, dear. But first," the mother added with steely determination, "take this opportunity to ask Lady O'Brien if you mightn't take her out riding on the morrow. Although I hear tell her father, Lord O'Brien, has given the Earl of Drennan permission to court her." A worried frown crinkled the smooth forehead of the matron. "But that announcement carries little weight. And as they are not yet formally betrothed, there is still a chance of her making a match of it elsewhere, isn't there?"

"Yes, Mama," her heir replied blandly, and reluctantly headed in the direction of their hostess.

Many pleasant diversions were planned for the fête. Along with the usual hunt, there would be picnics, music recitals, boating on Kilkarney's lake, and a fireworks display had been planned to coincide with the letter of recognition arriving from Prinney. It was expected he would congratulate the newly named Earl of Drennan on his title and peerage. The earl, shortly thereafter, would be invited to visit the English court where he would present himself formally for the final nod of recognition from the Prince Regent. A moment, which would undoubtedly serve as his public acceptance into the haute ton and the uppermost echelon of English society.

* * *

Lady Beatrice found herself dancing in a country set comprising of herself and Beau Powers as the first couple. Young Lord Reginald Fortescue and his sister Lady Felicity were the second. The ball had just become very gay with dancing. A hired orchestra played above in the ballroom's minstrel's gallery and the newly cleaned chandeliers sparkled above the guests.

Beatrice was just about to pass under young Lord Reginald's outstretched arm when she was interrupted in mid-step.

Tommy Flanders, the footman, bowed before her.

"A gentleman has arrived, my lady. He says he has no card, but he insists on speaking to you in private," he said, frowning haughtily with disapproval. "He isn't on the guest list, ma'am. Shall I send him away?"

"No, don't. Perhaps it's one of His Grace's family who decided to make an unannounced appearance," she said hopefully, thinking how wonderful it would be if at least one of His Grace's relations had come. "We wouldn't want to offend him if that is so. Best show the gentleman to the yellow study. Oh, and leave me to deal with the matter of where to place him for the night, Flanders. You may, however, inform His Grace of our guest's arrival."

She added to herself that if the dungeons weren't already occupied with rat skeletons, she'd put the guest there. It was extremely rude to show up at the last minute and expect to be housed. Perhaps she could send him off to her father's?

Frowning over the matter, she finished the country set. She made a final curtsy, and cordially excused herself from her partner's presence.

The study was cool, despite the warmth of the lit peat fire on her right. She paused, uncertain if she ought to enter. For even with his back to her in the dimly lit study, she recognized him. The arrogant tilt of his head gave him away. When he turned, twirling a quizzing glass nonchalantly in one hand, leaning on the white and black marbled fireplace mantle with the other, she knew her first guess to be correct.

"Vi—Viscount Linley," she said, astounded at the sight of the man she had once almost married.

"Lady Beatrice," he said and gave an effusive bow. Taking up his quizzing glass once more, he surveyed her. Small, squinty, brown eyes covered by thick eyebrows stared at her. His youthful handsome face had changed, she noted. His once flawless skin was now full of large, pitted scars. The result, no doubt, of having caught some sort of sexual contagion from one of his favored soiled doves.

She felt his insolent scrutiny. It made her cringe. She felt as if she were some sort of loose woman of the streets he were about to consider purchasing for his personal pleasure, instead of an intelligent, highborn lady worthy of respect.

"Aren't you the thing, old girl," he drawled, his lips curling upwards in a slight haughty smile as he eyed the almost translucent blue pelisse of her Liberty silk. Its empire waist and silver slit underskirt outlined her feminine form.

"Not t'all the stiff, top-lofty spinster I left behind when I went to war, are you? Been having a good time, m'dear, whilst I was away fighting for our country?" He sneered openly. "Obviously, not given me another thought, eh?"

"You needn't play the martyred soldier with me, Viscount Linley. Last I heard you were with the China Tenth Regiment," she said coolly, referring to the regiment that was under the Prince Regent's personal patronage, and thus far had seen no battle.

"'Tis well known that the young aristocrats which comprise your regiment, Lord Linley, parade about in sunny Brighton in their meticulously tailored uniforms singing at the top of their lungs, playfully flirting with the ladies. 'Tis disgraceful, especially when one thinks of all the other brave, young men in the Union risking their very lives fighting against the French."

The viscount opened a box of snuff and lined some of the noxious substance on his sleeve. He sniffed it up his nose, delicately knocking the rest back into his box.

"All that may change very soon, m'dear. Indeed, I might smell gunpowder yet. There's talk that we may be sent to reinforce Wellington's troops in Spain. Dashed, if I can't buy my way out. But the commander won't release any of us to go home. Says we're less than a bunch of cowards if we try. So, my dear, you may get your wish yet."

"I see," she said, bristling with dislike at the manner in which he referred to her as "my dear." She'd never been his "dear" anything. Not even when they were almost betrothed.

She eyed him cautiously. "And what brings you here to Drennan Castle, Viscount? Are you known to the earl? Old school chums? Perhaps comrades dating as far back as boyhood days?" She doubted the earl would have developed, even at such a tender age, a friendly alliance with this overbearing bore. He had better taste than that.

"The new earl and I are not acquainted," Linley answered, moving as close to her as he could without actually touching her. He invaded her personal space, his eyes staring impudently down into the low neckline of her frilled bodice.

"Faith, you ought to be flattered, my dear," he whispered into her ear, so close to her she could smell the foulness of his brandied breath.

She wrinkled her nose. He'd obviously taken the liberty of helping himself to the earl's liquor decanter while he waited. His fake courage was evident in his overly familiar manners towards her.

"I came here expressly to see you, Lady Beatrice."

She felt her skin crawl, dreading what he would reveal next.

"Indeed. How, uh, delightful," she lied, flicking her fan open, using the silk screen as a barrier between them. The mantle clock ticked, the only sound in the semi-dark room as she waited for him to continue his revelations.

By the holy rood, she fumed inwardly. The viscount always did enjoy the dramatic. His cat and mouse games had always been one of his more vexing characteristics. One she had found utterly detestable. It was as if he took a certain joy in discomforting others.

She took a deep breath. All she needed was to be patient. Eventually, the pompous cad would tell her what had really brought him here. She waved her fan back and forth, an outlet for her nervous energy.

The mantle clock continued its rhythmic ticking till he at last complied.

"Mother wrote to me, urging me to pay you a visit. She says that you've changed," he said, a boyish tone of devotion in his voice when he spoke of his mother.

"Did she now?" echoed Beatrice in mock surprise. "And I always thought your dear mama disliked me so. I do believe she once even called me a . . ." She changed her voice and manner to match that of the large, haughty countess. "'A common, sheep-shearing shrew,' among several other equally unflattering phrases."

She stopped and shrugged. All of that horrid exchange was in her past. As far as she was concerned, it was never to be relived.

"But, Viscount, you didn't come all the way to Ireland to tell me that your dear mama believes I've changed. I refuse to believe it if you did. She and I were always on the verge of scratching each other's eyes out, as you well know."

"Lady Beatrice, you misunderstand," he said taking her hand into his own. His voice was firm with the high-handed manners of one born with a silver spoon in his tiny clenched fists.

"I've come back to fetch my bride. She who was deprived of me when I loyally enlisted in his Royal Highness's guard. And here she is miraculously waiting for me, still unwed, and eager for my touch. Is that not so, my dear?"

"It most certainly is not," she said, glaring at him with dislike, an angry smile on her lips. "Perhaps, Viscount, you've heard of the legend that tells of when Saint Patrick drove all the snakes out of Ireland and put a curse on all the other lowly reptiles here, as well."

She eyed him meaningfully as if he were one of the unwanted low life that had unexpectedly crawled out from under a rock. "If I were you, I'd make haste and rejoin my regiment. Before you catch some terrible wasting sickness," she advised with pointed loathing.

He waved a perfumed handkerchief languidly, as if to disregard the insult.

"I'm gratified to see that you're not completely

indifferent to me. Mayhap then I can hope we can come to some sort of understanding?" he asked, lightly grazing a finger along the line of her exposed shoulder blade.

She gritted her teeth at his touch. Why the devil did gentlemen always think they had the liberty to touch her? Couldn't they use words to make their meaning known?

She shrugged his hand off, raising one dark eyebrow at him for his audacity. No one touched her unless she wished it. He knew it better than almost anyone. There had been numerous times in their previous acquaintance she had demonstrated that very well defined point.

"Long loneliness is better than bad company, Viscount," she bit out. "And pray do not forget, sir, 'twas you who left and broke our engagement, not I."

The viscount drew back a little and smiled, as if the thought of leaving her to uncomfortably explain to a ballroom full of guests on the night of what was to have been their formal betrothal had been merely a highly amusing event. One he would have liked to have witnessed for his own personal entertainment.

"I do remember taking my leave of you," he said simply without any apology.

"Frankly, sir," she sniffed with indignation, "you left me t' hang the day of our betrothal. No doubt, you've now come looking for me tonight because you're once more in need of my fortune. I paid your bills once, sir, but never again. I strongly advise you to take your leave." She stopped, hesitating over her next move. Then in a stronger voice uttered her decision, "Or I shall be forced to scream and bring the entire household down upon your head."

"With your reputation as a conniving shrew, Lady Beatrice, I rather doubt anyone would pay you any heed." The lord sneered, laying a menacing hand on her.

"There, sir, you are wrong," a familiar voice said

darkly from the door. The Earl of Drennan entered the room.

He strode into the dimly lit study followed by two of his liveried footmen. The footmen stood guard, seeing to it that no one entered the room.

In one quick glance, the earl took in the contemptible sight of a young buck standing intimately near Lady Beatrice, quite rudely ignoring her obvious dislike. He raised dark eyebrows questioningly at the cad's audacity. He felt the strongest urge to give the viscount a facer for daring to come near her, let alone for having the temerity to touch her.

"And just who the devil are you?" he demanded. He felt as if the unwelcome guest were a footpad caught in the act of trying to rob him of one of his most prized possessions, namely the beautiful lady standing before him.

"I am Viscount Linley of South Dwighton," said the gentleman unwisely. "I've come to pay my intended, Lady Beatrice, my heartfelt respects."

"That, Your Grace, is a lie." Beatrice huffed, shaking herself free of the cad's hold on her. She was thoroughly tired of his venomous presence. She glowered accusingly at Linley, her fan almost breaking in her hands as she twisted the stays in anger.

"I have never in the past, nor in the present, ever been his, Your Grace!" she said with vehement loathing. It was as if Linley were speaking of an unlikely match betwixt herself and a veritable demon monster.

"I suspected as much," he said dryly, putting a white-gloved finger along the mantle as if inspecting for dust. "And knowing, Lady O'Brien, how meticulously you had all the rooms in the castle cleaned, I thought your ladyship might wish to have some help with removing this unwanted vermin."

"If it should so please, Your Grace," she said sweetly, deeply curtsying to his pleasure. "Your desire in this instance is entirely in accord with mine, sir."

He signaled to the footmen behind him to take action. They stepped forward and grabbed the viscount roughly by the arms.

The young aristocrat tried to shrug them off as they laid heavy hands upon him. Silently, with what little dignity he could muster, Viscount Linley walked through the study doors. The footmen flanked him on each side as they escorted him out of the room and to the front portal.

"Did he harm you?" James asked, his voice filled with concern.

"Nay," she said, shaking her head. She smiled at him. "Your entrance was perfectly timed. I'm fine."

"Shall I escort you back to our guests? It's a certainty that they have been pining away for their lovely hostess's presence. I've been practically besieged by every young buck in the ballroom demanding to know where you were, my lady. Demme, if the ball hasn't come to a complete standstill. No one, especially myself, are enjoying themselves without your lovely presence. I was hoping you'd return to us and enliven the room once more with your gracious smile and charm."

"If you please, Your Grace. Let us not tarry any longer then and keep our guests waiting. I dread to think that 'tis I who am depriving others of their merrymaking," she said, smiling at the fulsome compliment, her dimples fetchingly marking each cheek.

She walked with him into the main hall where the ball had carried on splendidly unaware of the unsavory episode that had just transpired in the study.

* * *

Before Beatrice retired for the evening, the earl

approached her, reassuring her that Viscount Linley would never trouble her again. "I personally took the precaution of having three of my outriders escort him to a nearby inn," he said. "They are under strictest orders from me to see the viscount gone on the morrow from Urlingford."

"Your Grace is too kind," she said, sighing with happy relief. She was grateful to be rid once and for all of the unpleasant aristocrat's presence in her life.

"Lady O'Brien," he said and hesitated, as if for once uncertain how to go about asking her. He shook his head. "I know I've been aloof since the night we were together . . . But I would like an opportunity to begin again. I wondered, that is, would you give me permission to call you by your given name?"

She smiled up at him, pleased by the request. "If you will extend to me the same privilege, Your Grace."

He took her hand in his and bringing it to his lips, said, "With pleasure, Lady Beatrice." He kissed it, smiling warmly down at her. She, in turn, wore a befuddled look of uncertainty.

"It's Lord James, my dear," he supplied for her. "Although I prefer being called Captain amongst my old acquaintances."

"Goodnight then, Captain James." She smiled at him, without a cloud of worry in her thoughts as she retired for the night.

That evening, snug and safe in her warm bed, Beatrice's thoughts dwelled upon the master of the house. She had to admit to herself the wonderful, almost heroic way he'd appeared when she'd been forced to defend herself against that loathsome toad, Lord James was, she smiled into her pillow, proving himself to be a most dependable and worthy friend.

Chapter 8

The day was crisp and clear. A little early morning fog rolled off the hills as a pair of thoroughbreds with their accomplished riders eagerly crested the highest point near Brightwood Manor's estate. The small stone manor lay mapped out below in its Tudor gray stone glory. Its one wing lay snugly situated in a cot wood of swaying trees. A small flock of longhaired sheep baa'd to each other as their herder passed with his collie dogs. As prime Irish countryside went, one could not ask for more. The rolling green hills and sparkling lake below provided a worthy view. This was Ireland at its best, green, prosperous, and tranquilly beautiful to behold.

"Tell me about those trees over there?" he asked, pointing to a group of green parasol saplings planted in a sunny sheltered part of her estate, away from the rougher winds blowing from the North Sea.

"They're our mulberry trees," she said, not disguising the pride in her voice. "They'll be used for feeding the silkworms I intend to import this summer from a Quaker farmer in England."

"Another one of your projects?" asked the earl, impressed by her numerous ventures, which he'd had the occasion to note during their ride.

She nodded and laughed, feeling carefree and happy. Since early that morning they'd been in each other's company, riding around the local parish together. A most welcome diversion for both of them, as neither had had much time for any form of solitude since their guests' arrival.

They had both unexpectedly had the same idea to awaken before the morning's breaking of the fast and take a quick ride before the others awoke. Upon meeting in the stables, they'd agreed to go out together.

Reluctant to part with his company, Beatrice proposed showing him her small local properties situated near his own vast estate. She warned him that the ride might uncomfortably jostle his injured leg. After calm reassurances that he was completely mended, they'd set off together.

"Most of the people in the village believe my aunt Mary left me a vast fortune," she said, amusement etched on her face at that bit of myth. As if her poor maiden aunt, the daughter of small landed gentry, ever could have acquired such vast wealth. Her late aunt had lived comfortably at a modest, genteel level. It was certainly not on the scale befitting that of a queen.

"Indeed. So I'd heard." The earl nodded. Davis had told him as much on one occasion. It had helped further spark his interest in her.

"Would you like to hear the truth of the matter?" she asked, a smile as warm as the sun above them lighting her face.

He nodded, bemused, enjoying the sight of her smiling.

"I'm the one who built my fortune. Aunt Mary's inheritance, of which I've received only a small annuity, helped me in the beginning." She paused, not certain she should be trusting him. The attentive way in which he listened brushed away her small hidden fears that he would ridicule her for entering into what was considered to be the exclusive domain of gentlemen.

"My first portion from my inheritance helped me buy a new breed of sheep. They're called angora with wonderfully long, soft fleece," she raptured on about her first venture. "From the money earned from their wool, I purchased the land for my mulberry trees. Then, this spring, I intend to buy the worms and looms necessary for the making of silk."

She stopped. Flushed with pride, she wondered if he now understood how hard she had worked by carefully investing her money. The hard work involved in preparing the land and researching the needs required for a silk-making enterprise had left her with no time for anything, or anyone.

"And thus your great fortune was created, which made you famous," he finished for her.

"Aye." She nodded solemnly.

"But how did you decide what to invest in? And how much?"

"I have expert advice available for me. At first reluctantly given, but as my reputation grew, so did the line outside my man of affair's door." She smiled, a little shy about how she conducted her business. For it was unusual, she knew, for a gentlewoman, unless she were widowed, to run an entire estate and business almost single-handedly.

She had always known that one day Brightwood Manor would be hers, the inheritance being passed down through the surviving heir, regardless of whether it be male or female. And why, she'd reasoned when she grew old enough to understand, should she wait until her beloved father had passed on to make the most of it? Why not create her own fortune and insure that no Englishman would ever rule over her estates?

From that day on she'd determined to learn as much as possible about running Brightwood Manor's holdings. She continued her explanation of how she'd developed her mythical wealth. "Then the day arrived when anyone in the parish, who had an innovative idea in farming, beyond using kelp to manure their fields, beat a well-trod path to Brightwood." She paused once more, knowing the true irony behind her next words. "They came because they wanted me to help finance them with my late aunt's inheritance, you understand."

"Not knowing that, in truth, it comes from your own hard-earned wealth," he said, giving an acknowledging nod to her cleverness. "But how is it that no one knows that it was you who created all this?"

She laughed, ready to reveal her most well-kept secret. "I hide behind a screen while the gentlemen are being interviewed by Master Randolph, my man of affairs. I listen and take notes of their conversation. When they're gone, we sit down and discuss whether or not the venture is worthy of further notice and financial support."

"And you trust this Master Randolph?" he asked, wondering how one gentleman of her acquaintance had come to be part of such an important secret, and yet not managed to change her evidently low opinion of men. And if he did not know himself better, he told himself with some self-derision, he would almost believe himself jealous of the trust she'd given her man of affairs.

"Aye, I do trust him." She smiled mischievously, the faint dimples he had first detected the day they'd met reappearing impishly around the corners of her mouth. "His wife told me that if Master Randolph ever gave me a day of grief, she'd play the devil and roast him herself over flaming coals on washing day."

"Why did she say that?" he asked, puzzled by the other woman's strange loyalty.

"Because, sir, I'm the midwife, who helped bring into the world five of their seven children," she answered with a smug smile of one who knows her worth. "Any more questions?"

"None. I bow to a far superior sex," he said and grinned back at her. His admiration lit his clear blue eyes as he enjoyed being in her confidence.

Beatrice tilted her head to one side. She found she liked the sight of him on his handsome mount. He had a good seat. She had seen as they rode up the hill that he sat tall and erect, fully in control of his horse. It had been a pleasure watching him ride.

Sitting here beside him, she felt a strange, happy pleasure course through her. At that moment under the dappling blue sky, surrounded by the green hills she so loved, it was enough. For once she didn't worry about her feelings towards him, about her independence, nor about that argument they had the night they made love. She simply leaned back into her saddle and enjoyed herself and the view, which lay before them.

His next words, however, destroyed that delicate illusion of blissful tranquility. It was as if the snake had suddenly made himself known in the Garden of Eden.

"Perhaps," he hesitated, "with your knowledge of money, you might be able to help me, Lady Beatrice?"

He drew his hand into his breast pocket.

"In what way, Your Grace?" she asked cautiously, her spine stiffening.

"Captain James," he smiled at her, "remember?"

"Captain James," she amended, running her tongue nervously across her lips. She wondered what sum of money he might request of her. She turned her gaze downwards, waiting for him to tell her what venture he wished her to partner. Mayhap she had been too hasty thinking that he might not be like other men?

"I'm afraid it concerns money—"

"Of course." She nodded, a frigid tilt of her head in acknowledgment. Her heart plummeted, a cold dread settling in her middle. What else could it be with men, other than money?

"Which came to me rather in a queer manner," he continued.

[159]

"I see," she said, waiting for his full explanation. The gentleman obviously had sought her out so that he might garner some financial advice, or ask for a loan. The castle was, after all, going to cost him a pretty penny to repair.

"Do you wish me to give you advice, Your Grace? Some pointers as to how to invest it in various ventures. Is that it?" she said, her voice taking on the same frigid tones that she used when confronted by a particularly annoying suitor.

"Not quite."

Startled, she looked up at him then and met his eyes, searching for an explanation. He looked guiltily down at his waist pocket.

"I think I best show you," he said, grinning like a young boy who was about to show off one of his favorite finds. He produced the gold coin he'd found in his bed.

She gave a soft gasp, recognizing it at once. It was the dreaded leprechaun's coin. "What I have need of is, well, someone who can translate this for me. Perhaps you can help me find out where it comes from and what that strange script says?"

He frowned a little in thought. "Faith, perhaps I really ought to give it to you? I did, after all, find it at Brightwood Manor amongst the bedclothes. Mayhap one of the members of your household has been searching for it and would like it back?"

"No!" She gasped aloud.

Noticing the look of surprise on his face, she amended. "That is, 'tis surely yours now, Lord James. None of my house has come to me concerning any such loss, and therefore, I'd prefer you kept it."

"Can you translate the inscription? I am most interested in learning what it says. Perhaps it has some special significance, which you can decipher."

"Oh, most assuredly," she said, fearful that anyone else should. If he were to ask around, someone might reveal the truth. "If you will but hold it up, so that I might read it."

He handed it to her. "It is written in the ancient language of Irish Gaelic." She smiled reassuringly, pretending to decipher the words written on its gold surface.

"Why," she said brightly, as if the news she had to impart was good, "'tis a fairy's coin, my lord!"

"A what?"

"A coin of . . . ah, good fortune," she lied.

He nodded, re-pocketing it. "It's just as I thought."

"Truly?" she asked amazed and curious as to how he had come to that unforeseen conclusion.

"Why do you say that?"

"It's brought me nothing but good fortune since I found it."

"Indeed," she said, secretly relieved. "I'm glad it's brought you such good fortune. I hope that the wee ones will let it stay upon you, Captain James."

"So do I." He nodded as he looked down at her, nudging his mount closer to her own. "And, Lady Beatrice, I believe it already has . . ."

Before she could say another word, he kissed her. His hands held her face up to him like a delicate flower, as his mouth, as gentle as a warm breeze blowing over blades of new spring grass touched her, beckoning a response.

She sighed and drew closer to him. She had intuitively known since that night that they both had been yearning for this moment. She may have turned down his marriage proposal, but that did not mean the attraction they felt for one another had ended. His gentle hands moved from her face down to her waist, strong arms wrapping themselves around her, half-pulling her off the saddle.

She leaned across to him, losing herself in the warmth of his embrace. Her mouth locked willingly with his, reveling at his firm touch. The passionate ember that she had thought long ago to have completely snuffed out glowed deep inside of her, burning.

He took her horse's reins and led her towards his own estates. On the edge, where the manor's property line joined the castle's, stood a small cottage. Next to it ran a cool stream that was well shaded by a cluster of trees. Stacks of cut planks and timber lay neatly in a lean-to nearby.

"When I first came to the castle, all of the rooms were in need of repair," he explained, dismounting. "I lived and worked here for a time."

He tied her horse's reins to a post.

"Would you like to come inside?" he asked, looking at her thoughtfully.

He left unasked the real question behind his invitation. *Did she want to come inside and be alone with him?*

She silently nodded, yes.

He placed his strong hands on her waist and helped her dismount, holding her a moment longer than was necessary when her feet touched the ground. She looked up at him, her eyes never leaving his face. She wanted him. She hadn't stopped wanting him since the moment he walked away from her bed.

"Come in," he said, opening the door, quickly checking to see if all was in order.

She hesitated at the threshold, fighting her fear of entrapment. "If I come inside, you won't force me to marry you, will you, James?"

He shook his head, almost laughing at the notion.

"By my word, I promise never to force you to do anything you don't want to," he said, smiling down at her, clearly amused at the idea. "You needn't fear,

Beatrice. You have my assurance that today we are merely friends . . ." He added softly, "And if you so desire, lovers. It's your decision."

With that promise, he impatiently picked her up and carried her inside. The cottage was very small. It contained but one room. A bed large enough to hold his manly frame dominated most of it.

He shut the cottage door with his back as he crossed the threshold, heading straight for the bed. It was made of wood, strung together by rope, a feather mattress and a crocheted quilt lay on top.

He carefully laid her down. He stood over her, his eyebrows lifted as he asked, "Do you wish to continue?"

"Yes, I want us to be lovers," she replied, nodding, her riding hat tilting precariously on her head.

She lay back, waiting for him to join her, letting her hat fall carelessly to the floor. Through half-closed eyes, she watched him latch the door. She knew she was safe; he would not force her into marriage. What happened next between them was to be entirely her choice.

He returned to her side and began kissing her. Her mouth opened willingly, enjoying the dance of their tongues as he pressed his lips against hers, his hands deftly unbuttoned her fitted riding jacket. He removed it and reached behind her, undoing her riding skirt until she wore only her corset.

"Now for the rest," he whispered into her ear. She shivered in anticipation.

He hooked his middle fingers at the top of the corset, peering down at the round globes of her breasts. He took in a deep breath and looked into her green eyes, his own shining with desire, as with ease, he pulled the corset down.

Her heart pounded in a breath of expectation as he stared at her, his eyes aglow with warm desire. He murmured before kissing her, "Beautiful, Beatrice, absolutely beautiful . . ."

He removed all his clothes and lay naked next to her. He behaved as if there was not a house full of guests waiting for them back at the castle, all that mattered was this moment, alone with her. As he kissed her, she felt the burning warmth increase and spread from between her legs to her entire body.

His hands and mouth slowly took their time enjoying the feel of her skin beneath his touch as he kissed every inch of her body, moving his tongue and mouth along every beautiful curve. With each caress, she forgot who she was, tossing away the hard-earned title of Spinster of Brightwood Manor.

She lay back and rejoiced in James's lovemaking with complete abandon. His fingers found their way into her moist heat, caressing her until she was wet and moaning at the exquisite sensations he was evoking. He moved to position himself between her legs and boldly she took his manhood in her hands and caressed him, as well. He threw his head back and groaned, shuddering at her touch. She guided him inside her, joining their bodies . . . and then they danced, moving in a rhythm as old as time itself. The heat inside her began to build, that delicious throbbing she could not control, spiraled as he thrust into her, increasing the tempo of their joining. She grabbed his waist, wanting all of him.

Suddenly, she felt an explosion of heat, the muscles inside her squeezing his manhood, her heart pounding against his chest, as she cried out, "James!"

He removed himself from her, letting out a cry of his own.

Afterwards, she lay next to him, her heart slowing back to its usual pace, as languidly she ran a finger along his arm and chest, recovering from their lovemaking. Her heart felt light and for a reason she was not yet ready to examine, she was at peace.

He went to the river and heated a kettle over the fire

of an open hearth, bringing the water back to her. She stood and washed in a large wood bucket. He handed her a linen towel to dry herself with.

"*Merci*," she said in French.

"My pleasure," he answered, briefly kissing her on the lips.

She wanted to say more, but could not find the words, knowing that perhaps it was best not to speak of it at all. He had promised not to force her into marriage and she was, for the moment, satisfied with that, her independence secure.

They redressed and left the small cottage . . . she didn't need to ask him how he felt. She could tell that he was as pleased as she . . . a smile on his face told all, as the scar above his eye crinkled with good humor. But before she could utter a word, he nudged their horses on the flanks, urging them forward. Gaily, they raced back to the castle.

*　*　*

The following days Beatrice was disappointingly not permitted much time in the earl's company. She often found herself in the middle of the ballroom, or even silently listening to music, surrounded by her numerous admirers. They followed her everywhere. She could turn neither left nor right without one of them inadvertently tripping over her layered skirts.

How tiresome it was to be so damnably rich! And as for the earl, Captain James, she mentally corrected herself. She hardly saw him at all. Those blissful moments they'd shared together were quickly becoming a faded memory. The ladies fawned over him, dowager and debutante alike, eagerly trying to further the cause of their chosen prodigy. Hoping against hope that one of their young charges would finish the little season with an early marriage proposal and save them the added duty of paying for a much costlier trip to the big city of London.

Leading the pack of coquettes was Beau Power's sister, the town cit, Mistress Laeticia Powers. For wherever the handsome earl wandered, so consequently followed the well-endowed lady in pink.

"Obviously thinks that color will make her look younger," she heard her aunt sniff in disapproval one morning as the dazzler entered the dining room wearing a gown of the brightest blush.

The diminutive widow in black had no pangs of maidenly discretion to keep her from letting the dasher know her thoughts. For Aunt Agnes, never one to talk about someone behind their back, made plainly known where the lines were drawn and which side she had chosen to champion.

"Beatrice, I thought only those of us who experience the horrors of drink would see pink in the morning," the aunt uttered ruthlessly aloud as the dasher brushed past them towards the sideboard where the food had been laid out.

Plates, serving spoons, and open mouths, were suspended in midair as everyone stared at the object of the older lady's derision.

To the selfsame widow's pleasure, the dasher's cheeks glowed a color similar to that of her gown. Instead of taking her usual place closest to the earl, Laeticia headed for the opposite end of the table. It was also the farthest from the tiny black dragon and her barbed jibes.

Beatrice noticed the friendly manner in which the other lady treated their host. She watched the petite pocket Venus stroll around the grounds with him that afternoon, a parasol in her white-gloved hands, twirling giddily.

She overheard Laeticia say breathlessly as they reached

the top of the hill where she had been practicing archery, "Tell me again about the time you and your soldiers bravely routed a battalion of Boney's men, Your Grace."

"Now, Mistress Powers, you exaggerate. Yet once again," the earl said, his voice tinged with amusement.

He corrected her, as he would a wayward child. "I said that my regiment took part in a campaign that helped rid our valiant commander of an artillery unit that had been shelling us to bits."

"Oh, yes, how terribly thrilling!" trilled the lady, placing her hand fetchingly upon his arm. "I do so adore hearing Your Grace recount how he commanded himself in battle. It's utterly too exciting for words." She dimpled up at him. "Là, it sets my little heart a-racing a pitter-patter right here."

The beauty placed his gloved hand upon the spot just beneath the frill of her bodice, so that he too might feel the excited beats of her heart.

"Ah . . . um . . . indeed," he murmured and quickly removed his gloved hand.

Beatrice clenched her bow and arrow. She'd been trying to concentrate, but failed miserably. Her arrow flew through the air landing in a patch of lawn far behind and to the left of the target.

"Here!" she said, thrusting her bow to one of her admirers, who faithfully stood by her side.

A piercing urge to go over and pull the earl away from the conniving hussy pricked her barely tamed temper. Firmly reminding herself once more that she was the property of no man, and in return no man belonged to her, she managed to rein in her rage. Not even the selfsame gentleman, who but the day before had made her feel weak-kneed and breathless from his passionate lovemaking, would give her reason to create a scene. She had promised her aunt that she would comport herself as a lady.

Resolutely, she turned her back on the couple. She held her hand out silently for her bow and arrow. Stringing it, she took aim and let the arrow fly. This time it hit the outer center of the mark.

Someone, it sounded like one of the debutantes, tittered nervously nearby.

She glared at the offender. The tittering stopped.

The devil was certainly having a merry field day with her!

Aunt Agnes had also been grimly observing the pair. It was quite evident that her niece did not understand what grave danger the other lady represented. She approached the crowd that surrounded Beatrice.

"Gentlemen, if you please," she said, trying to reach her niece.

But none of the dandies budged. Each prized the position that he'd hard won. They jealously formed a tighter knit circle around Beatrice.

Collapsing her black silk parasol, the tiny lady in black turned the sharp end upon the shapely young calves and buttocks that stood barring her way to her niece.

"I say, old girl," one of the dandies yelped in protest as the point struck a calf.

"Have a care, won't you!" protested another, receiving the sharp end in his nether regions.

The tiny poking demon paid little heed and continued brandishing her weapon until at last she reached the inner circle. Raising her parasol menacingly in the air, she dramatically banished the lot of them.

"Be gone!" she bellowed. Her long black shawl flapping up and down like flying bat's wings. "I wish to speak to m'niece alone."

Startled, fearful of another bruising poke, the tulips of fashion scurried off in different directions. The debutantes, whom they had previously ignored, suddenly looked quite pretty in their virginal whites, and by comparison to the tiny black terror next to them, quite harmless.

Agnes squinted up at her niece.

"Well, girl, what are you staring at? Are you going to sit there like a simpering school girl and let that trussed up pink pigeon have her way with your gentleman?"

"He's not my gentleman, Aunt," she replied stiffly, propping up her usual weapons of aloof indifference.

"Nor will he ever be if you don't change!" The aunt glowered at the pair heading in the direction of the lake below.

"You might at least try and steer him towards the altar before that London baggage stitches her initials on his pillow!" She wagged a finger at her in warning.

"What the Earl of Drennan chooses to do or not do, is none of my affair."

"Don't go about playing coy with me, girl." The aunt huffed, indignantly. "I saw with me own two eyes the way your mouth was mussed when you and the master of this great stone barn came riding back."

She nodded, her tiny gray head challenging her to deny the accusation.

"I know, therefore, something of a private nature passed betwixt the two of you. And I won't believe a word of it, if you tell me it didna! Come now, girl, you can't deny it."

"I won't," she said, her face reddening slightly at the confession. She felt like the veritable schoolgirl her aunt claimed her to be.

"You know, Auntie, I'm not a wee bairn anymore," she added defiantly, daring her aunt to question her actions. She was tired of being treated like a child still tied to her governess's apron strings. "Do remember next month I come into my majority."

"As if the whole world didna know it," bit out the tiny lady, fed up with the old maid's attitude her niece persisted in taking towards life.

She gave the young woman a derisive snort to let her know what she thought of that important event.

"So you'll receive at last the rest of your aunt Mary's money, won't you? Ha! And I suppose it'll be providing you a handsome husband and a brood of loving children to go with it, as well, m'dear?"

Beatrice chewed on the lower part of her lip.

Children. She'd not thought of that. Faith, her aunt had a way of finding her Achilles' heel. She adored the wee ones. They were the reason she'd chosen to learn to become a midwife in the first place. Aye, her aunt was right in that respect. She'd never given a great deal of thought to how she would feel if she didn't have a family of her own to love and care for.

And one could not go about having children without a husband. The devil take it, for that one needed a gentleman of equal standing or higher in society, if one was born to be a lady. Nay, she couldn't just go off and advertise for one and have him suddenly appear when she was ready to start a family. That would be as bad as letting her father arrange a match for her.

What she needed was a gentleman confidante. Someone she could share her ambitious dreams with, a husband who'd listen and encourage her in her ventures. And most importantly, not meddle. A partner in life, who like the Earl of Drennan would make both a good worker and a lover.

Her green eyes widened. She blinked, looking back towards where he and Mistress Powers stood by the lower south terrace at the bottom of the castle's hill. Even from this distance, she could see that they made a handsome couple.

Her eyes narrowed into dark green slits. She suddenly

realized that she did not care one bit for the view. Nay, not one bit.

"Aunt Agnes," she said decisively, turning to the tiny lady who'd shrewdly helped steer her in the direction she was about to take. "What shall I do?"

Chapter 9

Lady Beatrice O'Brien, the cool aloof Spinster of Brightwood, began a transformation that startled those who were well-acquainted with the serious-minded hoyden. Her conversation suddenly turned away from the more mannish topics that had usually peppered her speech, such as the market price of wool and the current blockade from America. Now it was much lighter, some would even say, provocative banter.

"Tell us the latest news, Lord Reginald," she said, lying languidly on a cushion beneath one of the large trees that bordered the grounds. The sun lightly dappled a path across her peach walking gown.

Young Reginald looked eagerly up at the dark-haired beauty. He had been reading the latest addition of the *London Gazette*, which had just arrived by courier. The earl had arranged for the papers to be delivered almost daily by coach. It was much to the pleasure of his English guests, who thought themselves to be almost at the end of the earth, being away from the center of the world—London.

"It's filled, my dear lady, with the superb news of Prinney's party for the disposed French royalty," he said, looking down at the gossip column. "What ho! Old Creevey has outdone himself this time! Just listen, my lady . . . ," he said, laughing with delight, enjoying the wicked bit of news he'd espied.

He stood up and dramatically took the posture of a

well-received lecturer dissecting the latest *on dit* from court for the public at large. "Apparently, all of London attended. But neither the Princess of Wales, or Lady Fitzherbert were seen at the celebrations at Carlton House, or as Creevey put it, 'the two wives stayed at home by themselves'!"

Everyone laughed. They were all *au courant* of the present situation between their corpulent regent prince and his two wives. The first was the Princess of Wales, whom the Prince Regent had tried to divorce. The second was a Catholic widow, whom he had tried to marry. Both endeavors had proved unsuccessful for the prince.

At present, their prince was involved with neither of the ladies, but taken up with Lady Hereford, now called *Madame Maintenon*. It was a title she'd earned after having married in secret, Louis the fourteenth of France at the ripe age of fifty-one.

"The Prince Regent is becoming a regular Henry the Eighth!" Beatrice commented and all laughed in appreciation at the jest.

The English court had become something less than noble since King George the third had gone both mad and blind. Only the threat of the war-crazed French Emperor across the channel brought any true feelings of loyalty the British now felt towards his successor, the Prince Regent. If nothing else, the deplorable manners of the "First Gentleman," as the prince was called, provided entertaining gossip during the war.

The earl, who happened to be passing by with Laeticia Powers on his arm, paused to listen to the conversation. He scowled jealously in their direction, hearing the outbursts of laughter following Lady Beatrice's pronouncement about the Prince Regent. He frowned. Why the devil wasn't she shocking them away? How unlike her!

The gentlemen seemed lately only too pleased to be in her company. And faith, she acted, for once, as if she were actually enjoying herself. That the lively inane banter surrounding her was actually interesting, even stimulating to hear.

But why not? He had found her wit to be quick, her ideas to be sound and enlightening. Faith, ever since their ride together, he'd been thinking of her various enterprises with nothing but respect.

She had accomplished what many a land manager failed to do, and on a much smaller budget and scale than any larger estate. She'd used modern methods to produce great abundance and profit from a small estate. Indeed, he'd begun since their conversation to consider plans of developing his own estates in the same manner as Brightwood Manor's.

"Your Grace," said Laeticia Powers, carefully trying to divert his straying attention away from the spinster heiress, whom she had decided to be her only true competitor for his interest. Although the afternoon sun had appeared briefly that morning, the air was cool around them. It whipped the ladies' skirts around their legs, causing some of them to pull their silk shawls more tightly around their shoulders.

Despite the breeze, Laeticia wiped her forehead dramatically. "Please, Your Grace, the sun is so hot . . . can't we walk over to the shade of those trees over there and rest?" She indicated a secluded grove of trees in the distance, away from Lady Beatrice and her circle of admirers. She knew they would not be heard or seen by any of the others. It was a perfect spot for a secluded conversation.

He paid her no heed, instead he intently watched Lady Beatrice.

"I said, if we stay here much longer, Your Grace, I shall get spots!" the lady beside him whined loudly. He sighed, reluctantly looking down at the pink confection standing next to him.

She suddenly reminded him of a toothache he'd endured as a child. Indeed, her demanding whining was fast becoming a nuisance. Why he had found this artless creature interesting for so long was short of amazing.

As they passed his man Davis, he pointedly nodded in the direction of the lady who clung to his arm. It was the agreed upon signal that Davis would help him get rid of whatever cumbersome lady was currently pestering him. In the last few days, there had been quite a few.

Davis surveyed the situation, and approached his master.

"Excuse me, Your Grace," he said bowing to the couple. "But I do believe, sir, that you asked me to come and fetch you if you were needed by the workmen. That is, if they had any questions, which required your attention."

"Ah, yes." The earl smiled. "And I take it that something is in need of my attention and direction?"

"Quite, Your Grace."

"Well, then, it's been a delight walking with you, Mistress Powers, but as you can see, I regretfully am being summoned elsewhere."

He made the obligatory bow to her and started to turn on his heels.

"But, sir," the lady protested, thrusting herself and her ample bosom in front of him, blocking his escape. Her blue eyes shone with determination at her objective. She'd seen this scenario played out before by other gentlemen she'd tried to attach herself to. This time she was determined not to be fobbed off.

"Surely you will walk me over to that grove of trees first, Your Grace?" she asked sweetly, her pretty, pale, blue eyes pleaded with him. He could not possibly refuse to escort her, thus abandoning her completely, to do so would be ungentlemanly. She looked expectantly at him to retake her arm.

The earl lifted his eyes heavenwards. The woman was incorrigible. He could either give her the cut direct, which he knew she did not deserve as he had previously encouraged her flirtatious advances, or he could give in and escort her to the willow trees. Having made his decision, he took her arm once more and continued their leisurely stroll around the lake towards the group of weeping willow trees bending picturesquely over the edge.

Amused by his master's predicament, Davis hid his mirth behind the long lace of his livery uniform. And to think this was the man Wellington had once called "One of the most courageous soldiers in Spain!"

Lady Beatrice also watched the couple make their way to the secluded grove of trees. The green sparkle of her eyes lost a little of their light, and with a pasted smile on her face, she turned away from the view.

*   *   *

That evening, the ballroom was lit with shimmering candlelight. The lovely chandelier hanging overhead had been one of the major feats of cleaning that Beatrice was immensely proud of having completed in time. The long dripping Venetian glass ornaments were bedazzling as their cut patterns shadowed the well-polished ballroom floor below.

Candlelit sconces with raised, golden, gilded arms and hand-blown glass protectors were lit along the walls adding an elegant glow to the room. These decorative lights had been recently ordered from Dublin and replaced the more ancient wall holders once used for torches. At the far side of the room, elderly dowagers sat warming themselves by an intricately carved fireplace, one of the few original ones left in the castle.

The earl was dancing with one of the debutantes when he caught sight of her. He held his breath and looked at the fairness of her white alabaster skin, her long, lustrous black tresses woven into an elegant style, emphasized the beauty of her oval face. She stood out among the ladies both in height, beauty, and wit. He hated that she was surrounded by her usual entourage of male admirers.

He thought her an exotic flower surrounded by lesser, more common varieties. For instance, the one hanging on his arm, Lady Anne Ferguson. Although in a very conventional sense, she fit the bill quite nicely for a harmless flirtation with her pale, blonde hair, and pretty, blue eyes. Undoubtedly, many would consider her a fetching English rose, a lady of fine breeding who would make some fortunate gentleman a worthy wife. But now, as he held the lady at arm's distance, listening to her lisping utterances of banal conversation, he could not imagine spending an entire evening in her insipid company, let alone a lifetime.

His gaze strayed back to the corner where the exotic flower sat holding court with those vying for her hand. Rumor had spread like wildfire that she had already turned down two proposals of marriage. A third was in the works for that very same evening.

The dance ended. He made the proper bow and returned his partner to her beaming chaperon. He walked over to a potted plant near the exotic flower, waiting for the next dance to be announced. Without any hesitation, he stepped directly in front of young Lord Reginald, whom he noted jealously, had already had two dances with her. Three would have bordered on scandalous, an open declaration of his intentions to ask for her hand. The earl could not possibly permit it, if not for her sake, then for his own.

He bowed to her. She smiled encouragingly at him.

"My dear Lady Beatrice," he said, his voice husky smooth with the pleasure of seeing her smile at him.

"Captain James. Your Grace," she whispered, correcting herself, self-consciously aware of others listening to their conversation, her heart thumping excitedly beneath her ball gown of silver damask.

"May I have the pleasure of this dance?" he asked, holding out his hand.

She nodded and held out a white-gloved hand, her dancing card dangling unheeded, from her slender wrist. Oblivious to the disappointed looks on the young gentlemen's faces beside her, she stood and took the earl's arm.

He led her out onto the dance floor where couples were taking their places. It was not until he placed his hand intimately upon her small waist that she realized they were about to dance the waltz, a scandalous new dance that required a gentleman putting his hand on a lady's waist.

She had only danced the waltz once before, and that had been at a small local assembly with friends, not in a grand ballroom surrounded by the jaded members of the ton watching on. They would not hesitate to laugh derisively at any misstep.

As if he sensed her nervousness, he smiled down at her. He gave her a squeeze of reassurance, urging her onward.

"It'll be fine, Lady Beatrice," he murmured, his superfine black waistcoat briefly brushing up against her as they prepared to begin.

He reached for her hand in a confident manner of one not afraid to run the gauntlet of the ballroom. "Let me assure your ladyship that I've only trod on a few slippers this night. And if you will but smile up at me, I promise to do my very best not to step on yours."

She did smile then and laughed, her worries of miss-stepping fleeing like flies before a swatting hand. *When I am in my dotage, she thought as the music began and the earl swung her out onto the floor, I shall remember this night as the one in which Captain James Huntington, the Earl of Drennan danced me into a dream.*

They spoke not a word as they box stepped. To Beatrice, words were not adequate to describe the joy of being held in his arms. She was oblivious of the envious glances of other ladies, only aware of that magic moment when her gloved hand touched his. Indeed, a magic as old as time itself seemed to have led them to each other.

She did not know how she found herself on the balcony, alone with him, but she walked willingly into his arms as if it were the place she most longed to be in the whole entire world.

"I've missed you," he whispered into her ear as they gazed down at the lake below them. Its sparkling moonlit waters glowed silver on the surface.

"Have you?" she asked, her heart pounding, as he came behind her and she felt him place his strong arms around her.

"I thought you were too busy with the other ladies to notice my absence," she remarked, recalling vividly the afternoons he had spent in the company of Laeticia Powers. She recalled the manner in which he had abandoned her the day after their amorous interlude at the cottage, leaving her in the company of the other gentlemen, when she wanted only to be with him.

She cautiously stood back a little from him. Maybe this was a mistake. She listened to his deep, manly laugh and wistfully she thought she heard a note of jealousy as poignant as her own when he spoke.

"And you, madam, could lead an entire regiment of men comprised solely of your numerous admirers.

Perhaps I ought to recommend to Wellington for recruitment your charming self? I'm certain, judging by the effect you have on most of the gentlemen here, it would prove most effectual in recruiting an entire legion of lovesick followers into joining up."

"Indeed, sir." She laughed. "And leave you here at the mercy of all these eager young ladies? I think not. Faith, it would be most cruel if I did so. For a gentleman may only take one lady to wife."

"Then, my dear lady, what do you suggest we do?" he asked, his voice suddenly deep and rough with open desire blazing in his brilliant sapphire eyes.

Caught off balance, she could find no glib reply.

"I—I don't know," she whispered, smelling the clean scent of his freshly starched silk shirt. She pulled back to look up into his ruggedly handsome face.

His bright blue eyes searched hers. A warm, throbbing excitement coursed through her. Her beloved pirate was about to plunder her heart.

"Don't you, my dear? And I thought that by now you understood how I felt about you . . . I told you at your father's house that I intended to make you my wife. And I still do."

"Yes, you did speak of wanting me," she said, a sudden fear constricting her heart, remembering his previous proposal, how he had tried to frighten her into accepting, by dangling the threat of scandal over her head. She turned away from him, gripping the balcony's railing, her knuckles white with tension. She was not certain how to answer.

He had spoken of his attraction for her, but not of those more tender feelings she'd always associated with marriage. That of respect and mutual fidelity mixed with the strongest of all feelings for the other person—love.

"And what is your answer?" he asked, his breath seductively warm upon her face. "Will you have me?

And become the mistress of this castle and all its many holdings, including me?"

She looked up at him uncertainly. She realized she wanted hearth and home as much as any other woman. But the fear, it was still there . . . she was still uncertain she could trust him. Was he like the others who had pursued her merely for her wealth? Did he care for her beyond what her purse strings could provide?

"I—I can't," she said, her eyes holding his with a worried, searching expression. Did he understand her reservations? Could he possibly wait till she'd sorted out these frightening emotions? Perhaps giving her time to build her trust in him and a future they would have together?

"Shush," he said, placing a finger over her lips. "You don't have to answer me now. I believe you need some time to think this over. We'll talk of this at another time, when you've had time to consider."

She nodded, relieved that he understood. He was giving her the time she needed to be certain that she was about to make the right decision. It would allow her to free herself of any doubting demons.

He whispered huskily, "While you think upon our union, consider this," and sweeping her into his arms, he kissed her. His insistent mouth possessed hers, his arms holding her body up against his until she trembled with desire and sweet longing, drawing him to her as she returned the kiss.

Unknown to the couple were two men watching from the tall, French doors that opened out onto the balcony. Their dark forms and softly spoken words were overheard.

Sharp, beady eyes focused upon the embracing couple.

A man in a stolen livery uniform wiped his nose across the clean sleeve, which would have pained the true owner if he'd known. He began to take meticulous notes. For a few gold coins placed in his unclean hands, he'd happily promised to spy upon the members of the household, thinking all the while of how to quickly destroy the couple before him.

Another set of eyes spied upon the couple, as well. But his eyes brimmed with tears of disappointment. Instead of continuing to stare at the couple, he turned and silently walked away from them.

*   *   *

That night in an inn of ill repute some five leagues from Drennan Castle, the same pair of cynical, sly eyes that had spied upon the earl and the spinster, made their reappearance. They squinted eagerly in the dim light of the taproom, adjusting to the pitch dark after coming in from the moonlight.

The room was crowded with thugs and cutthroats for hire. He searched for the man he'd come to contact.

He nodded to a few acquaintances. He had been here but three days ago, when he had been one of the men lounging around the taproom getting drunk, hoping to be one of the lucky to feel the cool roundness of a few coins greasing the palm of his dirty hands.

The bartender, wearing a white wig, conversed with a gentleman, a titled one by the looks of his elegant clothes. The gentleman, a dapper man, in mustard-colored waistcoat nodded to the informant as way of greeting, indicating a room to the right where the two could find some privacy for their conversation. For who knew which man in the room would be willing to betray their plans for a few well-placed guineas? A whispered word in the right ear could produce plenty of the desirable gilt. For their venture involved those of considerable wealth.

The squinty-eyed man entered the secluded room with eager anticipation. It was screened off from the rest by a mere curtain. The news he had to impart would stir, he was certain, the titled gentleman into action.

"Well, what news do you bring me, Snipes?" asked the haughty lord, hoisting an elegant red heeled boot up onto a nearby bench. "It had better be worth my while. I can't continue spending my gilt on the worthless tripe you've been feeding me lately. Has there been any further development between my lady and that gentleman?"

Snipes wiped the foam from the tankard across his sleeve before he spoke. His eyes focused upon the lord before him.

The aristocrat had paid him quite well to enter the service of the Earl of Drennan and to spy upon him and the young lady who had been acting as the mistress of the household. He regretted not being able to squeeze a little more money out of the lord for the spying. Perhaps if he told him of what he saw and heard, the fancy shirt would be willing to hire him for the other half of the job.

"Aye, my Lord Linley. There's been a development betwixt the two of 'em. You might even say of an intimate nature, if you gets my meanin'."

"Indeed," drawled the man, raising his quizzing glass to his eye, inspecting the commoner. The impertinent mercenary talked about his betters in such a knowing tone, as if he had the audacity himself to look up the lady's skirts.

"How intimate, Snipes?"

"What I meant, sire, is that the lady and him you told me to spy upon, were seen being very friendly towards one another and talkin' of marriage and such," said the man with a breathy smile of villainous intent.

He eagerly rubbed his dirty hands together.

"Now what do you want me and my partner to do about

it? I take it none of these goings on meet with yer approval? Been intending to have a go at the lady for yerself, eh, gov'? Want to get a little bit o' her between the—"

"Be careful of how you speak of my intended," the aristocrat said shortly, touching the sword at his side. "Or you may find yourself quickly being replaced by another, and quite permanently."

"Aye, for sure, m'lord. I was just makin' a harmless jest," said the brigand. He was confused by the gentleman's intentions towards the wealthy spinster and the newcomer, the earl.

"Do you wants me ter send for my friend now? He can help us, uh—escort her ladyship to you for any impending nuptials."

The aristocrat twirled his quizzing glass. A gleaming yellow smile of satisfaction lined the creases of his pock-marred face. He leaned his head back against the chair, contemplating his revenge against the woman who had spurned him.

He envisioned how much he would harm her and felt once more the pull of satisfaction in his nether regions when he dreamt of it. Aye, he would experience great pleasure in cowing the shrew's will to his. Demme, if he wouldn't take a whip to her if she didn't do as he wished.

"Yes, Snipes," he said, sipping his mulled wine. His eyes glazed with a madman's dreams. "It's time we put our plan into action. Contact your friend."

Placing a pile of gold coins on the table, he began to make concrete his own plans for the Spinster of Brightwood Manor to become his bride.

*　*　*

Under an almost cloudless blue sky, Lady Beatrice found herself floating along in a boat rowed by young

Lord Reginald Fortescue. Normally, she would have found the company of the young lord to be a bit overpowering, like too much perfume, cloying, overly sweet. But not today. Today was glorious no matter whose company she found herself in.

She had spent half of the previous night dreamily thinking about the earl and his proposal. She had not yet confided in anyone what had passed between herself and the handsome master of the house. Not even to her inquisitive aunt, who was usually so uncannily aware of all that occurred in the castle. No one knew of their meeting last night.

"Did you enjoy yourself last night, Lord Reginald?" she asked, lazily letting her fingertips dip into the cool water of the lake.

"Not exceptionally," murmured the young lord. Then not able to resist a tiny jibe, he added, "Not like some ladies and gentlemen in the assembly I can think of."

"Is that so?" Blithely smiling, Beatrice adjusted her parasol to her right shoulder. The lace silk sunscreen twirled fetchingly in her gloved hands. She did not realize what a pretty picture she made in her yellow poplin afternoon gown trimmed with white lace, her dark curls spread about her as she leaned comfortably back into a pile of pillows, her emerald eyes half-closed, dreamily thinking of the gentleman she'd kissed.

"Faith, I had such a glorious time last night myself. Captain James, I mean His Grace," she blushed, "took a great deal of care in planning for the ball, supervising nearly every detail of it himself. I do believe everyone had such a grand time dancing." She sighed blissfully, remembering the feel of his hands on hers as they waltzed.

"Including his exalted self," murmured the disgruntled young lord, jealously remembering the way he'd seen the lady and the earl together on the balcony.

"What was that you say?" asked Beatrice, suddenly sitting up and causing the boat to rock a little.

The young lord stopped his rowing and looked her directly in the eyes, water dripping from the oars. "It was noticed that your ladyship and His Grace did not return immediately to the ballroom after you finished your dance," he said, his face placidly shuttered from any revealing expression. "So I went looking for you, Lady O'Brien, supposing you had taken a stroll out onto the balcony for a breath of fresh air."

"I . . . uh . . . that is, I did," she said, a telling tinge of pink staining her cheeks. Suddenly, she recalled that if the earl had not asked her to dance, she would have with Lord Reginald.

She cast a questioning look at the young lord before her. Had he been witness to her and the earl's embrace? If so . . .

"Lord Reginald, I—" she stammered, but found she could not continue. It was far too embarrassing.

"Yes, Lady Beatrice."

"I, uh—that is—I regret missing our dance last night," she said. "And I don't want you to think that I don't esteem your friendship. It was intolerably rude of me to have forgotten you were next on my dance card."

"Not to fret, my dear," he said reaching for her hand.

She immediately stopped her ramblings. She looked at him.

"Lady Beatrice," he said, swallowing. "I want you to know that it is I who value your friendship. At one time I thought our friendship might develop further into something dearer, at least I thought that would happen. There had been for me a hope it would grow and allow us perhaps to contemplate a match between us."

He sighed deeply, as if lifting off a heavy burden that had been hanging over his head since they first met.

He thrust aside his mother's dire warnings of cutting him off without a guinea. He was a man, not a puppet. Now he intended to cut the invisible maternal strings that had been dictating his actions all week.

"I now realize that we would never suit. Lady Beatrice, it would appear you and I were meant to remain simply friends."

Beatrice leaned over the oars and kissed him on the cheek. "Thank you, Lord Reginald. I would like that. I have so few."

At that the young lord laughed. "And that is why, madam, almost every gentleman on this lake watching us right now would like nothing better than to hang me by my own cravat. And if I'm not mistaken, one gentleman in particular is glaring daggers at me in a rather dangerous manner. I hope he doesn't decide to call me out after this. I've grown rather fond of not having any holes in my tender hide."

"For sure now?" she asked laughing, highly amused at the thought. The idea of someone fighting a duel over her was absurd. Turning her head in the direction of the shore, she glanced to see of whom he spoke.

Her hand stilled above the water. She ought to have known. He stood there, imperiously watching them, lordly with impatience as he awaited her return to shore.

"Aye, so it is him," she said pleased, for it was none other than the Earl of Drennan.

She winked at the young lord. "And a grand sight he is, too, if I don't mind saying so, my lord."

"Are you contemplating a match then, ma'am?" asked the young lord, and strangely felt a tinge of envy for his rival.

She shrugged, sobering at the question, her eyes never leaving the shore where the earl stood watching. "I confess I am contemplating the question."

"Hmm . . . ," murmured the young lord, eyeing the

[187]

shore and the man. "I'd decide quickly if I were you. He doesn't strike me as a very patient fellow."

*   *   *

When they reached the shore, the Earl of Drennan came and stood in the knee-high water. He held his hand out for her as she stood, ready for the moment when she would step out of the boat and onto the pebbled shore. Unexpectedly, the bottom of the boat hit the sand. Caught off balance, she fell heavily against his sturdy chest.

He smiled wickedly down at her, and without any warning, swooped her up into his arms and carried her effortlessly to the shore.

"Did you thank young Lord Fotescue for the ride, my dear?" he asked looking down at her with a possessive gleam in his eyes.

"I did, my lord. Why?"

"Because from now on, my sweet, I intend to be the only one allowed to be alone with you in a boat."

"Indeed, sir," she said smiling, listening to the happy, steady thumping of his heart.

"Yes, vixen," he murmured into her ear. And when they reached dry land, he reluctantly put her down.

A group of young dandies made their appearance, boisterously insisting that they needed her ladyship to come settle an important dispute between them. Without a backward glance at their host, they proceeded to whisk her away.

*   *   *

On the morrow, the first planned hunt turned out to be a misty one. North Sea fog rolled into the hills and valleys surrounding the castle. A light, hazy rain had dampened the fields the night before. Spring flowers bloomed brightly in contrast along the sheep paths beyond the stone fence. One's blood raced with anticipation at the sound of baying hounds. It was, in Lady Beatrice's opinion, a glorious morn for a hunt.

She watched attentively the Master of the hunt come up the castle drive, a tall, dignified Irish gentleman about fifty years of age with gray sideburns and a portly figure. He was dressed in a striking, scarlet hunting jacket, black, polished hunting boots, and wore an elegant tri-corn with a single pheasant feather gaily saluting from the hatband. He carried a beautiful silver flask on his belt with the best hunting recipe in the parish, perhaps even the entire country.

She smiled and waved a hand in recognition. For it was her own father, Lord O'Brien, who served as Master of the hunt. She did not know by what miracle had brought about his leading, but she highly suspected it figured with her. The sporting lord rarely loaned himself and his hounds to anyone, no matter how important his consequence. He valued his hounds far more than his neighbors or any of the puffed-up English titled.

The servants stood about in the Earl of Drennan's livery, passing out hot tankards of mulled port or watered whiskey topped with cloves and a dash of sugar on lemon rinds to the assembled gentry.

Among the castle's guests were many familiar faces, those of Urlingford locals, among whom she had grown up hunting. Many came by and greeted her with smiles, nods, and a kind word.

Her father grinned at her as he passed on her left, begrudgingly admitting to the castle's hostess, "The brew's passable, m'dear. Although mind, it doesna have the numb blinding effect of one of me own. But I suppose that be for the best, as I donna want anyone knocked off his mount before we get started."

[189]

"Aye, sir, 'tis best we save that event for the hunt itself!" she quipped with a coquettish wave of her whip. This light remark brought about a scatter of chuckles from those nearby, who knew that before the day was out, several of the assembled followers would find either themselves, or their mounts, the fallen losers in the field.

Captain James, she noted with surprise, was mounted on a superb black thoroughbred that appeared to be a little high strung. The animal kicked out at another horse from behind him that had drawn a little too close.

He was elegantly attired in a black-waisted hunting jacket and sported a matching black hat with a modern brim. His white cravat was properly tied in the square knotted mathematical and held firmly in place to his starched white shirt by a sapphire stud. Although his mount appeared to be spirited, the earl looked completely at ease on the animal, and she noticed he remained admirably in control of the horse's movements.

She had thought that maybe he would forego that day's hunting due to his previous injury from the bog. The hunt would not be the simple easy trot into the countryside that they had enjoyed together when she had shown him the parish. The hunt required a great deal of stamina and skill. Not only because of the demands of the obstacles met in the field, but because it was not uncommon to remain mounted on one's horse up to six hours at a time.

One of the whips in charge of the dogs approached Beatrice and asked where the final rendez-vous place would be at the end of the day's hunt. She answered that they would stop at the castle for a repast at midday. She glanced again in Captain James's direction when she heard his horse give a snort of eagerness to be off.

He caught her glance and brazenly winked at her, tipping the brim of his hat.

She blushed, remembering the feel of his strong, sturdy arms beneath her when he had carried her away from the boat.

Her father gave the signal to release the dogs from their pens.

The hunters, who for the most part were seated on their own sturdy mounts, which they'd brought expressly for the purpose of this event, prepared themselves.

Beatrice watched her father lead. The whipper-ins were in charge of the hounds and the assembled hunters followed them down to the field below the castle.

Red foxes were frequently sighted by the old castle ruins, having dug sturdy dens full of numerous exits and entrances under the fallen stones. A more perfect place to find foxes would not be found in the entire parish. The castle was located near a thickly bracketed field not too far from ripe crops of grain. The foxes ate and hunted mice and ground fowl, which made it a perfect habitat for their game.

A forest grew along a quick running stream, which ran through the fields. It was perfectly suitable terrain for the horses to follow the dogs as they chased the line of scent of the chosen game.

Lord O'Brien gave the order to cast the hounds, which meant setting the pack loose in a set pattern in search of the scent. Upon casting, the huntsman blew his horn signaling the beginning of the hunt. Everyone waited with anticipation. From a bush down near where the ruins met a cornfield, a red fox slipped out from under the broken remains of a toppled chimney.

Espying the *reynard*, as the fox was affectionately called by the huntsmen, the Master of the Hunt lifted his hat in the direction of the fox.

"Tally ho!" he yelled out to all, immediately following the dogs on the field that were already in pursuit. Lady Beatrice and the others followed from behind. It was bad form to pass the Master and the dogs during a hunt.

The first obstacle in the form of a sturdy sheep rail loomed up quickly. Beatrice watched with admiration as her father and the whips jumped over the fence. The dogs ran rapidly beneath it. The rail did not so much as twitch or twang at their passing.

She rode a good, solid horse that day. It was a white mare, who was fresh and willing to go wherever commanded. Eagerly, she followed them, her horse jumping the rail effortlessly as she kept her seat.

The earl and Beau Powers followed, both of them successfully making it over. The next gentleman rider, young Lord Reginald Fortescue, was not to be so blessed. The back hooves of his horse knocked off the top post.

She turned to see two debutantes stuck behind the fumbling jumper. Their horses, now skittish from the falling post, refused to take the jump. It was only on their second attempt that they were able to follow over the post. It was at that moment the pace of the hunt quickened. The fox was spotted again. It appeared as a red dot off in the distance, racing across the stream. The hounds were a grave danger to his brush, as his tail was so fondly called.

"Grand day for a hunt, Mistress O'Brien!" called out one of the tenant farmers. He tipped his hat as she passed him leaving the field.

She waved a hand in greeting at several of the workers who had gathered in the field to watch the gentry.

"Yes, it is, Master Flanagan!" She nodded in agreement and with a click of her tongue set her horse at a brisk trot to catch up with her father and the hounds. The hunt then raced across the muddy path near the brook where the previous night's rain had left pools of wet and muck.

She could not help but laugh out loud as she witnessed dainty Laeticia Powers, who had been trying to keep up with the earl, receive a direct hit from a flying clod of mud from the rider in front of her. The pocket Venus had not been paying attention to the path ahead and took the flying mud clod squarely on her face, dirtying her dainty nose, mouth, and chin. She now wore a mask of splattered mud and dirt.

Not surprisingly, young Lord Fortescue gallantly rode up to the pretty blonde and offered her his monogrammed kerchief with which to wipe her face.

Upon entering the woods, they met their next obstacle, the dark running stream. The horse in front of Beatrice, a dappled gray quarter horse, which belonged to one of the whips, balked at the water.

Her own mount hesitated only briefly, she was proud to say later, and effortlessly sailed over the stream. Others, including Captain James and Beau Powers, did not manage quite so well.

She watched as Captain James came up from behind. He looked a little ruffled and dirty from his own mount's balking and leaving him on the ground. But with a tip of his hat and a happy smile, he rode on.

It was at this point by the water's edge that the hounds lost the fox's scent and the riders took a needed pause.

Hunting flasks were passed around as all shared a word or two about how they had so far fared. Already some of the hunters had given up and returned to the castle.

The quest for other game and another run took them until midday. At this point, her father and the whipper-ins called an end to the hunt and a return to the castle.

She did not know how it came to pass, but as she

was turning towards the castle, her horse stumbled near the stream. She dismounted to check the animal's hooves and legs. She had to be certain it was not lame.

Captain James and Beau Powers reined in their mounts. James lightly dismounted. Self-conscious of the handsome gentlemen watching her, she made a few quick brushes at her riding habit and tidied a thick strand of hair back into place. She was not aware of how pretty she looked when she did so. The sparkling stream and green forest served as a picturesque backdrop behind her.

"Lovely day, isn't it?" said Beau Powers, removing his hat gallantly and smiling down at her from his gelding, Aries. His own handsome blue eyes shone with amusement at how the earl had tossed that lucky coin of his and won the privilege of being the one to dismount and help the winsome lady.

Blushing, secretly delighted that the two most handsome and dashing gentlemen of the field had stopped to check on her, Beatrice answered, "Aye sir. 'Tis as grand a day as we could wish for. Lord O'Brien, to be sure, ought to be pleased. Monsieur Le Reynard led us a merry chase." She watched as the earl checked her mount for any possible injuries.

"And how are you, my lady?" he asked when he'd finished his inspection.

Lowering her eyes, she smiled, dimples appearing, "I'm fine, Your Grace. 'Twas kind of you and Master Powers to stop and keep me company."

Nodding, he said, "I think it's safe for you to remount. May I offer you a leg up?" He cupped his hand under her right foot at the ready and pushed her gently up into the saddle. Then he swung up on his own mount. His sapphire blue eyes shining with delight at the beautiful, dark-haired lady whose hunting hat was now coquettishly tilted to one side.

"Uh—hmm." Beau Powers coughed discreetly, reminding the couple of his presence.

"Thank you, Your Grace," murmured Beatrice.

"The pleasure, my dear, was all mine," he answered, tipping his hat. The trio turned their horses in the direction of the castle. Upon their arrival, a sumptuous feast, presided over by the ever-efficient Davis, was served soon afterwards.

Chapter 10

Blissful thoughts of happiness were not, however, what occupied Aunt Agnes's keen mind at supper that night. She had been closely observing the one person at the table with whom she was well acquainted, her niece. And she was worried. Beatrice had not taken more than a few nibbles of food off the full plate set before her.

Her young niece was not known to eat like a little twittering bird. And knowing that her niece had planned the menu, Aunt Agnes quickly dismissed the notion that the food somehow had not agreed with Beatrice.

"Are you feeling well, my dear?" she asked from across the table as a footman collected the still full plate. "I've noticed that your cheeks have been frequently flush of late. Perhaps you caught a chill when you were out hunting today with your father?"

"No. I'm feeling quite the thing, Auntie." The niece sighed, looking with mooncalf eyes in the direction of the earl who sat at the opposite end of the table. "You needn't concern yourself with me," she reiterated, merely glancing at the beef pudding the footman set in front of her.

"If you are certain," answered Aunt Agnes, glancing slyly in the direction of the most eligible bachelor in the room. The earl was at that very moment lifting his crystal goblet of wine in a silent toast to her niece.

Beatrice, a radiant smile on her face, lifted hers in return.

"Quite fine," she replied blithely, sipping her wine,

never taking her smiling eyes away from that of his.

"Oh," her aunt beamed with delight, "I'm so relieved to hear it, my dear."

But a fairy tale ending was not how the evening concluded. After dinner, it had cut Beatrice to the quick to see Lady Powers try once more to monopolize the earl's attentions. The dasher's full white arms stuck to the earl's coat sleeve as if she had sewn herself to him. It had been a near impossibility for Beatrice to enjoy the gifted tenor they had hired from Dublin for the musical entertainment they had planned. She was too occupied by the other lady's presence.

The dapper tenor, stood before the assembly with an elegant, pointed beard and mustache. He had been requested to sing some Irish ballads. Both she and the earl thought that it would be a fine treat for their English guests, who had never heard many of the songs before.

When Master O'Shaunasee sang a haunting, love ballad in ancient Irish, tears sprang into her eyes. She felt deep within herself a tender swelling of emotions, as if the gentleman had brought forth the words written over two hundred years before expressly for her. It made her sad and wistful for the earl. She had to admit to herself she had felt attracted to him from the first, when they met in the bog and his body had brushed up against hers, sparking an ember in her heart she had thought would never catch flame. It continued to burn until finally it culminated with their lovemaking. Her heart had known all along, but she had denied what it told her, that she was in love.

She wanted to believe he loved her. That somehow he knew of the burgeoning love she felt for him. But the past few days had made it difficult for her to speak to him and they had not been alone since the blissful moment they shared together in the tiny cottage. She felt tears of frustration well in her eyes as she yearned to be alone with him, to confide her love.

[197]

"Here, Bea'," whispered her aunt, handing her a handkerchief when the last note had faded away. A few tears glistened in her own clear, gray eyes.

"Dearee me," the old lady said, wiping them away. "That gentleman could sing in a choir of angels."

"Aye, Auntie." The niece nodded, wiping her own. "Master O'Shaunasee's voice is a gift from God."

At the end of the recital, the usually reserved crowd of predominantly English listeners thunderously applauded the thin, dapper Irishman before them. They stomped the floorboards with their enthusiasm for more. The tenor obliged and sang another song, this one a merry tune. It was accompanied by the billows of the Irish pipe and required the clapping of hands in rhythmic unison.

Afterwards, many of the titled guests jostled forwards vying for a moment with the talented performer, trying to entice the singer to come to London. Invitations were given for him to visit their salons and perform there as their own special prodigy.

Master O'Shaunasee, with great finesse, refused their offers. He replied that he preferred living in the only capitol he had ever wanted to know as home, Dublin.

"Besides," he smiled at the admiring ladies, twirling his waxed mustache, "I could never abandon m'wife and five wee bairns despite the great honor of your delightful company."

* * *

Beatrice felt a hand on her shoulder. It was the earl. His dark eyes looked down at her. "I must speak with you," he whispered urgently into her ear.

"Where?"

"The south terrace. Meet me there in five minutes."

She nodded agreement, as the young gentleman she had sent to fetch her a glass of punch appeared by her side.

Although it was early spring, the wind off the lake was not as chilling as it might have been. It gently brushed against her skirts as she made her way to the terrace. She wore her favorite shawl over her shoulders, its long, fringed ends dangling down her back. Her evening gown of white silk gave her the appearance of a bride.

"By Jupiter!" the earl said as he stepped out of the shadow of a willow tree where he had been silently observing her approach. "You put the very stars in the heavens to shame tonight, my dear Lady Beatrice."

She smiled, pleased by the compliment, enjoying the gleam of open admiration on his face as he stared at her.

She had received many fulsome compliments from her entourage of admirers concerning aspects of her beauty. Her various body parts had been eulogized and rhapsodized in such verse and rhyme that even that old bard, Shakespeare, would have been pleased. But none of these fawning compliments meant as much to her as the words the earl had just said. For she knew that they were spoken sincerely.

She stepped into his arms then, contentedly sighing as he held her there. The sparkling moonlight glittered off the water below and bright, silver stars above shone benevolently upon them. She rested her head against his chest.

"Lady Beatrice," he said, his scar crinkling into his smile. "The time for you to give me your answer has come. I have, I believe, been most patient in that respect. Indeed you must congratulate me for not tearing into young Lord Reginald Fortescue's hide the other day for daring to take my betrothed out alone on the lake. I held myself back, behaving in the most virtuous manner for you, my dear."

She smiled to herself, and said in a teasing voice, "I

[199]

am not yet your betrothed, sir. Pray do not forget, I've not yet given my answer."

He turned her around to face him and kissing her brow said, "Then do not keep me in suspense any longer. I must know that you are completely mine."

Looking into his ruggedly handsome face, the one she had grown to hold so dear since that fateful day when his horse had thrown him. She knew she must confess to him what held her back from accepting him.

"Indeed. But I too need to know something, sir," she said, her heart pounding with fearful dread at the response she might receive. She looked him squarely in the eye and asked plainly, "Do you love me?"

"Do I love you?" he repeated releasing her, stunned by the question. He held her away from him so that he might see her face more clearly in the moonlight.

He laughed shakily. "You have not gone and fallen in love with me, have you, my dear Lady Beatrice?"

"Yes," she said softly. "I have," she murmured.

His smile disappeared. He brushed a hand agitatedly through his hair. Her declaration of love came as an unexpected surprise.

"I know that from the first I wanted to marry you. Both for your beauty and your intelligence," he said, speaking honestly from his heart.

"Yes?" she asked, urging him on.

"Sink me," he said, shaking his head to clear it. "I don't know if I am in love or not." Then he smiled, his teeth flashing in the dark, and he took her by the shoulders, forcing her to look at him.

"I have been acting like a veritable schoolboy would these past few weeks. And truth to tell, my dear, the feelings you've evoked in me are a far cry from that of an untried youth in his first blush of love," he said looking back into her eyes. His own sparkled, recalling the passion she always managed to stoke in him on several occasions.

"No, I do not know if I love you," he admitted. "What I have come to understand about this obsession is that I want you to be completely and utterly *mine* in every sense of the word. I want you, make no mistake about it, my dear. I want you at my table and in my bed, as suits my wife and bride."

He looked fondly down at the intelligent woman before him, a lady who had as much business acumen as any of his male overseers. And what if she were made to see the profitable side such a match would offer? Perhaps then she could be persuaded to agree upon their marriage, realizing the benefits outweighed the more sentimental matters?

"And through this union, when our two lands are finally joined together, we will both become more profitable, my dear, using each other's strengths in building a secure future for our heirs. Our estates will no longer be rivals in trade, but joint ventures in the valley, working together to build a solid dynasty." He smiled smugly down at her, thinking that that final bit of logic would turn his offer in his favor. He was mistaken.

She sighed unhappily. His answer was not what she had hoped for. It brought no warm glow of reassurance that would melt away her fears. Fears that he wanted her only for her money. It only caused her to become further alarmed.

She avoided looking at him. He would probably in due time forget about her and return to London. He was, it would appear from all that talk of joining lands and creating a dynasty, proposing a marriage of convenience, just like all the others.

"A marriage of convenience, for a dynasty," she said sadly. "Isn't that what you're proposing? I feel much like the goose that laid her golden eggs for the giant. I see a future, were I to marry you, where I'd become, in time, nothing more than a fascinating Irish bird caged in Your Grace's drawing room for you to display to visitors."

She looked at him. She saw that he would not deny this supposition of his wanting to possess her merely to own her lands and wealth. Her heart throbbed with dull sadness. He obviously did not love her.

"You're famous, you know, Your Grace?" she said, the hurt evident in her trembling voice. "All of Urlingford, and probably a good deal of Dublin, is already talking of your triumph in snaring my attention. I do believe even our haughty English guests have found some source of amusement in watching the Spinster of Brightwood fall in love with their handsome earl. I'm quite certain we'll be the topic of dinner conversations for months to come."

She knew that their guests had secretly been making bets amongst themselves as to whether or not their earl would win her. She wouldn't have been surprised if the local gaming dens in Dublin and London had her and the earl's name written on their betting sheets. She knew she had been a constant source of amusement in the past for such ridiculous betting. But whereas before she would have laughed, she now no longer found it to be very droll. It hurt.

"My lady," he said, trying to stop her before she destroyed the last bit of tenderness that existed between them. "I do care for you. Don't deny my suit. You and I could be very happy together, my dear."

"I do not know if we would," she said. "As you do not love me, I rather think one of us would be most unhappy." Tears began to well in her eyes. They stung, but she refused to wipe at them. He would not see her weak with regrets.

"They'll say you tamed the Spinster of Brightwood Manor, you know," she said pulling her shoulders back straight and looking him directly in the eye. "You ought to be delighted. Your well-planned strategy worked to some great effect, sir. You won my heart, but not my hand."

"Lady Beatrice," he said, moving towards her, trying to think of how he could undo his dreadful blundering.

Shaking her head, she moved away from him. She had heard enough. She felt more miserable than she had ever felt in her entire life. Her heart ached with the knowledge that he did not love her and that she had been a fool to believe that he might care deeply for her.

She picked up her skirts, and without a word, walked to the terrace stairs. She left him standing alone in the moonlight, looking down at the water's edge, contemplating where his second proposal had gone wrong.

Behind the locked doors of her bedchamber, she sobbed her heart out, refusing to answer the soft knockings as her aunt pleaded to speak to her. The oak door remained firmly shut until the following morn when her maid discovered her missing from her bed.

* * *

The first Beatrice knew something was amiss was the moment a rough, large hand clamped itself tightly over her mouth, awakening her.

"Don't breathe a word," a low, menacing voice muttered in the dark.

She felt the sharp end of a knife pricking her exposed neck above her night shift. She tried to open her mouth and bite down upon the hand held over her, in preparation for a scream, but another sharp poke stopped her.

"Try it and I'll gullet your ladyship like a carp. I swear I will," the rough voice whispered menacingly into her ear.

Her bedchamber was pitch dark. With the exception of

the low burning embers in the hearth, it contained little light. She could not make out the face of the man beside her, only his dark, burly form leaning threateningly over her.

The smell of cheap whiskey and fish left her no doubt as to the man's true identity. He was undoubtedly a hired mercenary, sent to either rob her of her purse, or worse . . . She shivered, suddenly afraid.

It was not unheard of for heiresses as young as twelve to be kidnapped and ransomed, or worse—forced to marry against their will. If this were the case, she had much to fear. She knew of too many men who might be desperate enough to carry out such a villainous deed.

"Well, my lady," said the voice of the man holding the knife. "What will it be? Will ya cooperate or shall yer maid find ya stiff in the morning in this 'ere bed?"

She nodded her ascent to do as he asked.

Her life, she did not question, was in grave danger. Although it did occur to her that whoever might have paid for these men to enter her room might be vastly displeased if they killed her. With a sharp knife pointed at her throat, she wasn't willing to take any such chances of risking the mercenary's wrath. Listening, she heard someone else rummage through her clothes press. He muttered a curse as he stubbed his toes against the oak wood and brass hinges.

The other mercenary dragged her out of the bed. She gave a frightened squeal as he gagged and blindfolded her. He grunted and threw her over his broad shoulders. She felt him take heavy, swaying, shuffling steps towards the open French doors leading out to the balcony.

"Be quick, we haven't all night," the man whispered harshly to the one going through her things.

She felt a cool breeze coming through the French doors. It was spring and she could smell the roses that she'd planted below, blooming in the mist.

"Now ya better keep still," said her abductor. "Or I'll drop ya to the ground below to be dashed t' tiny bits at the slightest hint of a kick."

She immediately stilled. The only way they could have entered her room was about to become the same way they would leave it. That could only mean she was going to be carried down a steep ladder to the ground below, a sheer drop if ever there was one.

Frightened, her heart leapt to her throat. The pulsing fear paralyzed any thoughts of escape. She was glad her kidnapper had blindfolded her, for she then wouldn't witness the frightening feat. Her balcony was a good two stories above ground level. It hugged a steep cliff that dropped to the terraced lawn below.

She felt the shaking of the ladder. The late evening wind blew up her long night chemise, and above the sound of the creaking trees, she heard the grunts of her captor as he carried her slowly down.

Jangling step-by-step, he carried her. She remained perfectly still, not wishing to cause them to fall. She clutched his clothes with a fierce grip.

Upon reaching the ground, the man deposited her on her feet. He tightly bound her hands and pushed her forward. She heard the sounds of horses pawing the gravel impatiently, the jostling of leather, and the squeak of a carriage door as it opened.

Her captor helped her up the conveyance's steps and then thrust her none too gently onto the leather squabs. She bruised her right shoulder as she accidentally hit the side of the carriage door, letting forth a muffled squeal of protest.

She listened to the man yell, "Give way, Jack, we've got her!" Then she heard the horse's quick *clip-clops* as the vehicle picked up speed, rocking her to and fro along the bumpy road.

The crack of the ouster's whip sang overhead as he urged the horses onward. She must have fallen asleep,

[205]

for suddenly, she found herself in the motionless carriage.

A familiar male voice spoke, giving commands. It sent warning tingles up and down her arms. This was a man she knew! A villain who'd dared to do this evil deed.

"Pull the hood off, Snipes. I wish my intended to behold her bridegroom," she heard the self-satisfied aristocrat say.

The blind removed, she watched as the carriage door opened and he stepped into the light of an upheld lantern. She gasped aloud at the loathsome sight of his face.

"Why it's you! Viscount Linley, a cad of the lowest order, if I ever met one," she said, her voice trembling with all the contempt she could muster.

"How dare you let these cutthroats touch me?"

"No, m'dear, you're sadly mistaken, 'tis really none of my doing," he said, as if the entire plot had been of no consequence to him. "You know perfectly well you brought this sorry state of affairs upon your own pretty head, my dear. Aye, if only you had listened and obeyed me, none of this sorry business would have come to pass." His yellow teeth glistening in the lamplight, he smiled with complete delight.

"Upon my word, look at you, Lady Beatrice. Quite a bedraggled mess, aren't you? But I forgive you this unseemly attire," he said, sighing over her state of disarray. "I hear 'tis normal for one of such a shrewish temper as yourself to go gallivanting about the countryside in the most peculiar attires."

"It's almost shameful when I consider how different this meeting might have been, if you had only greeted me more warmly the last time we met to discuss our impending nuptials," he said, whipping out a lace handkerchief and a box of snuff. "We wouldn't have had to go through this added expense of forcing you to marry me. Quite tiresome, really, hiring mercenaries."

"You worthless snake!" she spat. "I'll make your life a living hell if you go through with this."

She sprang at him, her sharp nails ready to scratch his eyes out. Suddenly, she felt a forceful thrust backwards. Her lunge was squarely stopped by the forceful hands of her original captor.

Snipes held her in place, his grip like metal bands wrapped around her upper arms. She winced, stopping all futile efforts to fight.

"Nay, my dear, I think that once you've enjoyed the pleasure of my warm bed, you'll be begging me to keep you," the viscount said with a cruel laugh, angry by her attack.

He hadn't counted on her resisting him. She should have been begging for mercy. He brutally grabbed a handful of her hair. Pulling her head back, he forced a punishing kiss on her mouth, drawing blood as he raked his teeth across her tender lips.

Satisfied that he had proven his dominance over her, he daintily wiped his mouth and gave a nod to her captor, who then hauled her into the inn in front of them.

"Our honeymoon hideaway." The viscount, who walked beside her, leered as the mercenary pushed her roughly in front of him.

"By the by, there's no need to try crying out for help. Indeed, you'll just make yourself hoarse. No one will pay you any mind. We've paid the innkeeper and the servants enough money to keep them deaf and dumb for days. Of course, once we're married, we'll be paying them off with your dowry. A husband's prerogative, I believe, to use his wife's blunt."

"You lazy villain. What is that you really want my money for?" she asked, rubbing her sore wrists as Snipes released the cords.

He nodded in the direction of the two hired thugs who had helped him kidnap her. One stood at the door, blocking her path, lest she try to make an escape. The other swaggered over to the bar and bought himself and his partner tankards of ale for jobs well done. Two rougher villains, she had never seen in her life.

"My friends, although normally of understanding natures, are none too patient where money is concerned. To be candid, they persist that I pay back my gambling debts. The proprietor of one of the clubs I frequent, I'm afraid, quite adamantly persuaded me. I, in turn, hired them to kidnap you. So you see, being the gentleman that I am, I was forced to do what I must." He eyed her significantly. "I have no choice but to marry you and make all your money mine."

She shook with rage, but kept her thoughts for once, to herself. She reminded herself that she had to keep her wits about her if she didn't want to find herself leg-shackled to this inbred maniac.

She smiled amiably at him. "I'll strike a bargain with you, Viscount. If you set me free, I'll pay off all your debts myself." She walked over to him as if she were fully clothed and heavily armed, instead of half-unclad and badly bruised.

"Think upon it carefully. For if you let me go now," she whispered in her gentlest, most persuasive voice, "I promise not to let the earl murder you."

At this, her captor laughed, a deep, hearty chuckle. "But he's got t' find you first, my dear. And truth to tell, I don't believe he will. Nay," he shook his head once more with smug certitude, "I know he won't."

* * *

It was in the early morning hours before the breaking of the fast that the Earl of Drennan was first alerted that

[208]

something might be amiss. The precise moment was when Aunt Agnes came charging into his room unannounced.

He lay abed in his nightshirt as she barged in. His manservant, Davis, tried to restrain her from awakening His Grace.

"Go away, madam. My master is still abed and would not appreciate being disturbed."

"Your Grace!" cried the woman in black, pushing Davis's hands aside with a hearty shove. Her frightened, wrinkled face appeared by his bedside.

"Something dreadful has happened. M'niece, Lady Beatrice, she's missing!"

"What?" he said sitting up. "What do you mean missing?"

"I mean she's up and disappeared! She and some of her clothes, her maid tells me, are missing! And I don't know what to do!" wailed the lady.

"Her room's a mess, clothes thrown about every which way. Not at all like her. And . . ." The old woman's voice trembled with final certainty that something dreadful had happened. "And on her bed we found a sharp carving knife!"

She sank to the floor beside him, her hands clasped in pleading. "I'm begging Your Grace, you must help me. Something dreadful has happened to her. I know it."

"What?" he asked aloud, knowing full well she would not be the first wealthy heiress to be taken and kidnapped.

He then looked sharply at Davis, remembering vividly the scene between Lady Beatrice and Viscount Linley. The way in which the young aristocrat had proclaimed that he'd come back to fetch her, resonated in his memory.

"His betrothed," he said in a chilling, ominous voice that frightened the old lady next to him. "That's what that cad had called her." *Not if I have a word to say about the matter,* he thought furiously, throwing back his bed linens.

He turned to his man and gave orders that horses were to be saddled and ready to depart within the half-hour. "Fetch my firearms and sword," he said fiercely, barking out the command as if he were back on the battlefield. "And two days' provisions for all the men who'll accompany us."

"Aye, aye, Captain." The corporal saluted and hurried to do as he was bid.

The battle had been declared and he knew on which side his master was fighting. It was that of his beloved lady, the Spinster of Brightwood.

"What's all this ruckus?" asked Beau Powers dressed in a light blue-and-white-striped morning jacket as he watched the young earl dash past him. Surveying the riding clothes and weapons of the other gentleman through his quizzing glass, he raised his white-blond eyebrows in concern.

"Demme. You ain't having a hunt without me, are you, James? No one told me, and I so enjoy a good hunt."

"No, Beau," answered the earl with a taut grin. "I'm merely preparing to rescue a damsel in distress. Lady Beatrice, it would appear, was kidnapped last night from her bed. And I am, as it were, acting as her errant knight."

"Now that does sound rather exciting," said the Beau, dropping his quizzing glass into its habitual pocket.

"Would you mind terribly, old boy, if I joined you? Hunting a villain sounds much jollier than hunting a fox."

"If you wish." The ex-captain nodded, secretly pleased to have his friend by his side. It was well known that Beau Powers was an excellent shot. And he might be in need of a good marksman.

"We leave as soon as our mounts are fetched and saddled," he warned the dandy.

"That eager, are we? Sink me, but this is going to be rather jolly. Haven't had an opportunity to use m'braces since some brigands tried to rob m'house in Cork last fortnight," said the gentleman rushing up the stairs at a full charge.

"Humphrey!" he bellowed urgently to his man, who stood sleepily in the hall, in his nightclothes. "A hunt's a-foot and I don't intend to miss it. Quick, man, to my aid! Go fetch my pistols!"

*   *   *

Moments later the Earl of Drennan, Beau Powers, and several other members of the household, were seated on their mounts ready to go after the kidnappers.

After a quick survey of the local taverns, they discovered that their notion, that Viscount Linley was the one who had kidnapped her ladyship, was correct. Various carriages bearing his family crest had been seen speeding away from the castle the night Lady Beatrice was taken and had been sighted on the side roads nearby.

"It would appear that they're heading towards Scotland," said the earl, upon receiving further intelligence at one of the inns.

He passed a small bundle of coins to the innkeeper, a man he had rightly surmised had no trouble giving out information for a price.

"There are three hired cutthroats traveling with the carriage. To his knowledge the viscount has had no opportunity as yet to marry Lady Beatrice," his voice tellingly cracked upon saying her name.

They barely rested that day in their pursuit. They took a few hours to gather information before recommencing the chase. When her father, Lord Patrick, had been sought out and informed of his daughter's kidnapping, he had come to them immediately, his white beard bobbing with dismay and fear.

"I received my sister's note an hour ago. I came as soon as I could," he said, his eyes watering with worry. "M'lass . . . tell me, is she all right?"

"It's difficult to say," the earl answered honestly. "We're hoping to receive more information from those I sent out. It is hoped they'll ferret out their final destination."

"Then all is not lost." The father sighed. He patted the earl on the shoulders, seeing the desperate determination in the younger man's eyes. "I know you'll get her back, lad. And she'll be waiting for you."

"I know she will," answered the earl, his face stoically hiding his pain at losing her. How stupid he had been!

Over the last couple of hours he repeatedly replayed over in his mind the night she had turned down his proposal. He knew now how differently he should have acted, the words he ought to have said, and the way he should have said them. But that illusive dream of reconciliation meant nothing until he got her back. Would she already be forced into a marriage? Would the viscount harm her? These tortuous questions and others plagued him as he rode on in a fury.

* * *

It had been two days since she'd been kidnapped. During that time Beatrice had been in and out of more four-wheeled conveyances than in her entire lifetime. She'd lost count how many times they'd switched. They never stayed in one place long enough for her to find a way to escape, or to be found. She'd almost begun to despair of ever being rescued, let alone be allowed to lay down her weary head and get a good night's rest.

As she stood stretching herself in front of the newest inn, another dusty carriage was brought forth. She listened to two of the ousters discuss their journey.

"The viscount can't keep up this bruising pace forever," the one said to the other. "I 'eard the Earl of Drennan is offering a goodly sum to anyone who'll help return her ladyship to 'im."

"Aye," replied the other. "Bet he pays up better than this empty-pocketed beef-eater will. Stiffed me last week of m'pay, he did . . . said he'd pay me back what he owes me when he weds 'er."

Beatrice's hopes soared. Here was a way out of her predicament!

She could bribe the ousters into aiding her escape, by offering to pay them double the amount of the award the earl posted. If only that would help her get free!

She smiled and raised a hand to catch their attention. But before she could open her mouth and make her offer known, the viscount came up from behind and grabbed her arm. She grimaced, biting down on her lower lip in pain.

She cast him a hateful stare. She was fast becoming tired of being bruised and pinched by brutish male hands.

"Lady Beatrice," he said. "I've good news, m'dear. The local friar and I have just finished having a little chat. He understands my urgency to wed you, seemed almost sympathetic in fact. Told me I'd be doing you a service. Apparently, it's not every day a shrew is redeemed from the fires of hell. The friar said he'd find it agreeable to perform that sacred rite that will make us man and wife. He's even amiable enough to do the deed tonight for a small, but tidy sum."

He frowned a little at the thought of the small bundle of coins he'd had to pass over to the friar. But what did that matter? He leered down at her with smug satisfaction.

"Is that not delightful news? Now we won't have to

travel all the way to Gretna Green. We can wed here at our ease, without any further unseemly interruptions."

"No," she gasped involuntarily, "he can't marry us!"

"Ah, but he will," the viscount countered, placing his riding whip up against a smooth unblemished cheek.

"You know, I begin to grow tired of your protests, Lady Beatrice. After we are wed, I suggest you rid yourself of that disagreeable temper of yours, or pay the consequences by forcing me to scar that oh so delicate, milky skin."

She flinched, closing her eyes against the threat, and blocking out the vision of his sneering lips and his pasty, pocked face.

The ousters, who avidly stood watching, enjoyed the viscount's show of power over her. She could hear their hearty laughter join with the viscount's at her cowing.

Her heart sank. She knew she could no longer count on receiving help from that quarter. They were in league with the devil. She would have to devise another plan of escape, and quickly.

* * *

Later that evening, one of the serving girls, Mary, brought up a white-laced wedding veil with word that the viscount wanted her to wear the delicate confection. Looking it over, Beatrice knew that unlike the simple white wool dress that had been loaned to her by a local baker's daughter, this veil had come from someone of her own rank. The delicacy of the silver inlaid lace, beaded with precious diamonds and pearls, bespoke of a bride endowed with great class and wealth.

If only . . . she shivered. She would have been a happy bride once. Her regrets concerning the earl were too numerous to dwell upon. Now here she was, waiting to marry the blackguard who'd kidnapped her. A man she despised. She had no one to blame but herself. Her own, stupid pride.

If only she had accepted the earl's proposal, none of this would have happened. Tears slid down her cheeks for what might have been. Aye, she could have married Captain James, the Earl of Drennan, and been happy. Even if he only felt a certain amount of possessiveness for her. But then that would have been better than the loneliness she'd felt before he'd come into her life.

Aye, they could have shared so much together. But what good were her regrets doing her now? She had to shake off this self-pity and put her quick wits to use. And these blasted tears were of damnable little use to her. She wiped them away furiously.

Think, Beatrice, she told herself. *Think, m'girl, and get yourself out of this dreadful mess.* She looked down at the elegant confection.

The veil—maybe someone had . . .

"Where did this come from?" she asked suddenly, looking over the elaborate headpiece for clues. "Did the viscount's mother send it?" Even as she asked, she hardly believed that the woman who had once hated her could have provided such a thoughtful and sentimental gift.

"Nay. It be from Dovehill Hall, ma'am," explained the maid with some pride. "From the young lady what got married to old Lord Langtry last month."

"And how did she come to know of me?"

"Oh, ma'am, when the viscount came here last week for their wedding, he stayed with his lordship and Lady Langtry at Dovehill Hall, as their only guest."

"He stayed there?" she asked, curious to know more of the Langtrys, not being acquainted with the name. "You wouldn't happen to know what they talked about, would you?"

"Aye, my lady. I'm sorry to say that I do," the maid

whispered as if it were still a secret. "Told them of his plans concerning you, the viscount did. And all about how he planned to marry you."

The servant gave a slight shudder. She'd not quite forgotten that night, how the young lady had almost fainted at the sight of old Lord Langtry, her intended bridegroom.

"To be sure, it be right peculiar at the hall. They act different than the rest of us, the quality do." The maid had the good graces to blush, remembering belatedly that her ladyship was quality herself.

"In case you didna already know, the young lady was married to her husband, Lord Langtry, for a great sum."

Astonished by the queer way the maid referred to her ladyship's dowry, Beatrice asked, "How so?"

"Her guardian, Squire Lynch he be, offered her to his lordship in exchange for a pile of gold coins. I saw it m'self. It filled twenty-five leather purses, it did."

"My word." Beatrice blanched, realizing that they were discussing none other than Squire Lynch's orphaned ward, Lady Kathleen. She was the young heiress she'd met long ago at the village church in Urlingford.

"But Lady Kathleen is barely fifteen. He couldn't have married her off. Her trustees would never have permitted it. She's clearly under age."

"She's fifteen as of yesterday, ma'am. They took her to Gretna Green to tie the knot. And then brought her back here, so as to avoid the law. Lord Langtry being the magistrate here and all. There'll be no trouble, ye understand?"

"The poor child," she said, nodding.

She did understand. And it made her own present predicament seem not nearly as sinister. Poor, poor, young Lady Langtry would now never have the opportunity of knowing that heady feeling of falling in love. Her youth had quite literally been stolen by her greedy uncle.

"I hope her husband treats her well and that she's found some happiness," she said fingering the veil, feeling the finely crocheted threads of lace.

"Here, ma'am," said the servant pointing to a small piece of paper tied to it with a sliver of white ribbon. "It looks as if she wrote you a word to go with it, don't it? Probably wishing you the best for your own future happiness."

"No doubt," Beatrice answered weakly, for every moment they spent in this tiny airless room was bringing her closer and closer to that which she most dreaded. She looked down at the small parchment of paper, unfurling the scroll.

It simply read: *Take heart. I have sent word concerning your whereabouts. Trust no one. Signed, Lady Kathleen Langtry.*

She crushed it to her bosom, her hopes soaring with relief. Help had been sent for. She would soon be rescued!

"What'd it say, my lady?" asked the maid trying to peer over her shoulder. "I can't read none m'self. It all look like chicken scratching to me, it does."

She spread the paper open for the maid to see. She had to keep the simple woman's confidence until she was rescued, or they might move her away to yet another hiding place.

"See the message is as you thought. Her ladyship merely wanted to wish me well with the viscount."

"Well, ain't that nice." The maid nodded as she hung the veil beside the dress that had been chosen for her to wear. "I always thought she was a sweet, young lady, I did. Not like some I hears that likes to try and castrate a gentleman." She nodded at the famous shrew. "Not that I think the viscount is likely to put up with such tricks once you're married."

[217]

Pretending to pay avid attention to the servant, Beatrice prudently dropped the short missive into the hearth's fire. None would know of her impending rescue. She had now only to pray that the earl and her father would find her.

* * *

Beatrice paced her tiny, shabby chamber. It was nearing the dinner hour and soon the wedding would take place. There was still no sign of the earl and her father.

Nary a sound of dissent came from below. Indeed, if she were to go by the boisterous laughter she heard, it sounded as if all the visitors to the inn were celebrating the impending nuptials.

Mary approached her with the borrowed wedding gown. "It's time you were dressed in your finery, my lady. They say they intend to hold off serving dinner until you and the viscount are wed. Aye, and for once even the priest has arrived beforehand to see to it the deed's done."

"Let him wait," said Beatrice, wringing her hands, worriedly looking out the tiny window. Where were her promised rescuers?

"What'd you say, my lady?" asked Mary, giving her a sly glance, her voice sharpening. "Listen well, your ladyship, the viscount told me 'imself he'd come up and fetch you if you didn't hie yourself t' him in good time. Aye, and if I was you, I'd be setting m'thoughts on how to placate your new husband. From what I understand, he'll not likely make ye a gentle one."

Beatrice dumbly nodded at that bit of advice. She needed no one to remind her of the feel of the viscount's riding whip brushing against her cheek, or of his violent threats. She closed her eyes against the fear roiling inside, willing her heart to cease its frantic hammering.

"Help me prepare," she whispered, fingering the bridal veil, her hopes secretly lying with its owner.

*   *   *

Lady Kathleen Langtry looked at her dour companion, Mistress O'Grady. The grim-faced lady in plain black was more like her prison warden than her paid companion. The woman, who had once been the housekeeper of this large manor house, had been told by her husband to keep an eye on her. And keep an eye on her she did.

Every word and action Lady Langtry made were duly noted in a little black book the woman kept by her side. There was not a word or gesture the plain woman did not note and criticize.

Her husband, she shuddered thinking of the crippled old man her uncle had married her off to, knew everything she did and every word she said. It was almost maddening. She had overnight become a prisoner in what was supposed to be her home. Before her marriage, she had been simply a neglected orphan living unobserved in her uncle's house. Now she was the child bride of an old, lecherous lord, who had incarcerated her in this gloomy tombstone of a manse.

She leaned her head back against the stiff, red sofa and inwardly sighed. Her golden blonde curls contrasting against the bright red material of the lounge chair as her sad blue eyes looked up at the ornate ceiling above her. But she had a plan.

She may not have been able to help herself out of such a grim state of being married to an old man she did not care for, but she would do her utmost to try and save another from the same, dreadful fate. She had devised a plan to help the Spinster of Brightwood Manor not marry that villainous fop who'd attended her wedding dinner. It was the same horrible night she'd heard of the criminal plot to kidnap the rich heiress and force her into an unwanted marriage.

"Mistress O'Grady," she said innocently turning to the other woman. "I should like you to tell the stable boy to saddle my horse this afternoon. I intend to go riding today."

"Indeed, ma'am," answered the other, her coal-black eyes looking down at the china doll figure of the young lady who had overnight become the mistress of the house where she had always reigned supreme. "I don't think that's a very good idea, my lady. In fact, I'm quite certain that Lord Langtry would object to it. He thinks it's very bad for your health to go riding about in the country."

"But you're wrong, Mistress O'Grady. I have already spoken with him," the young mistress said firmly, knowing ahead of time what her reply would be. "I have already obtained my husband's permission to ride this afternoon."

"Then I shall have someone accompany your ladyship," O'Grady replied smoothly, her dark eyes narrowing ever so slightly.

It was well known that the housekeeper did not know how to ride, and would not be able to keep up with her ladyship if she tried, the young lady being a horsewoman of some skill. She had counted on her companion not riding.

"That will not be necessary," she said, feeling the test of wills between her bare fifteen years and the others odd fifty.

"But I insist. His lordship would want someone to accompany you, Lady Kathleen. You are still young and unknowing of the world and the dangers others may represent to you, especially gentlemen. I, therefore, feel it to be my duty to send at least our stable master with you," the companion reiterated more firmly.

"As you wish," answered the child bride sweetly. Everything was going according to plan.

* * *

That afternoon, dressed in her oldest riding outfit, the same ill-fitting one her uncle had given her when she first came to live with him, Kathleen sat calmly astride her horse. He had taken all her beautiful riding clothes and sold them to pay off his gambling debts. Before she lived with her uncle, she had a stable of horses and ponies of her very own. That was before her parents had died in a typhoid plague and left her to the negligent care of her loathsome uncle, Squire Lynch, and his corruptible solicitor.

"Why are you wearing that rag?" asked Mrs. Ryan appearing beside her. "I thought his lordship had ordered you to burn all those old clothes."

"My other one is still being fitted by the modiste," she lied. "I have no other riding clothes to wear. So I put these on."

"Very well," answered the grim woman. "I suppose if you keep to the back roads, no one will see you."

"Indeed not." Kathleen nodded, and picking up her riding whip, walked around the frowning woman towards the stables.

Instead of entering the stables, she walked beyond them to a small wood where a gardening hut stood on the edge, well-screened from the main house.

She opened the door and stepped inside. In the half dark, she took off the old riding dress, and stepped into a pair of boy's breeches, pulling an old blue peasant shirt on. She wrapped her hair up into a broad, leather shepherd's hat pulling the floppy brim low over her face.

"What goes on 'ere?" she heard the gruff familiar

voice of the stable master behind her. "And who might ye be, lad?"

"Uh . . . I'm the new house boy, Jeremy O'Conner, sir," she said stammering, holding onto the brim of her hat in a manner she hoped the stable master would not find peculiar. "I brought you word from the big house, master."

"Oh, you did, lad," said the stable master. "And what is it?"

"The uh, lady, the one what's always dressed in black?"

"Aye, that be Mistress O'Grady," he said impatiently. "What's she want?"

She tried putting on her best servant accent. "She, uh, said that you weren't to wait no more for the young mistress. She up an' changed her mind, she did . . . decided she didn't want to go riding after all. But they wants me to have a pony to fetch some needles and thread in the village for them."

"They did, eh?" The stable master nodded. "Very well, you brought your message, lad. Here, I'll give you a hand with that black pony there. Buttons, he's called, lad."

The stable master went and fetched a saddle for the pony. He strapped the saddle onto the small mount and gave her a hand up.

Smiling, Lady Kathleen kicked her heels into the pony's flanks and departed, heading towards the tavern where she'd heard the earl and his men were waiting for news concerning the kidnapped Spinster of Brightwood.

Cautiously, she approached the inn. Word of mouth had made it known about the parish that a small fortune had been posted as reward for news of the wealthy spinster and her kidnappers. It had not been difficult to learn where the gentlemen searching for her had decided to rest before continuing their frantic search.

She arrived just as the gentlemen were preparing to

leave the inn. She dismounted and tied the pony to a post, pulling her hat low as she approached the group of gentlemen and outriders drinking and talking at tables that had been set outside beneath the shade of a large oak tree.

She eavesdropped on their conversations. It was evident that they were still waiting for news. Several of the gentlemen were in deep discussion as to where they should look next. Two of them were, she noted, the earl and a handsome gentleman of fashion, an Englishman she'd never seen before.

The stranger was almost as tall as the earl and just as broad shouldered. His hair, the color of a shining new guinea, was neatly cropped in the Corinthian style. She had never seen a real dandy up close before, and skirting the other gentlemen came as close as she dared to this manly perfection.

She must have been staring openly, for next she knew a sharp pair of sapphire eyes looked down at her.

"Looks as if you've snared yourself another admirer, Beau," said the earl with a hint of amused laughter. "The lad here with his mouth hanging open apparently finds you quite fascinating."

Kathleen pulled harder on the brim of her hat, her own blue eyes staring up at the two gentlemen, her cheeks blushing with shame. She'd been caught.

The nonpareil looked down at her with a kindly smile. "What is it, lad?"

"I, uh, have a message for you two gentlemen," she said, swallowing nervously. "A noble gentle lady sent me here to give it to you."

The earl grabbed her roughly by the arm. "Did this lady, by chance, have long raven hair and green eyes the color of new sprung grass?"

"No-o," she squeaked, her arm feeling as if it were in a vice.

"Release the lad, James, you're frightening him,"

[223]

said the nonpareil, noticing her evident distress.

He looked down at her with a reassuring smile. "Tell us the rest of your message, lad. Does it perhaps concern the one we seek, Lady O'Brien?"

She silently nodded.

"I was sent to give you this," she said, almost whispering, as she stared up at his mouth. It felt unreasonably good to see this handsome Corinthian smiling down at her with approval. It had been a long time since anyone had shown her any sign of friendliness.

"Where is it?" the earl asked.

"The lady writes that she espied Lady Beatrice one league from here, at a country inn called the Blue Bonnet. That's where she's been taken," answered Beau in a rush. "They intend to marry her off to the viscount tonight."

Kathleen grabbed hold of his arm, her eyes pleading with him.

"You must hurry and rescue her before it's too late, sirs. My mistress told me that they've sent for a priest."

"But surely she can protest the marriage to the clergy?" he said, as he noticed her look of panic and worry.

"Not this one," she replied, shaking her head. "I know this cleric. For the right price, he'll say they were properly married."

"Thank you," he said, and reaching into his horse's satchel withdrew a purse of money. "Here, take this to your mistress. The reward is hers. And thank her kindly for us, for she may have saved my beloved's life."

"Aye, my lords. I will give her your thanks," she whispered and pushed the satchel back into his hand. "But she didna do it for the reward, kind sirs. Rescue Lady O'Brien away from those evil villains. That is all she do ask of ye."

She noticed the dark circles around the earl's eyes and the haunted look of determination. She felt reassured that this lord was determined to succeed in rescuing Lady O'Brien. She was relieved. This man would surely save the kind woman who had always treated her with gentleness and compassion.

"May God speed you on your journey, Your Grace," she said to him, and turning, she bowed and walked back to her pony. It was as she remounted using both of her hands that her broad leather hat, which had managed to stay safely upon her head, blew off.

Two pairs of amazed male eyes stared at her long golden hair as it tumbled down her shoulders. Her eyes met those of the astonished dandy's. She gave him a saucy wink and a coquettish laugh that she could not keep from bubbling up, and galloped away.

"Heavens, a girl!" Beau muttered aloud, almost choking on his ale in surprise.

James watched, in admiration, the retreating back of the brave, young woman disappear down the road.

"Beautiful and brave . . . just like my Beatrice," James said, his words bitter with regret. He knew now he loved Beatrice with all his heart and soul.

He'd behaved like a complete idiot. Marry in order to establish a dynasty? Balderdash! What had he been thinking? That was not the way he should have spoken to her. He should have taken her into his arms and told her he loved her. Damn his eyes!

He wanted to tell her as soon as possible how much she meant to him, how his heart pounded at the very sight of her, how she made his blood run hot at her very touch, how he greatly admired everything she did. There were so many things he should have said.

He was head over heels in love. If she didn't believe him, he would dedicate his entire life proving it to her if he had to. But first he had to find her and set everything right. He had to! Nodding to his men to hurry and prepare for their departure, he quickly set off.

* * *

Through the fine silver net of her veil, Beatrice saw that the inn had filled with men. A fire had been lit and the priest, in clerical white, stood waiting with the viscount for her appearance.

"Some of our customers asked if they might not see you tie the knot," whispered the maid to her as she paused. "The viscount gave his consent, saying the more witnesses, the better. Less likely for his claim upon you to be challenged that way."

Silently, Beatrice acknowledged the servant's words, her hands clutching the bouquet of wildflowers the maid had thrust upon her.

No doubt, the viscount was making doubly certain that his word would not be questioned concerning the wedding rite. Aye, she felt the invisible rope he'd made around her neck tighten. Soon there would be no way of escape. She looked at the rough men lounging about in the half-darkened room staring at her as she approached. They were grouped about in one big, brown and black blur.

One of the men, his face partially hidden by the shadows, nudged another, who appeared to be the tallest man in the room. She heard him say to the ruffian wearing a gypsy scarf about his head, "Isn't she the bonniest bride you ever did clap yer eyes upon, sir?"

The deep voice, it was a familiar one . . .

She turned to stare. But could not make out the face in the shadows. The voice was one she would dearly love to hear again. It sounded so much like her father's.

"Aye, sir," The tall man nodded in a cultured accent. "And a delightful feast for any man's eyes."

Startled, peering at the man from beneath her veil, she looked up at him.

"Please, dear God," she whispered aloud, praying. "Let it be . . ." And when she opened her eyes, she met those of the tall man staring at her.

Blue eyes like the ocean before a spring storm stared back at her. The gypsy saluted her. She gasped, almost losing her balance as she tripped on her next step.

"Courage, my lady," he said, his hand immediately at her elbow steadying her. He nodded her forward, to continue her journey to where her detested bridegroom stood impatiently waiting for her.

"Have no fear for me, good sir. I fully intend to play my part and see this through," she said, her eyes never leaving his, her courage drawing from his.

"I thought you would, my dear," he said, audaciously kissing her slender hand.

The squinty-eyed man beside him, one of the paid mercenaries, put his hand on the tall gentleman's shoulder, trying to keep him from touching the bride. But the tall man ignored him, swinging his tankard into the air shouting out, "Another toast t' the bride, gentlemen!"

"To the bride!" all the men shouted, raising their tankards to her.

The cleric, Father Rathbourne, stood in front of the lit hearth, where above it two small swords lay crisscrossed on hooks for decoration. The cleric gave her a benevolent smile as she reached him, and the viscount. He was, she could see, a bit tipsy. His fat pudgy nose and round cheeks were rosy from the brew that everyone had been passing liberally around.

She felt the viscount's cold hand grab hold of hers. The boisterous talking quieted, and all eyes focused on the scene before them as they awaited the cleric's opening benediction over the couple.

"Dearly beloved, we have come together in the presence of God to witness and bless the joining together of this man and this woman in holy matrimony," he intoned in churchly solemnity. "The bond and the covenant of marriage was established by God so that man might create a union."

As the cleric continued invoking the holy virtues of marriage, Beatrice cast her eyes about the room, looking for a familiar set of beloved colt-blue eyes. They were not difficult to find, for they immediately met hers.

"Will you, Viscount Reginald Adolph Philip Linley, have this woman to be your wife?" she heard the cleric ask, breaking with tradition by asking the groom first, his bleary eyes trying to focus on the page before him.

"Will you love her, comfort her, and keep her, in sickness and in health? And forsaking all others, be faithful to her as long as you both shall live?"

"I will," answered the viscount coolly, giving her hand a crushing squeeze.

"Will you, Lady Beatrice Kathryn Margaret O'Brien, take this man to be your beloved husband, to live together in the covenant of marriage?"

Lady Beatrice, a smile on her face as gracious as the sun coming over the green hills of Ireland on a fine spring morning, looked at the cleric as if he had just said something highly amusing. She then turned around, her emerald eyes set on those she loved most of all in the world and answered in a strong voice. "I most certainly will not."

She removed her hand from the viscount's clasp.

"Are you certain, Lady O'Brien? Perhaps, my lady, you would like to, uh—to reconsider?" the cleric squeaked, glancing fearfully at the glowering red face of the pock-marked groom.

"No," she answered simply. Her smile, if that were

possible, brighter than before. "I most certainly will *not* take this man for my husband, Father."

"Didna you hear the fey, lass?" someone in the room heckled. "She gave her answer. She didna want 'im."

"Aye! We all heard her, Father. She donna care for the white faced codfish you've presented her," another added. And at this jeering barb, the tall man stepped forward, offering his arm to her.

"She's done with you, sir," the tall gentleman said, looking down at the viscount from his greater height. He gently led her over to the older gentleman, who had previously commented on what a pretty bride she made.

The old gentleman grinned from beneath his long silver beard, merry green eyes the same color as hers twinkling.

"Da!" she said, her voice hitching with joy and recognition as she tenderly looked at her adoring parent. His large arms grasped his beloved daughter about the shoulders in a fierce, fatherly hug.

"My darlin' lass," he murmured, holding onto her as if afraid they'd once more be separated from each other.

"Take your hands off her!" growled the viscount, drawing down one of the small swords from the mantel of the fireplace.

At the sight of the drawn blade, weapons from all over the smoke-filled room were produced. The viscount and his men, although more numerous, were outmaneuvered by the pub's Saturday night crowd. Looking at the winsome bride and her handsome supporter, the tall gypsy gentleman, they quickly sided with them.

He, the obvious leader of the group, took off his cloak.

"It's you!" spat the viscount in recognition as he found himself eyeing his nemesis, the Earl of Drennan. "You'll pay for this meddling with your life!" he cried lunging madly forward, thrusting his blade at his enemy's heart.

Captain James, quick on his feet, side-stepped in time to save his vulnerable breast. The blade, nonetheless, sliced easily through his blue, wool shirt, exposing his bronzed flesh.

"Here, man!" yelled out Beau Powers, realizing his friend stood in perilous danger. He pulled down the remaining sword and tossed it to him.

All eyes were upon the two opposing gentlemen.

The squinty-eyed mercenary who stood next to Beatrice slowly drew out a hunting knife from his belt, in preparation of throwing it into the earl's exposed back.

Beatrice, seeing the blade, quickly seized her father's blunderbuss from his belt and trained the ancient weapon upon the mercenary's scowling, wrinkled face.

"Have a care, sir," she said proudly eyeing the familiar weapon. "It donna look like much. But 'tis known to have shot down a bigger man than you."

The viscount, legs spread apart, knees bent, growled, ready to skewer her beloved to death.

The sizzling sound of two blades meeting sang in the air as Captain James met the thrust with a counter parry of his own, knocking his adversary's blade to one side. The blades sliced the air and all drew back to give them more room.

Beatrice's hand shook as she watched.

"Hand it here, lass," her father said taking the weapon from her. "We donna want to be paying the pallbearer for two bodies, now do we?"

She quietly nodded. Her eyes never left the forms of the two men battling in front of her.

The earl was a trained swordsman who had picked up the art of fencing during his service from a Maltese fencing-master in Valleta, Spain. Sweating, his hand gripped the hilt of the small sword, he feinted and lunged. The lunge was parried, and as he made a rapid extension of his sword arm, his well-toned body and legs tightened as he tried to reach his opponent again.

Only while he maintained this attack was his life safe. The moment it slackened, or his attention wondered, the viscount's blade would most certainly dart forward and swiftly kill him.

He beat against the viscount's blade, thrusting first, over and under, his strength and the long reach of his muscled arms to his advantage. The viscount's pencil-thin figure and years of advanced training made it more difficult for him to find a target wherein he might wound him.

The earl may not have had the private tutoring of French fencing masters all of his life like the viscount, but he'd had experience and control from the battlefield. The blades met harshly, jarring his long fingers, and only in the nick of time did he beat the second thrust, which the viscount made as he advanced.

The viscount sneered mirthlessly. His snarling thin lips parted, his temper flaring into blind rage for revenge.

The blades slipped apart. He prepared to end the earl's life.

James seized the moment and leaped forward with lightning speed, slicing a line through the viscount's upper exposed breast. Red blood bubbled heavily to the surface staining the white chemise of his silk shirt.

The viscount cried out, dropping his weapon.

The earl kicked the small sword aside with his foot. It slid across the plank floor and landed at Beatrice's feet. Jumping over it, she rushed forward into his arms. He held her fiercely to him, his heart pounding with relief and joy as she covered his face with kisses.

Lord Patrick leaned over the wounded viscount and

said with disgust, "He's not dead, just fainted. More's the pity . . ."

A maidservant appeared with fresh linens and the local surgeon, who had been sent for, during the rencontre.

Beatrice tended her beloved James. Several haggled cuts across the hand and the thin jagged line on his shoulder bore witness to where the viscount's sword had lightly scored during the battle. There was a mad shock of delight and pleasure for James when he discovered the light of love still shining in her emerald green eyes.

Beatrice tenderly bound his hand herself, disinfecting the wounds with strong spirits and binding them tight with clean linens and sweet kisses.

"Beatrice," he said, stilling her hands by holding them, "please, darling—please put me out of my agony. I know I've behaved like an absolute cad and each of my past proposals were cocky and full of arrogance. I was a fool and rightly deserved your refusals . . ." He paused in his speech to tenderly brush aside the strands of her black hair, which had managed to escape from beneath the wedding veil. "I love you. I have since the very first. My brave darling, will you do me the honor of marrying me?"

"Yes," she said, smiling at him through tears of joy, "I will."

"The third time is the charm, then," he said, kissing her and pledging, "I vow to prove my love to you, my darling, every day for the rest my life."

* * *

Two weeks later, after the banns were published, the new Earl of Drennan was seen driving a high-sprung, open carriage drawn by two fine matching-white horses, to the Ryan family's farm to pay visit to his betrothed's goddaughter. The little girl, who was to be named Beatrice Ann Ryan, was to be baptized in the castle's newly renovated chapel on the next day.

His lovely bride-to-be, wearing a cream-colored morning gown with a straw bonnet trimmed in leafy green ribbon, smiled up at her groom as she sat next to him.

A shout was heard by a young boy with the signature Ryan red hair as they approached. "They're here!"

Maureen stepped outside, carrying her baby daughter in her arms. Her large brawny husband, Paddy, appeared at the door. The husband nodded to his eldest son to hold the horses' reins for the earl. Delighted to be in charge of such a fine pair, the young man did as asked.

Descending, James greeted the family and shook hands with the patriarch, an elderly man who sat in a rocking chair nearby smoking on his dhudeen pipe.

"Go fetch us some ale, Mary," said Paddy to his capable daughter standing next to him, "so we might toast the earl and his new bride."

James handed down Beatrice from the carriage, and much to the amusement of all who watched, refused to release her.

"You know what I want," he murmured into her ear when she tried to remove herself.

"Very well," said the bride with a small sigh of pretend exasperation,

She kissed her groom willingly on the mouth in front of the large brood, which caused the entire clan to cheer and applaud in approval.

James took from the back of the carriage, two large baskets filled with preserves, tea, and hard to find spices and salt to the father of the family.

"We never forgot your kindness in sending us a

hamper when we were working on the castle," he said. He looked fondly at his bride, remembering the day he mistook her tiny aunt for a fairy. "It was unforgettably delicious."

"'Twas nothing, Your Grace," said Paddy with a blush. "It was all m' fine wife's idea. She wanted to show Lady Beatrice her gratitude for helping her birth our little Bea Ann. We don't know what we would've done without her help, fine midwife that her ladyship be."

They stepped inside the farmhouse sitting room. Mary arrived with a large tray filled with tankards of ale, which she passed around.

"To Your Grace and your fine bride, Lady Beatrice," said the father of the large red-haired brood. "May you both enjoy good health and have many children. Slainte!"

To which all loudly responded, "Slainte!"

In turn James toasted the Ryan family and his wife's new goddaughter, who was soundly sleeping in her mother's arms, unaware of the presence of the important guests.

Beatrice brought forth an off-white christening gown made of fine, Irish lace, beribboned in white and seeded with small pearls, a matching bonnet dangled from her hands by the ribbons, and everyone exclaimed over its elegance.

"My mother made this for me for my christening," she said. "I thought I would loan it to my goddaughter for tomorrow."

"So delicate and lovely," murmured Maureen, reverently touching the lace. "It's a real honor, my lady. And our Bea Ann will look like an angel when she wears this tomorrow."

Looking down at the sleeping baby with wisps of red hair, a dreamy smile appeared on Beatrice's face as she thought of the children she and James would have together.

They were going to have a wonderful life, working on the castle and manor estates, while raising a family.

She briefly wondered if the fairies knew of the happiness they had given them when the magic coin passed into her hands? Had they seen the love grow between them?

She was soon to have her answer.

James put his left hand into his right pocket and brought forth his lucky coin, tossing it freely into the air as was his habit. And as he did so, and many in the room swore later when asked to retell the tale, it mysteriously shimmered and disappeared into thin air.

"The devil take it. I've gone and tossed it away," he said when it did not land back into the palm of his hand.

"No, Your Grace, you haven't thrown it away," said the winsome beauty by his side. "The fairies have merely taken back what was rightfully theirs. They were just waiting for the right moment, didna you know?"

The ex-soldier who had inherited a title, rebuilt a castle, and fought for the lady beside him, dreamily smiled. "Faith," he said in brogue, "And I wish them joy of it. For I've got the real treasure right here in m'arms."

"Aye, then what are you waiting for? Why don't you kiss me, then?" The ex-Spinster of Brightwood Manor smiled back.

And the valiant lord obediently complied.

Author's Biography

Engaging, romantic frolics are how author, Beverly Adam, describes her Regency Romance series: *Gentlemen of Honor*. The redheaded writer currently resides in California where she revisits history on a regular basis as a romance novelist and biographer.

Made in the USA
Middletown, DE
12 March 2015